STICK TOGETHER

Also by Sophie Hénaff in English translation

The Awkward Squad (2017)

Sophie Hénaff

STICK TOGETHER

Translated from the French by
Sam Gordon

MACLEHOSE PRESS
QUERCUS · LONDON

First published in the French language as *Rester groupés* by
Editions Albin Michel, Paris, in 2017
First published in Great Britain in 2018 by MacLehose Press
This paperback edition published in 2020 by

MacLehose Press
An imprint of Quercus Publishing Ltd
Carmelite House
50 Victoria Embankment
London EC4Y 0DZ

An Hachette UK company

A CIP catalogue record for this book is available
from the British Library.

ISBN (PB) 978 0 85705 581 1
ISBN (Ebook) 978 0 85705 578 1

10 9 8 7 6 5 4 3 2 1

Designed and typeset in Minion by Libanus Press Ltd
Printed and bound in Great Britain by Clays Ltd, Elcograf S.p.A.

To my own little gang,
again.

"Like phoenixes floundering in the ashes."

Eva Rosière,
Laura Flames and the Awkward Squad

PROLOGUE

The Vaucluse, November 24, 2012

Jacques Maire walked along the canal which ran through the centre of L'Isle-sur-la-Sorgue. He was counting the ducks. The water-parsnip, which turned the limpid stream a shade of green, swayed gently in the current, dipping in and out of view in the shimmering light. Boats rocked back and forth in the peaceful flow that urged him to slow his pace.

With the calm, collected smile of the village do-gooder, Jacques returned the distant "bonjour" of the local librarian, before passing beneath the plane trees on his way to the boulangerie. In the main square, the marble plaque on the war memorial caught his attention. It had been defaced. A drop of golden paint, still wet, trickled from the final vowel of a new name that someone had added.

Jacques Maire: August 17, 1943 – November 25, 2012.
November 25, 2012.
Tomorrow.

1

Commissaire Anne Capestan was doing battle with the latest in a long line of shoddy printers allocated to her team by the ever munificent police quartermaster. The machine maintained that it was running low on ink, even though Capestan had only just replaced the cartridge. After pressing every single button twice, the commissaire admitted defeat. She did not have anything particularly important to print. Not least because she did not have anything particularly important to work on. Or any work at all, in fact.

After a glittering start to her career that saw an Olympic medal for shooting and more badges of honour than any young officer before her, Capestan had joined the Brigade des Mineurs, without knowing that the posting would test her emotions to their very limit. During her time there, on a case that was horrific even by the Mineurs' grim standards, she had shot down a suspect. There were no two ways about it. She was the star pupil who had gone off the rails; "a loaded Kalashnikov with an innocent smile," as her colleague Eva Rosière had delicately put it. After narrowly escaping the sack, Capestan now found herself at the head of a team of down-and-out officers, an idea dreamed up by Buron, the big boss of 36, quai des Orfèvres, to clean up the Police Judiciaire by chucking all the undesirables onto the same scrapheap.

A month ago they had successfully solved their first case, something that – far from earning her awkward squad the respect of their peers – had only served to intensify their disdain. Grasses. Traitors. That was their reputation after hanging a fellow officer out to dry. Not an easy label to remove, and it weighed heavily on Capestan's mind. On her pride, too.

As for Commandant Lebreton, he had adjusted to the situation with his customary calm. He was no stranger to the scorn of his colleagues. A glorious spell at R.A.I.D. had been cut short when he came out as gay, and was speedily transferred to working in internal complaints with the I.G.S. – a role where you might as well wear a sign reading "Judas" instead of a uniform. In such a place, crippled with grief following the death of his husband, he had found it harder to stomach the bigotry. One accusation against his superior later and he was fast-tracked to Buron's custom-made dustbin. Right now, he was tipped back in his chair, feet crossed on his desk, leafing through a Sunday supplement from *Le Monde*, taking a break from the futile task of investigating the boxes of cold cases blocking their corridor. A loud voice from the next-door room made him lower his magazine, listen for a second, raise an eyebrow, and continue with his article.

The commotion involved the umpteenth difference of opinion between the volcanic Eva Rosière and the unsinkable Merlot. They argued constantly, not always about the same thing at the same time, but that never seemed to concern them in the slightest. This time they could be heard having a heated discussion over a game of snooker, the most recent contribution from Capitaine Rosière, the novelist-turned-screenwriter-turned-millionaire. Her spell at number 36 had come to an end when the top brass finally tired of her grindingly unsubtle parodies of them in her television series, "Laura Flames". Ever since tipping up at their makeshift commissariat on rue des Innocents, she had taken charge of the refurbishments, exercising decreasing levels of restraint. The day before, when Rosière had floated the idea of buying a football table to keep Dax and Lewitz amused, Capestan had asked whether she was planning on charging a membership fee for the commissariat or if it would be pay-as-you-play. Merlot, eavesdropping next to them, had appeared to scrutinise the question without grasping the sarcasm. Rosière, a careful strategist despite her boorish air, had backed down. No doubt a temporary retreat, Capestan had thought to herself.

The commissaire moved away from the printer into what had become the billiards room following the arrival of a full-sized table a few weeks ago, complete with fringed rectangular lampshade, four leather armchairs, a cue rack and a magnificent oak-topped bar with a set of matching stools.

"It's official, Anne, no-one else will want to join our squad now," Eva had said with finality. "May as well furnish it properly – makes the space less dreary." Dreariness was now the last thing Capestan associated with the commissariat; space was the second last.

Merlot, measuring in at a full cubic metre, stood rooted to the spot, a look of alpha pride written across his face. The former Brigade Mondaine capitaine, a well-connected but booze-addled freemason, was standing firm during Rosière's thunderous diatribe, snooker cue in one hand, red ball in the other. His jacket was flecked all over with blue chalk marks.

". . . it's all the same . . . Take rhino horns. One day, some limp-pricked so-and-so runs into a rhino and says, 'Whoa there,

I'd like me a horn like that, please. I'll just grind it up, guzzle it down, and away we go!' And, ever since, the not-so-cocksure of the world have been wiping out the entire species just to get a bit of life back in their loins."

At her feet, Pilote, Rosière's dog, listened reverently. He turned to Merlot, awaiting his response.

"Exactly, dear girl. Vitality! I quite agree . . . Vitality is the root of such giant scientific strides!" the capitaine said, nodding impressively and almost blinding Lieutenant Évrard with the tip of his cue.

The lieutenant, dismissed from the gambling task force after developing a certain weakness for blackjack, was perched on the side of the table, drumming her fingers on the polished wood as she waited patiently for the conversation to end. She had her back turned, more or less on purpose, to Lieutenant Torrez, who had stowed himself away in an armchair in the corner of the room, his billiard cue leaning against the armrest. Capestan strolled over to him.

"Who's winning?"

"The argument or the snooker?"

"The snooker."

"Me, in that case."

"Who are you playing with?"

"Me," Torrez said, frowning.

Yet again, no-one wanted to be on Torrez's team, preferring instead to play three on one. This was an improvement on the month before, when he couldn't enter the room without its occupants running for the hills. His shady reputation as a bringer of very bad luck was definitely subsiding, albeit slowly. Baby steps.

Everyone, including Torrez (especially Torrez), was continuing to exercise a healthy degree of caution. Only Capestan went near him in a carefree manner, refusing to be affected by this superstitious nonsense.

The buzz of a sunbathing cicada rang out of the commissaire's pocket. Her mobile. Buron's name flashed on the screen. A whole month had passed since the directeur of the Police Judiciaire last called, and that was only to notify her that his promise of a brand-new, fully functioning car had been honoured. Brigadier Lewitz, a lunatic behind the wheel, had needed just one day to write it off. After that, Buron had advised the squad to keep a low profile while their colleagues and the media cooled down, despite the commissaire's protests that their profile had never been high in the first place. But even she had to admit that the team could do with a cooling-off period.

If Buron was getting in touch today, perhaps that meant good news.

Capestan picked up.

"Good morning, Monsieur le Directeur. To what do I owe the pleasure?"

The sound of a Schubert sonata drifted from Orsini's stereo, tuned as ever to Radio Classique. For once, the capitaine was not listening. He was busy flattening a page of the newspaper *La Provence*, engrossed by the headline: "L'Isle-sur-la-Sorgue resident Jacques Maire murdered in middle of street."

Orsini pulled a pair of scissors from his pencil-holder and carefully cut out the article. Then he opened a drawer and picked out a red cardboard sleeve, sliding the document inside. He flicked over the elastic ties, took the lid off his black marker pen and let it hover above the card for several seconds. He did not know what to write.

Eventually, he laid down the pen and returned the sleeve to the drawer, blank.

2

Swathed in the gloomy trappings of winter, the capital felt murkier than ever. A thin film of greasy drizzle forced the Parisians to walk with their heads lowered, eyes darting across the pavement, defeated by the day before it had even begun. With her chin tucked into a big flecked scarf and a thick black poncho draped around her, Capestan picked her way through a forest of pedestrians' umbrellas on rue de Daguerre. She strode towards rue Gassendi, which, because of the crime scene, was at a standstill where it joined rue Froidevaux.

The body had been found two hours earlier. Capestan, whose desk was piled high with lapsed files, wondered what she had done to deserve such a fresh case. This certainly marked a return to the fray.

As always, the rubberneckers were craning to catch a glimpse of the action from behind the security cordon, doing their best to jostle past the obstinate police officers. The commissaire slipped past these nosy onlookers, presented her badge with a smile, and crossed the barrier, trying to make out the tall figure of the number 36 boss. In addition to the local police force and the forensics teams, she spotted a couple of lieutenants from the Brigade Crimi-nelle, who were no doubt itching to take on this case, as well as a

B.R.I. van that for some odd reason was parked at the top of the street. Throw in her own attendance and it was clear from all the heat in tow that this was no ordinary murder. The directeur's summons were suddenly all the more intriguing.

Buron, hands deep in the pockets of his khaki duffel coat, looked less than impressed as he contemplated the hustle and bustle. As Capestan approached, a smile vanished as quickly as it appeared.

"Good morning, commissaire."

She pulled back her hood to widen her field of vision before answering.

"Good morning, Monsieur le Directeur. What have we got here? Plenty of personnel, at least."

"Yes, plenty. Too many," Buron said, turning to survey the hive of activity.

Capestan thrust her chin back into her scarf.

"Why did you invite us to the party?"

"The victim is a big gun from the B.R.I., so I already know full well how they are going to play this. Same with Crim. They'll dredge up a lot of old bad blood, root around every gangland police file since Mesrine's glory days, and refuse to follow up any lead that doesn't fit the B.R.I. bill."

The murder of a top-flight officer . . . Leads that didn't fit the bill . . . Capestan was not sure she liked the sound of this.

"Monsieur le Directeur, please tell me you're not asking us to investigate another inside job. Other officers have got their knives out for us as it is."

Capestan had never been too bothered about her reputation, which was just as well, all things considered, but in the long run, being the object of so much bile was hard, even for someone with her thick skin. It required a lot of courage, or a lot of blithe indifference, to keep a clear head in the face of such disdain.

"No, I'm definitely not suggesting that this is an 'inside job'; I'm simply asking you to explore all possible eventualities, just as you would for any investigation. Having said that, yes, you do risk encountering a certain amount of . . . intransigence."

Buron let out a small sigh and rubbed his gloved hands together. He seemed determined to speak frankly:

"If I'm honest, my decision to assign you to this case has not been wildly popular. Crim. are saying they don't need any support in their investigations, and are already pretty upset to have the B.R.I. on board, let alone you and your other black sheep."

Capestan flicked a sodden curl off her forehead.

"I can well imagine," she said. "But I don't get it – did the public prosecutor's office request us?"

Buron shook his head and frowned, flexing his fingers in the morning air. In the directeur's language, this meant: "No, not exactly, there are still a few tiresome administrative hoops to jump through." Capestan translated this into the only term that was fit for purpose: "No." The public prosecutor's office barely knew her squad existed, and Buron, the Directeur of the Police Judiciaire, was enlisting their services on the sly. The commissaire kept coming back to the question of why she was there. Without wanting to be overly humble about it, she knew they had nothing to bring to the table on a case like this. Something about Buron's decision did not make sense.

"I'm sorry to keep asking, but why us, Monsieur le Directeur – ?"

Buron cut her short as a huge mountain of a man walked past, his muscular torso wedged into a black leather jacket. His dark features were handsome, but he wore a closed expression. Buron touched the man's elbow and drew him to one side. His hulking frame cast a shadow the size of a skyscraper. Recognising the directeur, he stopped abruptly and stood to attention. The directeur nodded his approval before addressing Capestan:

"Commissaire, allow me to introduce you to Lieutenant Diament from the B.R.I. Varappe Division, isn't it?"

The officer straightened even more, clearly proud to belong to this legendary elite squad, whose officers abseiled down the sides of buildings, dangling from their ropes as they sprayed bullets into the hideouts of hardened gangsters. Given the size of this officer, Capestan had some sympathy for both the ropes and the gangsters.

"Yes, Monsieur le Directeur."

"I gather that you, lieutenant, are tasked with ensuring clear communications between the B.R.I., Crim. and Capestan's squad, correct?"

"Yes, sir," he replied, his voice quieter this time.

"Pleased to meet you, lieutenant," Capestan said, giving him a friendly smile and holding out her hand.

The man shook it and nodded, studiously avoiding eye contact with the commissaire. Aside from the irritation at being subjected to these tedious pleasantries, Capestan also detected a hint of sadness in the lieutenant's eyes. Probably something unrelated to the job in hand, she guessed.

"As soon as the crime scene investigator has finalised his report, the lieutenant will forward you a copy. He will keep you up to speed as the various enquiries develop, and you will share any findings with him too, commissaire. For this case, I want the head honchos at number 36 to cooperate with complete transparency. Can I count on you? Lieutenant? Commissaire?"

Diament consented with a martial nod of the head. As for Capestan, she shrugged cheerily to show her agreement.

After the lieutenant had taken his leave, Capestan, who was rarely one to let things drop, returned to the question of why she was there.

"So," she said, turning to Buron. "Why us?"

The directeur motioned to her to follow him. They headed towards the body, which was now covered with a canvas sheet, and tugged on some paper overshoes. Perched on a ladder, a forensics officer was lifting fingerprints from a street sign. His colleague waited at the bottom, screwdriver in hand. The sign no longer read "rue Gassendi", but "rue Serge Rufus, 1949–2012, Bastard Commissaire".

Suddenly it was clear why Buron had called her.

3

Paul's turn in the limelight had not lasted. It had hardly been a long time ago, but he was still starting to get the impression that his star was fizzling out. Maybe it had already well and truly faded and no-one had bothered to tell him, leaving him like the spouse who is the last to find out when their partner cheats on them. At least that was how the unexpected call from a production company had left him feeling. A reality T.V. show was on the cards. Reality T.V. Next stop: oblivion.

Of course he had wavered, if only for a second. A long, humiliating second. Any prospect of a return to the big time held a powerful, Kaa-like allure. But Paul had quit the profession, that side of it anyway. True, the idea of a comeback appealed from time to time – if a real opportunity presented itself, no doubt he would handle things differently. But for now, he had a theatre to run and an army of stand-up comedians to keep in line.

Rolling up the sleeves of his beige shirt, he sat down at his desk to check his emails. There was a deluge from Hugo, one of his new recruits, whose desperation for praise could only be construed as part of a broader existential crisis. He bombarded him with messages. Paul sat deep in his chair, savouring a moment's peace before picking up the telephone. He rubbed his cheek and jaw with a mechanical motion to see whether his morning shave had been up to scratch.

As it so often did, his focus turned to the framed poster on the wall in front of him. He was twenty years younger. At his side were his two childhood friends and fellow members of The Donkeys, one of the most popular comedy trios of the 1990s.

They had shot to fame, some might say deservedly, through a blend of talent, hard work and luck. At the time, their success had seemed assured – eternal, even. It was the logical consequence of their teenage years, where the correct jeans and a few missing buttons had been enough to cement their cool-kid status. The comedy scene was essentially about replacing your pals, who would laugh at your jokes no matter what, with the paying public. A television deal followed, and before long it was all about the partying. Fame obeys its own rules. Little did he know that he would spend the rest of his life wondering what might have been if his fifteen minutes had only lasted a bit longer.

The Donkeys captured the spirit of the times. But the times changed, and before they knew it, it was all about stand-up. The trio split up. Paul had invested in a theatre, in the belief that he would always need a venue to perform in. Not so. He could barely cover his costs. People recognised him in the street; they just no longer paid to watch him perform. They would bang on about his old sketches, which they always seemed to get mixed up with other acts anyway. Audiences are like that – you think they love you, but their memory is short. Proof that, deep down, they don't really care at all.

Gradually, Paul had started booking undiscovered comedians, and one thing led to another. Even if they did remember which way their bread was buttered, the young bucks had a habit of looking down on him, convinced that their material was startlingly new, original and relevant. He had been exactly the same at their age.

Paul snapped out of his reverie. Time to call Hugo, that little brown-noser. At least his shows brought in a bit of cash. As Paul leaned forward to pick up his mobile, a text flashed up on the screen: *Hi. Are you at home?* It was his wife. His ex-wife, rather.

His eyes welled with unexpected tears. He sank back in his chair and caught his breath, trying to gather himself and make them go away. His jaw was clenched and the guilt came flooding back. He could not help glancing back at the mobile, staring at it as if it might talk to him and explain, as if it could make everything go away, or promise him another life.

When he left his wife a year earlier, he had cast off his last lifeline, his last friend. His rock. The only person he had ever loved.

Her absence haunted him, while her presence in the city tormented him. Her sweetness, her strength, her calibre; and then of course her face, her body, their nights together.

Leaving her had been harder than losing all his past glories. Before, he had felt overwhelmed by the currents; now, he was gasping for air on the sand.

He unlocked his telephone and with an uncertain, almost superstitious, motion he typed: *Yes.*

Then he waited.

When the three notes of the doorbell sounded, he could not suppress his smile.

4

Standing before the door, Capestan clenched her fists in the shelter of her pockets, almost willing it to stay shut. Of course, the news had to come from her. She had made no attempt to duck out of it, however hard she had to try to block out the untimely surge of anger inside her. Luckily, her sadness and empathy were overruling it for now.

So, she was about to see him again. And she was also about to see his new place (when he left her, he had played the true gentleman and let her keep their flat). To be fair, he had not *played* the true gentleman; he had *been* the true gentleman, as always. She knew full well that this apartment represented the final slice of a chunky – though depleted – family fortune. Paul had taken only his grandparents' furniture, along with the washing machine and the dishwasher. Not hard to read between those lines: I was the only one who used them anyway.

But then he had taken off at the first sign of trouble, citing a whole load of convenient, moralistic prattle. It was the day she had shot that scumbag dead – she had let off her weapon before, but only to injure – leaving her career in tatters. She had shown no remorse and refused to pass comment, reluctant to justify her actions, least of all go into detail about what had actually happened. A few minutes later, Paul had left.

Capestan heard the sound of footsteps. She tensed up. Everything around her faded away.

The door opened to reveal the most handsome man she had ever seen. Her husband. Paul was dazzling. It was as if all the light in the city radiated out from within him. He was a firework, while all around him were L.E.D.s. His mother had never been able to conceal her pride when she saw him: "His father and I weren't too far off: we chose Newman's first name, but he ended up a dead ringer for Redford!" To which his shady father would say: "Yup, he sure looks like an actor." Soon enough, the compliments subsided and the pride was notable only by its absence.

The very same father who had died earlier that day. Murdered. And it fell to Capestan to pass on the news.

Paul's smile, as he opened the door, vanished the moment he saw her stony expression. She was only there as a messenger and the news she brought was deathly serious. The long-awaited reunion was to be cool and heavy.

"Hi. Can I come in for a minute?" she said, breaking the ice.

He hesitated momentarily then made as if to kiss her on the cheek, before Capestan's stiffness made him reconsider. Instead, he moved aside to let her through in silence. She squeezed past him, noting the familiar musk of his Kiehl's aftershave.

"Thank you."

Capestan stepped into the apartment and – more as a matter of pride than politeness – resisted the urge to make a sweeping glance of his new digs.

"It would be better if we sat down, if you don't mind."

Something about her tone and the unusual nature of this first encounter in a year reinforced Paul's suspicion that something was up. He knew his wife well enough to be absolutely sure that she was not playing with him. He offered her the sofa and took the armchair opposite. Capestan sat down without taking off her coat. As she clasped her hands together, her eyes darted down to the scar on her left index finger.

She was looking for a way in, for the right phrase. Her line of work meant she was no stranger to these sorts of situations. But never with Paul. He was watching her patiently, with an almost military air about him. He looked resigned and hardened, ready to absorb any shock. Capestan felt awful for him. She heard her voice working of its own accord, harsher than she would have wanted:

"I have some terrible news, Paul. Your father . . ."

She looked down for a second, and when she raised her eyes, Paul already knew. He was just waiting for confirmation. She gave it to him.

"He was murdered this morning."

Paul sank back in his chair and stared at a point beneath the coffee table. The palm of his right hand stroked the brown leather of the armrest. Drifting between the effect of the news, his regrets and the need to keep a strong front, he refrained from reacting at all. His legs were shaking slightly. Capestan pretended not to notice.

To avoid watching her husband suffer, or pressurising him with eye contact, she took her chance to check out the decor. As expected, the apartment was warm, masculine and cheerful. An enormous oak bookcase dominated one wall of the sitting room, full to bursting with books, comics, D.V.D.s, rugby trophies, action-figures and small drawings, mainly seaside scenes, scattered around at random.

There was no table in the dining area, but a relatively tidy desk, and behind it a well-appointed open-plan kitchen.

Despite the solemnity of the situation, Capestan was still a police detective. A sort of automatic probe was retrieving information, scanning the surroundings and analysing the data. And nothing in this large room suggested the presence of a woman, nor a newborn or soon-to-be-born. No indication that he was even receiving visitors. Paul seemed single. Capestan felt a strange joy flood into her stomach and flush out the bitter remnants of her anger. It would be back soon enough. She resented this joy. She hated herself for feeling it in the first place.

In the kitchen, the corner of a back-to-front frame poking out from behind the big dresser caught her attention. She recognised it from a past so distant that it seemed improbable. It was a collage she had made for Paul's thirtieth. It was one metre by two, and 3D. A compilation of photographs, cinema tickets, pebbles, concert stubs, seagull feathers and other little tokens of their jaunts together. Back then, he was a star who wanted for nothing, and presents had ceased to excite him. But this unhangable object had rooted him to the spot. It had made him so happy. No-one had ever made him anything. Fifteen years later, Anne still wondered why he had been so taken by it. Both of them were bashful in the extreme and would never have dreamed of advertising their relationship in such a way, so the collage had spent years in hiding in their various apartments. But they could never bring themselves to chuck it, or even put it in the cellar.

In spite of everything, she felt herself softening, and looked back at Paul. His golden locks flopped down over his honey-coloured eyes.

He was not crying.

If she had been in his shoes, she would not have shed a tear for that man either. Yet his features were drawn with grief and his jaw was clenched.

Perhaps Anne was meant to say something. Perhaps she should have consoled him; perhaps she wanted to. But she stayed where she was, choosing to hold back.

He stared at her, seeming to search for a word or phrase before giving up too. In the end, he heaved himself out of his chair and headed for the kitchen where he filled up the water in his machine and grabbed two cups.

"Coffee?"

"Yes, thanks."

Silence was clustering around the room, stifling the space and putting up barricades between them. The vestiges of their love flitted about like ghosts. They could not find the words because the words no longer existed.

Paul set the cup down on the coffee table in front of her along with half a sugar lump and a teaspoon, before returning to his chair to drink his own.

After a long while stirring his coffee, he took the initiative.

"You're not leading the investigation?"

The underlying aggression, along with the resignation, in his tone did not escape the commissaire. She kept it brief.

"Yes."

He let out a short sigh and drained his coffee.

"You didn't like him."

The circumstances demanded a degree of tact, but there was no point denying an undisputable truth.

"No."

"Don't dishonour him."

Capestan instinctively nodded in agreement, then regretted it straight away. Keeping that promise would be impossible.

5

Capestan had no intention of dragging her feet over this case, much less letting another team solve it on her behalf, leaving her the honour of turning up at Paul's in her jackboots to reveal the murderer's identity, which would inevitably involve sharing a long catalogue of his father's enemies and misdemeanours.

She was already thinking about the crime scene, or more precisely her analysis of it. The body on its side, knees bent, bullet wound to the forehead, arms behind his back. The murderer had made Serge Rufus kneel before looking him in the eye and shooting him. Zero pity. Proof of a hunger for power and revenge, or was it the cold indifference of the sociopath? Then there was the sadistic embellishment of the street sign.

They were looking for a dangerous, determined killer.

Back at the crime scene, Capestan had also registered the many police officers milling around, ready to pick them apart later. Dozens of them, all with enormous archives at their disposal, computers loaded up with the latest software, and easy access to warrants. They had the bit between their teeth and a B.R.I. legend to avenge. Capestan was going to have to rally her troops like never before.

The clack of the door when she entered the commissariat chimed perfectly with the sound of the cue ball striking a red. But not everyone was idling in the snooker room; some were through in the sitting room, where Rosière was instructing Lebreton and Lewitz as they erected a two-metre-high Christmas tree next to the fireplace. She was being indecisive, and had been for some time if the weary expressions of her hauliers were anything to go by. Merlot, slumped on the sofa with a magazine in one hand and a glass in the other, was encouraging their industriousness with a series of carefully thought-through remarks.

"The base is wobbly, my friends, shore it up, shore it up! I have a good eye for this. Must my sense of decorum suffer – "

"Suffer?! If only it suffered in silence from time to time," Rosière muttered, her head tilted to one side to gauge the effect of the branches in the mirror. "There, that's perfect! The lights will reflect and it'll look magnificent."

"Precisely as I said," Merlot said. "Hold fire, I have here an article of the utmost interest on the – "

"Excuse me, Merlot," Capestan interrupted. They did not have any time to lose. "Something's come up. Lewitz, can you gather the troops, please?"

Lewitz headed to the door into the snooker room and poked his head inside:

"Team meeting."

He returned alongside Dax and Évrard, with Torrez following a few steps behind.

"So what's the news?" Rosière said, her chubby fingers counting the patron saint medals that were resting on her sizeable upper body. "A transfer to the back of beyond? An opportunity to stand in for the moving targets down at the shooting range?"

The commissaire waved at Rosière to rein in the sarcasm.

"There was a murder this morning in the fourteenth arrondissement, and we've been given partial control of the investigation."

A guilty rush of misplaced glee ran around the officers. Sure, a man was dead; but then none of them knew him, and a fresh case would do their status no end of good. Only Rosière applied any scrutiny to Capestan's words.

"What do you mean by 'partial'?" the capitaine asked.

"Crim. are taking the lead and the B.R.I. are helping out. We – "

" – we're the dogsbodies who get made to feel like traitors all day long. Fine, I see how it is. I'll sit this one out, thank you," Rosière said, before scooping up a cardboard box full of baubles.

"Eva . . ." Capestan started.

"She's right," Lebreton said with a resigned shrug.

"Plus when we do start investigating, it'll turn out to be another inside job . . ." Évrard said, smiling sadly.

The excitement was already long gone. Not surprising, really. For a while now, any dealings with number 36 had been met with a barrage of insults. One guy had even spat a few inches from Évrard's trainers. If the rest of the team had not rallied round her, she would definitely have slipped back into depression and joined the long roll-call of absentees. They always came back, but the disappointment clung to them like ticks on a tired dog.

Merlot, after taking a deep breath to revive his vigour, brandished his magazine:

"As it happens, I was reading an exceptional article in *Marie Claire*. Listen here: 'Animals lend their sense of smell to science and the police.' That's the title," he said, by way of clarification for Dax and Lewitz. 'Pigs have a higher number of olfactory receptors than humans, dogs and mice, according to a recent study. This

33

gift is put to good effect in Israel and the United States to root out drugs, weapons and landmines. French customs officers are trialling pigs from Brittany.' And that's not all! It goes on: 'Trained to detect the odours of gunpowder and drugs, five rats have entered the ranks of the police in Rotterdam, Holland.' Rats and pigs! Honestly! Can you imagine such a thing?"

A dismayed Capestan looked on as everyone resumed their trivial activities as if nothing had happened. They had given up without so much as hearing her out. A few bits of bunting was all they had to show from this sustained period of empty-headed torpor. They were wallowing.

"Imagine them in which investigation, Merlot? You all seem quite content slithering about in your leisure centre like earthworms. Police rats for who? I don't see any police around here!"

"Commissaire – "

"What? You're a whisker away from turning up in your pyjamas! I'm warning you, either you listen to this brief, or I'm closing the commissariat. You can lounge about in the café downstairs like everyone else."

Her voice was shot through with anger – the pressures of the day were starting to take their toll. Now she had got them listening, she just needed to pique their interest, while maintaining an air of authority.

"Buron gave us the call-up for sound reasons. We won't be working *for* Crim.; we'll be working *in tandem* with Crim. I don't know if a policeman did it, Évrard, but what I do know is that the victim is a policeman. You'll know him, no doubt, at least by reputation: Serge Rufus."

Now she had their attention. They focused on the whiteboard

that had been pushed aside to make way for the Christmas tree. She picked up the marker pen, removed the lid and wrote "Serge Rufus" in big letters, before turning to her team to get the meeting properly underway. She had to keep the momentum going to avoid losing them.

"Prior to retiring, Serge Rufus was one of the top commissaires in the Brigade Antigang. Now, we know that number 36 will do everything in their power to defend their colleague and pulverise anyone who stands in their way. They look out for their own. Our job is to fly the Swiss flag and remain entirely neutral. And maybe explore leads that the people at H.Q. – deliberately or not – might choose to neglect."

"Will we have access to the same info. as the others?" Évrard asked.

"In theory, yes . . . a B.R.I. officer has been tasked with ensuring all developments are shared between each department."

"So if we solve the case before our high-and-mighty colleagues, that would go down as a win?" Évrard asked, ever the incorrigible gambler.

"A thrashing, I'd say!" Merlot said, reassuring his partner.

"A pasting!" Rosière added, more to make amends than to amuse the others.

Everyone gathered round to hear the rest of the details. Merlot was already occupying the best part of the sofa with his usual expansiveness, while Évrard, Dax and Lewitz squeezed in along-side. Lebreton stayed standing, back to the wall, and Rosière had pulled up her padded armchair to close the circle, the dog keeping guard at her feet. Torrez was sitting on a stool in the corridor, leaning forward to keep track of the discussion.

"We're obviously not organised-crime experts, so we are starting with a handicap. If this does turn out to be a settling of scores from the Brigade Antigang's past, we won't have the case history to hand, nor will we have the same understanding of the terrain. But as we've seen before, we do have some – more unexpected – talents, right?" Capestan said, trying to breathe a bit of pride back into the group.

"Yes, we do!" Dax blurted out, slapping his pal Lewitz on the thigh.

The sound of the buzzer interrupted this sudden surge of ambition. Lebreton crossed the room to welcome their visitor. When he opened the door, he was surprised to discover a figure on the landing that towered even higher than he did. It was not every day that he had to look upwards to make eye contact with someone. The figure in question was standing bolt upright, and would have taken up the entire doorframe if he had decided to come inside. As it was, he simply introduced himself and held out an envelope:

"Lieutenant Diament, Varappe Division. Here is a copy of the facts pertaining to the Rufus case. We're still waiting on the autopsy and ballistics reports, but here you have the photographs of his residence, a summary of the door-to-door enquiries, and the records of a few suspects. I'll keep you updated."

Without any further ceremony, the lieutenant performed an about-turn straight off the parade ground, then pressed the button to call the lift, ignoring Lebreton, who raised his eyebrows and settled for a "Thank you", before calmly closing the door.

Back in the sitting room, everyone had turned to face him. Dax and Lewitz were in hysterics:

"Did you hear that guy?! 'Varappe Division' – it sounded like a fart! Hey," the latter said, holding out his hand. "Brigadier Lewitz, Ping Pong Division."

His friend shook his hand.

"Lieutenant Dax, Nintendo Division."

"I'm Évrard, Long Division," the lieutenant said, numbers on the mind as usual.

"Merlot, Gut-Rot Division!" the capitaine said, in a rare show of self-abasement.

The four of them fell about laughing, red in the face, as Lebreton brought the envelope over to Capestan. She opened it and glanced through the documents inside, passing them around the team. As she did so, a yellow Post-it on one of the final sheets caught her attention.

Someone had scribbled on it: *Why don't you go and comfort the son and leave the case to the grown-ups.* A sudden surge of anger overcame Capestan and her cheeks burned. Her heart rate went into overdrive and she had to breathe through her nose to suppress the blazing fury. She scrumpled up the note and continued studying the file with her mind split in two: one part analysing the information, the other smarting at the humiliation and already plotting her revenge.

"The telephone records start in June and finish in August. Is that it?" Lebreton said with surprise.

The last three months were indeed missing. Same for the bank statements. Every document had been gutted of all significant content.

"No. I get the impression that the go-betweens aren't going to excel at fair play," the commissaire said, trying to tone down the aggression in her voice. "No matter. We don't need them to think, and we can fill in any gaps on our own. Even so, there's plenty of info. for us to make a start. So, we've got Serge Rufus shot dead: bullet between the eyes; middle of the street; hands cuffed behind his back. Even if the autopsy report isn't ready yet, extensive bruising on his face suggests that he'd been beaten, maybe even tortured. For thrills? For revenge? To get him to talk?"

She did not know the answer, but Capestan was sure of one thing: whatever methods were used, it was extremely unlikely that anyone managed to extract a single word from that man.

"Rue Gassendi might not be the busiest street, but there are still far too many people around – day and night – for him to have been beaten up outdoors. Unless it happened in the Montparnasse Cemetery just over the road? Then they took him to the pavement outside his flat, specifically to shoot him. The blood stains are unambiguous – they pulled the trigger there, in front of the sign. Burn marks around the bullet's entry point would appear to indicate the use of a silencer. Even without the ballistics report, we can hedge our bets on a 9mm. The cuffs aren't standard-issue for the French police, they're Ukrainian," the commissaire said, holding up a different sheet. "Both the method and the apparatus have led Crim. to suspect the members of a gang based in Kiev. Three years ago, Serge stuck two of their guys behind bars and a third in intensive care. The last one never got out. This lot have a reputation for harbouring bitter grudges. The B.R.I., however, is not discounting other leads or gangs. Serge and his men have upset a lot of people, all of them nasty pieces of work. Of course, this needs to be taken with a pinch of salt bearing in mind where it's come from."

Crim. and the B.R.I. were always going to max out the organised-crime route. It would take months – even for two or three groups – to trace everything back, study timelines and list potential mercenaries. Capestan's squad was never going to compete with them on that front. They would have to focus their efforts elsewhere.

First up, there was the street sign. Not a single mention anywhere in Diament's paperwork. Hardly revealing in itself – the assumption had to be that number 36 would look into it further down the line. Weapons, blood, vendettas . . . high drama first, anything out of the ordinary second. The sign was there to mark the ending, to provoke fear, to make the victim sweat. There were plenty of sadists in the organised-crime world, but this ironic, stylised touch hinted at a certain refinement, a wry premeditation, that were not the hallmarks of your average mafioso. This plan had needed a thinking cap, albeit a sick one.

"At the crime scene," Capestan said, returning to the board and pointing her pen at one of the photographs lying on the coffee table, "someone had removed the street sign and switched it with another bearing the name of the victim, his dates and his profession: 'Bastard Commissaire.'"

"When was the sign put up?" Évrard asked in her soft voice.

"No idea. The cemetery is right there – maybe there'll be C.C.T.V."

"Let's ask the Varappe guys. They'll be able to yank the cameras down with their Spiderman web-shooters!" Lewitz said, slapping Dax on the thigh.

"We'll definitely ask if they have any footage. Number 36 might pass it on to us once they're done with it."

"The killer knew the stiff's date of birth . . . that's something, isn't it?" Rosière said.

"Yes, you're right, that is odd. Dax," Capestan said, turning to the lieutenant, who was still looking very chuffed about his Spiderman comment, "can you check online and see how readily available this information is on the Internet, or whether you have to hack into official sites to get it?"

"Where can you get a sign like that made?" Lebreton asked, peeling himself away from the wall. "A D.I.Y. shop? A printer's? A website?"

Rosière was flicking back and forth through the documents.

"The victim's wife died several years ago," she said after a while, "but he had a son: Paul Rufus. I can't find a statement from him. Has anyone told him yet? They don't seem to have questioned him."

Capestan lowered her head and gazed at the tips of her boots. It was time to tell them the real reason they had been assigned this case, not to mention come clean about the potential conflict of interest that might cloud her judgement at any moment. She sighed. There was nothing she hated more than revealing even the smallest detail about her personal life. She was all about discretion and a keenly guarded sense of privacy – years in the police spent rummaging through other people's lives had made sure of that. Here, honesty had to prevail over her secretive nature. The commissaire looked up and said blankly:

"It was me – I told the son. Paul Rufus is my ex-husband. Which makes the victim my former father-in-law."

For a few moments the room was dominated by a collective flutter of poorly disguised glances.

"Well, that's great!" Évrard said, immediately regretting her outburst. "No, sorry, that's not what I meant. It's just that in terms of information, backstory and perspective, we'll have a massive advantage over the competition . . ."

"In a way," Capestan said.

"What was he like, then, this super-cop? Clean? Bent?"

The commissaire felt her gaze drift out the window. She would not have gone so far as saying "corrupt", no, but there was definitely some shady conduct. Although, back then, her attention had been on other things. On other people.

6

École Nationale Supérieure de la Police de
Saint-Cyr-au-Mont-d'Or, Rhône, February, 1992

"Capestan, Commissaire Buron has saved your arse after yet
another screw-up and I've got no idea why. Maybe he's taken a
shine to it. Not me, though. An order's an order, and I expect it to
be obeyed."

"No disrespect, commissaire, but your orders – as with your
insinuations – sometimes seem inappropriate."

It was said without any insolence, nor the slightest timidity. At
barely nineteen, Capestan was by far the youngest in her year, and
despite excelling at pretty much everything, she had some way to
go when it came to diplomacy. She knew she should be better at
holding her tongue, and reproached herself frequently, albeit
never for long. Those were the kinds of skills she would have plenty
of time to work on when she was fully fledged. Anyway, Serge
Rufus, the most objectionable of her instructors, left little room
for manoeuvre. Either you let him squash you or you stood up for
yourself: there was no room for half measures.

The two of them were crossing the training ground, making
for the sliding security gates at the entrance. Seeing the vast earth
embankment stretching out before them, Capestan searched for a
way out of this wearisome conversation.

"I don't care much for your tone, Capestan. I'm not your

primary school maths teacher – I don't take kindly to being heckled by piss-artists at the back of the class."

Rufus's last sentence fell on deaf ears. Capestan was no longer aware he even existed. As the light suddenly transformed into a Texan sunset, Anne was spellbound by the arrival of a demi-god in a thick navy turtleneck and Carhartt jacket. As he walked straight towards her, their smiles broadened together, already free of any doubt. When he was just a metre away, he stopped. Capestan stopped. Serge Rufus stopped.

"Hi, papa," the demi-god said.

"Paul, what the hell are you doing here?" the commissaire spat.

He was the son of a shit like Rufus. The realisation dampened the mood like a cold shower, but not for long, as every last drop evaporated in the warmth of Paul's eyes. Paul. He handed his father a folded piece of paper.

"From your informer. He didn't want to give his name. It seemed urgent, a meeting or something. Given the welcome, though," he said, turning to Capestan, "maybe I'll give it to your colleague instead. She's much more smiley . . ."

Capestan's mind was already miles away. Her endorphins were running wild and she was too stunned to speak, think, react in any way, let alone take the piece of paper from him. In that split second she had waited nineteen long years to experience, Anne fell in love with an angel-eyed poser, a gleaming, superhuman show-off with the puffed-up ego of a peacock.

Serge checked Paul's movement. She saw a flash of fear in the son's eyes, the automatic recoil of his wrist and a tensing of his jaw. Capestan's brain kicked back into action. Party over. Serge Rufus was a brute, and no-one would be more aware of that fact than his son.

7

"He ordered it off this site," Dax said, pointing at the screen.

The flashing website that he had just hacked promoted, among other things, custom-made pint glasses for the newly retired and mugs with badly framed, heart-shaped photographs. The street sign page offered a wide variety of materials and inscriptions: *New Baby Boulevard, Strictly No Moaners, Just Married Street*, etc. But there was another section where you could type in your own message. To announce a murder, for example, and terrify your victim in the process.

"Can you see if he left a delivery address?" Capestan said, knowing already that the killer would never have been so stupid.

"Oh yeah, of course!" Dax said, who would have done the same in his shoes.

The young boxer thumped the keyboard and scrunched up his nose, willing the pages to load faster. No-one was ever quite sure what Dax would strike upon, least of all Dax. This I.T. whizz had left a lot of brain in the boxing ring. His technical skills were intact, but it was still safe to stay by his side to focus his efforts. That said, Capestan did not want to be patronising, so just before returning to her desk she threw out one last request.

"If you know how to find a credit card number or some bank

records, maybe another transaction or two, then go right ahead. Pile up the data and we'll whittle it down later. Happy hunting!"

The lieutenant shuddered with delight and grinned at his desktop. It was no "Call of Duty", but it wasn't far off.

Get one over on the big dogs at number 36, catch the killer, then deliver the news gently to Paul. Capestan was desperate to do her duty. A mixture of determination and sorrow was threatening to overwhelm her, so she let the adrenaline guide her research as she kept tabs on the team. After all, the last thing they needed on top of their other setbacks was a gloomy boss.

The front door clicked open and Rosière's dog, short of leg but full of gusto, flew in and made straight for Merlot's crotch. The capitaine let out a hiccup of surprise as the hound's mistress boomed across the room:

"Pilou, for Christ's sake, don't be so vulgar! Hey! What is that?"

A rat with brown fur, no doubt piqued by the dog's intervention, poked his head out from the capitaine's jacket pocket, whiskers twitching from side to side in search of an explanation. Merlot stroked him reassuringly with the back of his hand.

"This is my rat. I'm training him up for active duty."

The dog, remembering his place, trotted back to his mistress's high heels. Rosière, bedecked in a gold-trimmed, plum-coloured winter coat that served to upgrade her from buxom to virtually boundless, gritted her teeth and gulped. Then, desperate to focus both her eyes and thoughts elsewhere, she performed a half-turn and presented a cardboard box from under her arm as though it were a holy relic.

"An advent calendar from chez Mazet! Hope you've got a sweet tooth, children! Cost me twenty bucks, but it's the best. Be warned, though – first person I catch munching a praline or a bonbon without my express permission will be unwrapping a slap the next day," she said with a menacing look at Merlot, who was already rubbing his hands.

She hung her coat on the brass hook attached to the wall behind her desk and sat down in her Empire elbow chair, scanning her immediate surroundings for a spot worthy of her latest glorious accoutrement, eventually settling on a narrow console to her right. Rosière meticulously centred the box, opening it up like a photograph frame to reveal row upon row of pretty, illustrated, minuscule doors. With a broad, satisfied smile, she turned to Capestan for an update.

"So, my darling, what's new? Any developments with Operation Ex-Father-in-Law?"

Despite – or maybe because of – the casual tone, the "darling" could not suppress a smile.

"We're still waiting on the autopsy and ballistics reports. Torrez is studying what we have of the victim's accounts, and Lewitz is on telephone records. Dax has just found the website that the sign came from – it's the only one that offers the enamelled model in the right size and colour. He's poking around backstage to see what's in the customer baskets."

"There's a shop in passage du Grand-Cerf which is a registered parcel-collection point," Dax said, jabbing a thick finger at a page with Google Maps.

"Good work, lieutenant," Capestan said as she stood up.

Lebreton gave an appreciative nod and instinctively smoothed down his black jacket before wandering over to the screen.

"It's really close. Shall we get down there?" he asked Capestan.

"Yes, you go ahead. I have to stay here to greet our 'liaison officer'."

With a tenth of a smile at Rosière, his usual partner, Lebreton twitched the scar that ran down his cheek. The capitaine was already on her feet and putting her coat on. Pilou began pirouetting like a dog that had not seen daylight for three long minutes, his tail fanning the air, the wooden desk, the waste-paper basket and anything else it came into contact with. He only settled down when he saw Rosière standing there holding his lead.

Capestan was back over with Dax looking for the date of the order.

"Order placed anonymously October 5, delivery October 20," she called to the others before they left.

"That's one premeditated murder. What about payment?"

"Disposable prepaid card."

"Oh yeah, like phonecards for mobiles," Rosière said. "I remember them cooking up that scheme for credit cards, too, the idiots. As if the police didn't have enough crap on their plates. Here, guys! Who wants to buy some dodgy stuff without any trace whatsoever? 'Your trusty bank – here to help you commit fraud more easily.' Bloody hell, I've had it. Now we have to hope our gun-slinger went to pick up the parcel in person and that the owner remembers him. Shame it isn't super-recent . . ."

As Rosière and Lebreton made their way out of the commissariat, Lewitz joined Capestan in the sitting room. He was holding the sheet of telephone records. A few of the numbers were underlined.

"Seems Rufus wasn't much of a chatterbox. The calls are never longer than two or three minutes and, to be honest, there aren't

47

many in the first place. Anyway, I looked into the recurring ones: a G.P., a kidney specialist and a dentist, then there's his shooting club, the house of his former colleague, Léon, and one Madame Georges, who was his cleaner. I called her up for some questions, and she confirmed that no, he wasn't very talkative, but that he was fairly straight-up. He didn't go out much, watched T.V. for much of the day, never saw people. There are also several calls to his son, Paul Rufus, but they always hung up after a second. Can't have been too rosy a relationship," Lewitz said, somewhat embarrassed. "The only number that sticks out is this one," he added, pointing to a mobile number. "It belongs to a Denis Vérone. Reckon it's the actor?"

Denis Vérone was one of the members of Paul's old comedy group. His career had really taken off. Rufus must have resorted to getting in touch via a roundabout route.

"Yes, he's an old friend of the son. Right. The most recent date will be the most revealing. Dax will try and get his hands on them when he's finished with the sign."

A blast on the doorbell, so brief it was almost insulting, rang across the room. Diament. Capestan went to let him in.

He held out some documents without even a hint of a smile.

"The B.R.I. has remanded two suspects in custody," he said. "I've included the details. We'll be looking to conclude things very quickly now."

If he had anything to do with it, at least. After closing the door to the sound of the lift opening, Capestan rested her forehead against the frame. Two suspects in custody already. Her squad had barely warmed up and number 36 were ready to wind up the case there and then. Her anger lodged in her throat. The door opened again, forcing Capestan to step back.

This time it was Orsini, the old-school capitaine who was chummy with journalists the length and breadth of France, keeping them happy with a constant flow of police misdemeanours. He was just back from a long weekend.

"Good morning, capitaine. Was your trip a success? You timed it well – we have a new case."

"Good morning. Yes, lovely, thank you," Orsini replied, summoning all the enthusiasm he could muster.

He carefully folded his trench-coat over his forearm, clearly intrigued.

"About this case, then?"

8

Leading up from the Fontaine des Innocents, the ever-bustling rue Saint-Denis, once famous for its sex shops, was jam-packed with vintage stores and stalls selling trainers. Only a few flashing signs remained, as if to keep up appearances or to humour the tourists, or the Sunday-morning pervs who had supposedly popped out for the croissants. After walking down it at a lick, Louis-Baptiste Lebreton and Eva Rosière were now crossing rue Turbigo, entering a new arrondissement. Here, the naughty shops had made way for chichi little hipster cafés. Before long they were at passage du Grand-Cerf, an arcade that led to the Montorgeuil neighbourhood. Recently done up, and graced with one of the highest glass roofs in Paris, the Grand-Cerf was a hidden gem filled with characterful old shops, whose giant signs – including an elephant, some spectacles and even a giant papier mâché crab – traced a journey outside time. Lebreton loved this spot. His husband, Vincent, had run a tiny firm of architects there. This was a special time and place where his love could live on.

The Christmas decorations and bright lights, which at that time of year only accentuated the beauty of the place, stoked the fire of the commandant's grief. This would be his first Christmas as a widower. The rising tide of festive cheer and frenetic activity was closing in on Lebreton from all sides. He was desperate to skip December and go straight to January, when he would crawl like a castaway onto the first bit of beach before collapsing on dry land. That way he could resume winter without having to grit his teeth through the family gathering. But no, there was no avoiding this wretched season, and he would just have to wait before he could resume the steady rhythm of his daily suffering.

Late in the autumn though it was, a celestial light still tumbled through the glass overhead, bathing the passage in a peaceful atmosphere. Only the footsteps on the chequerboard floor and the muffled voices of the odd passer-by reached the ears of the silent police officers. They stopped in front of the shop mentioned by Dax. It was closed, contrary to the opening hours supplied by the lieutenant.

"Well, we should have seen that coming," an exasperated Rosière said. "A cock-up from Dax – surely not . . ."

Lebreton studied the sticker in the window.

"It's O.K., they're opening in fifteen minutes."

"Fine. Hold the phone, those cushions are gorgeous!" Rosière said, before disappearing into the shop opposite. The bell rang and, with an exasperated sigh, the commandant followed his colleague inside.

They re-emerged several minutes later, Lebreton armed with two plastic bags of multicoloured cushions, narrowly missing a chirpy little girl whizzing past on her scooter, relishing this dreamy cut-through as her mother waved at her to slow down. Each with a broad smile, the officers stepped into the parcel pick-up point just as the owner was opening up.

He welcomed them with a broad smile full of false teeth, topped with a carefully sculpted brown moustache. The man sold nothing but socks, so every customer was key, especially those with a demonstrable appetite for retail therapy.

"Good morning," Rosière said, presenting her I.D. "We're here to congratulate you on your memory, hopefully. About a month back, a package from persorigolo.com was sent here for collection. It was pretty heavy and about this size," she said, holding her hands fifty centimetres apart. "Any chance you remember the person who picked it up?"

The shopkeeper wore a cunning, enigmatic expression as he answered:

"I'm not sure . . . It was a long time ago . . . Maybe . . . Maybe I'll need some help to jog my memory . . ."

Rosière stared at him for a moment, incredulous, smiling before letting out a sharp peal of laughter.

"Am I imagining it or does this guy think this is 'Starsky and Hutch'? He's got the vintage cardie, alright . . . A barefaced attempt at bribery! You don't see that in the box sets nowadays – I should know! No," she said, wiping away a tear, "I think first you'll carry out your duty as a citizen, then you can enjoy the rest of the episode. It's the one where Starsky goes through your accounts with a veeeeery fine-toothed comb."

Outraged that his perfectly legitimate request had met with such ridicule, the shopkeeper turned to Lebreton, as if appealing to him to witness this cruel injustice. The commandant eased into his good-cop role, the one who treats the well-intentioned with respect and offers them the chance to restore their dignity.

"Forgive my colleague, I think she might have misunderstood. And she is prone to overreaction," he said with a glance at Rosière, imploring her to take it easy. "You strike me as a man who picks up on each and every detail. Of course you'll need some time to gather your memories. Just let me know when you feel your concentration is at its peak."

Lebreton took out his notebook and a pen, then stared at the man with a serious expression. He was hoping that this about-turn would be enough to mend any damage done by Rosière, whose quivering lips suggested she was a whisker away from all-out hysterics. If the man lost his temper, he would refuse to play ball and there would be no way to get him to cooperate. The officers would go away with nothing but a bit of faint amusement.

Thankfully, the shopkeeper raised a hand to his forehead to help himself focus. The commandant had presented him with an honourable way out, and he felt inclined to repay him with some information.

"Yes, a man did come. Darkish hair, medium build and weight. He had square glasses with thick lenses. Beard, fairly long hair at the back – quite early '80s in style."

"Do you know a wig when you see one?"

"No, it was real," the main said with a confident nod.

"This is great, thank you. Can you come by the commissariat later to do an e-fit?"

The man puffed with pride, delighted to be of service.

"If you think that will be necessary, then of course. The shop closes at four o'clock today. I could come straight after that?"

"Perfect, thank you very much," Lebreton said, scribbling the address on a page from his notebook and handing it to him. "See you then."

The commandant touched Rosière's elbow, ushering her to the door. She had had to turn towards the shelves of socks as her sniggering got the better of her.

She was sitting on the *métro* fidgeting with the new passport she had just picked up from the préfecture. The photograph was fine, even if it did make her look almost transparent. Surname: Évrard; first name: Blanche. White, but blank, too. Was it a premonition, or was it her parents' way of keeping their young love free of any obstacles? She often wondered what had brought them to christen her with a name that only accentuated her colourless character, erasing what little sense of self she had in the first place. Évrard sighed. She was making progress, though. The passport, her first ever, was proof of this. At last, the noise around her was starting to get quieter.

On the seat opposite, a middle-aged woman had been staring at a scratch card for six stops. As long as she left it untouched, anything was possible and all her problems might disappear. So she made it last. How could it be that so many people's sole hope resided in a tiny piece of cardboard whose single purpose was to inflict defeat?

You know the answer to that, Blanche. Stop thinking about it right now. But the recovering gambler in her was desperate to find out the numbers lurking beneath the silver.

9

A few hours later, Évrard walked into the small room where Dax was working on the e-fit along with the witness. The shopkeeper did not even notice the newcomer.

"How about the eyes, bigger or smaller?" the lieutenant asked, his hand on the mouse.

"A bit bigger. But then he did have deceptively thick lenses."

The man was choosing his words with a lot of care, as though he had registered that Dax might not be the brightest spark. He seemed eager to get it over and done with.

"Does this seem like a good resemblance, sir? We can move onto the nose if you're happy?"

Évrard found Dax attentive and amiable, as always. He applied himself. She skirted round the desk to look at the screen and immediately understood the witness's reservations. Ever the bluffer, she managed to ask the lieutenant for an explanation without betraying her emotions.

"Do you consider this system more reliable?"

Dax, concentrating hard on his portrait, answered without looking up from the screen.

"The Police Judiciaire refused to give us any e-fit software. Apparently it costs a bomb. So I set up an account on this. First twenty levels are free, you see. Working well, wouldn't you say? Realistic, no?"

Leaning in for a closer look, Évrard was inclined to agree.

"Seems spot-on to me."

In the sitting room, Capestan was thumbing through the article from *La Provence*.

"This is extraordinary! It can't be a coincidence."

"No," Orsini said. "The M.O. is too close, as are the dates."

The staging of Jacques Maire's murder in L'Isle-sur-la-Sorgue had the same complexion as Commissaire Rufus's in more ways than one. It was now up to them to scrutinise this killing and find the link between the victims.

When Orsini brought this article to her attention, Capestan had been examining the profiles of the suspects that number 36 had just placed in custody. The weapon used to shoot Rufus had been used in the murder of a fence a few years back. At the time, the two men now under arrest had been questioned and released without charge. No clear link with Rufus, but Capestan did not think for a moment that she had all the documents at her disposal.

Orsini's article was a game-changer. This identical crime in Provence turned their inquiry on its head, giving the team a strategic advantage. How would they ram this home? Sharing the information was not just the honourable thing to do; it was the responsible option too. These were murder investigations, after all. Plus it would give them the chance to rub something in their rivals' faces for a bit. Keeping quiet, however, would let them get their noses well and truly in front. Tempting. So, should they tell Diament? Buron? Capestan barely had time to consider it. The telephone was blaring out. It was the landline with its particularly aggressive ring. Buron, no doubt. She excused herself with a nod to Orsini, who went back to his office to work on the lead.

It was indeed the directeur:

"Capestan, have you hacked into a business's website without permission from the public prosecutor and without covering your tracks?"

"Errr, that's not . . . impossible," the commissaire said, looking across the room at Dax.

"Not impossible? Not impossible? Did you or did you not give the order?"

"For the hack? Yes, absolutely. I was only hoping the break-in would be more discreet."

"Now there's a fine example of contrition and regret, Capestan! 'I didn't think I'd get busted.' You sound like a bloody teenager!"

"There's an element of that," the commissaire said with a grin.

"We won't be able to use any information you found. A formal complaint has been lodged, you know."

"We'll add that one to the pile . . . In the meantime, we've just hit on an interesting lead. The street sign sold on the site we hacked links Rufus's murder with that of another man in the Vaucluse. Same method."

This revelation nudged Buron's disgruntlement into the background.

"Go on."

Capestan summarised the article from *La Provence*. She also brought him up to speed on their findings relating to the enamel sign. She could sense the cogs turning in the directeur's head down the line.

"How did you make the link? Provence is a long way away. Cases like this are out of our jurisdiction."

"Orsini is an avid collector of press cuttings."

"True, I'd forgotten that."

"We're currently making up an e-fit, which I was intending to send over to Lieutenant Diament."

"No. As I've already said, any such e-fit will have been obtained illegally from a hacked website. I think it would be unwise to compromise all the teams' investigations, Capestan. Just yours is quite enough."

"What about the other case – do we hold onto that info. too or shall we play the game?"

"Hmmm, the other case . . . Listen: the B.R.I. and Crim. have their own lines of inquiry that are proceeding very nicely. Let's not spread ourselves too thinly. Look into that yourselves, for the time being."

"Monsieur le Directeur?"

"Yes, commissaire?"

"Are you going to come out with it straight away, or will I have to guess like last time?"

She could hear Buron's smile broadening into the receiver.

"There's nothing to guess, Capestan. This is simply about considering other leads and methods. At the moment, the B.R.I. are making like Scorsese – they've only got eyes for De Niro. At least your rabble brings a bit of variety."

"My rabble, as you insist on calling them, have – "

"Yes, yes, I know. By the way, you're getting a new recruit tomorrow."

"A new recruit?"

"D'Artagnan. He was let out of the psych. ward this weekend. He's one of yours, no doubt about it. He got a mention in the paperwork when your squad was set up."

D'Artagnan. Real name Henri Saint-Lô. His nickname stemmed from his belief that he had started his career as a musketeer to the king, making him immortal. Quite literally a man for the ages.

After hanging up, Capestan went to the kitchen to make a cup of tea. While the kettle was coming to the boil, she went to the terrace to join Lebreton who was sitting in a deckchair with his long legs stretched in front of him, smoking as he read the autopsy report.

"Anything?" she said.

"Nothing we didn't know already, apart from a bit more precision on the time of the murder: between 6.00 and 6.30 a.m. And yes, he was beaten up, with fists and with the butt of a pistol. One, maybe two people."

A squeak caught their attention. It was Merlot's rat, who was wiggling towards his bowl at the foot of the small rhododendron. The two officers watched as he took a few sips. Lebreton tapped his cigarette on the ashtray at his feet, and, between drags, said drily:

"It could have been a pig."

Capestan stared at the rodent for a few seconds.

"True, we did escape lightly," she agreed, before changing the subject. "We're going to have a meeting tomorrow morning, bright and early. Orsini has come across another murder with exactly the same M.O. as Rufus's. He's looking for additional info. and we're going to review it. The article is in the sitting room if you want to take a look in advance."

"Yes, of course. Just let me finish this first," Lebreton said, waving the autopsy report.

Back at her desk, steaming mug in hand, the commissaire began rummaging through her papers for the profile of the fabled musketeer. Eventually she found it and switched on her lamp to study it.

She was so engrossed in her reading that she did not hear Dax approaching, forcing the lieutenant to alert her of his presence by knocking her desk like it was a door. Standing tall with his shoulders straight, he handed her a document that he was clasping in both hands.

"The e-fit, commissaire. It's ready."

"Thank you, lieutenant," she said with a smile.

Her smile vanished the instant she set eyes on the image. The man did indeed have brown hair, a beard and glasses, and was an average height, but he was also covered in long green fur, and armed with a sword and scabbard. A speechless Capestan simply pointed at them as she glared at Dax.

"Oh, don't worry about those – that was just to give Évrard a laugh," the lieutenant said, squirming a little. "It's 'World of Warcraft'."

"'World of Warcraft'?"

"Well, since we don't have any Police Judiciaire software to make up e-fits, I used the system for creating avatars on 'World of Warcraft'. It's an online game set in a fantasy world. Come on, you must have heard of it? There are elves, orcs, gnomes . . . You can create some awesome characters! And because the shopkeeper couldn't remember what clothes the guy was wearing, I thought it might be funny . . . O.K., I'll redo the body. But I can't guarantee I'll find a shirt and trousers . . ."

"They didn't give you the software?"

"Nope."

Capestan – raging inside about this latest example of institutional miserliness, yet another insult from the powers-that-be – examined the picture a second time. Overall, the image screamed online video game, but the finish was strikingly realistic. Dax was surprising her more and more.

"It was an ingenious idea, lieutenant. Super work, well done."

Swelling with pride, Dax made to return to his station.

"Just one thing, though – you didn't delete your tracks after hacking into persorigolo.com, did you?"

"Well no, you didn't ask me to."

"True, true, I didn't specifically request that. Next time, though, especially for the telephone records – stay under the radar. Always. That must be your default setting."

"O.K., noted," Dax said, literally noting it on a Post-it to be stuck on the edge of his screen: *Delete illegal hacks always.*

Just the sort of aide-memoire you want lying around when a suit pops in for a visit.

Rosière, strapped in to a fluffy, mauve sheepskin dressing gown, placed the water bowl on her marble kitchen floor. The dog, somewhat disorientated by the change to the timetable, sniffed at the bowl for an explanation and, not finding one, stared at his mistress with one ear pricked up.

"Olivier's meant to be calling, but he's hopeless when it comes to figuring out the time difference . . ."

Olivier, Rosière's beloved son, after years cheering up the house with his happy-go-lucky presence, had moved to Tahiti. The end of the earth. Every time he called was a huge moment for her, and Rosière needed a clear mind to make the most of their conversation. She had received an email the day before to book in the chat on Skype. With her hair done up and a notepad and pen next to her Mac, Rosière was ready. Christmas was fast approaching, so she would need to note down the flight times so she could send her boy the tickets.

The computer beeped and she was online straight away. Her son's handsome face filled the screen and his smile, despite being slightly pixelated, lit up her sitting room.

"Hi, maman! How are you?"

"Fine, and you, sweetheart?"

Olivier was great, working like crazy, kite-surfing every morning. He looked well for it.

"So, when are you getting here?" Rosière asked.

"O.K., so, this year it could be tricky, maman. It's our busiest period – we have to bring in temps and everything. The physio. practice is open every day, except for the twenty-fourth and twenty-fifth. I can't turn down the work, you know? Otherwise they'll just replace me."

"Yes, of course, of course, don't worry, sweetheart. It's work, it's important," Rosière said, reassuring him despite her blank tone.

After a few awkward niceties, the conversation ground to a halt. Rosière put her Mac on standby and leaned down to stroke her dog. After a while, she scooped him up and held him in her arms.

Not for the first time, she wondered if it was better never to have known true happiness, or to have experienced it in all its perfection, only to be crushed at moments like this.

10

"Fair maidens and young squires, the heralds were not mistaken – I am here!" the man announced in a tone that was genuinely swaggering rather than theatrical.

Short and sharp, he had removed his felt hat on entrance and was observing the assembled officers from the doorway. He wore a sardonic smile as he twizzled his moustache, before greeting them with a slow bow.

"I wish you good day and beg of you – once and for all – do not address me as D'Artagnan. My name is Saint-Lô."

A stunned silence fell over the team. No-one had heralded anything – they were simply getting ready for their meeting when the appearance of this sudden, excessive character had stopped them all in their tracks.

The natural, welcoming atmosphere that prevailed in the team had been thrown into disarray thanks to the new arrival, who seemed determined to take charge of the greetings himself. Blind to any notion of brashness, Saint-Lô strode into the room, hat clasped behind his back, before shimmying effortlessly over to the window to scour the square below. His every movement was as precise and supple as quicksilver.

"Surely it has not eluded you that the great Henri IV was butchered in this very quarter?"

Their building did indeed look out on the rue des Innocents to the north, but to the south it backed onto rue de la Ferronnerie, where a stone memorial marked the spot where the erstwhile king had been assassinated by that mad giant Ravaillac.

"Just down there."

Straight away, Dax and Lewitz looked at the floor, as if the king's blood-soaked carriage would suddenly emerge from the parquet.

"I was a mere fledgling when it happened – there was nothing I could have done. Nothing," Saint-Lô said with a mournful shake of the head.

Right, thought Capestan. Looks like Saint-Lô's stint in the psych. ward may not have had quite the desired effect. He turned to her, pre-empting her opinion.

"I know exactly what you're thinking . . . You consider that . . ."

Saint-Lô paused, then held his hand aloft to imitate the flash of a plume.

"'Treatment has been unsuccessful'."

He stowed away his hand before resuming, his tone a tad weary now.

"No, it did not. For I have no reason to be healed. I know who I am, and no manner of internment will deny me that."

"Yes, of course, capitaine, no problem," Capestan said, trying to calm him.

"Let me finish, I beg of you," Saint-Lô said, not aggressively, but with an unshakeable determination to bring his prologue to a close. "I tolerate such treatment without remonstrance as a way of preserving my post and my pay. You may imagine that hospital, at the very least, taught me to hold my tongue in order to keep the peace. But no. If I have learnt anything these last years, it is that silence is futile – we hunt witches even though we fear them. So I shall live as I see fit, and your petty opinions about my person will in no way alter my conduct. Scorn and rile me all you like . . . you are but the thirtieth brigade to gain my allegiance."

Capestan reflected for a moment on the countless philosophies that taught that age went hand in hand with wisdom and inner peace. This man appeared to turn that notion on its head. Buddha's thousand reincarnations had produced a bona fide idiot. Anyhow, this charade had gone on long enough – a more recent crime demanded the team's attention. Only time would tell whether Saint-Lô would deign to offer his services.

"Right, thank you for that introduction, and welcome, capitaine. We have an investigation underway. Are you in?"

Surprised and disappointed by the abruptness with which his swashbuckling entrance had resulted in a bloodless draw, Saint-Lô simply nodded.

"Yes, of course. If I am able to help, then help I shall."

"So long as you've got a head on your shoulders, then you can help."

Rosière, who was busy wrapping a Christmas bauble in sparkly tissue paper, could not resist a whispered aside to Lebreton:

"Not that that's a strict requirement – just look at Dax . . ."

Lebreton had set up the whiteboard in the narrow gap between the fireplace and the Christmas tree, which was now staggeringly bright thanks to each member adding their own decorations. The resulting hotchpotch would not have convinced many luxury stores or perfumeries, but here it somehow worked. Capestan had slotted some photographs into the frame of the mirror, showing the two victims, Serge Rufus and Jacques Maire, as well as the e-fit. She waited until everyone was in position before kicking off proceedings.

"We're in no doubt that both victims were killed by the same man, possibly him," she said, indicating the two photographs and the e-fit in turn. "Ignore the green fur, it's the other bits that count. We need to figure out what links this little group. But before all that, what's the latest on Rufus, Merlot?"

Due to the considerable extent of his network, the capitaine had been put in charge of dredging up any hearsay, nocturnal pastimes or unusual liaisons on the part of Commissaire Rufus.

"As with many of his Antigang colleagues, Rufus was in constant contact with all manner of disreputable types. For the most part, his informants were pimps, racketeers and armed robbers, along with a few lapsed gangsters. Nothing especially original, at least no big Mafia names in his notebook. Since his recent retirement he seems to have turned his back on the criminal underbelly. All in all, his Parisian activities struck me as perfectly ordinary. On the other hand, I am yet to rummage through his previous postings: Lyon, Biarritz, et cetera. For that I shall have to touch base with my other associates."

Capestan thanked Merlot with a smile before inviting Lebreton to carry on.

"The autopsy report is incomplete, but it does confirm the preliminary findings: Rufus was beaten for several hours, wearing handcuffs throughout – they dug into his wrists. No sign that he was gagged. There is therefore a strong possibility that our guy was trying to make him talk. But about what? That's the bit we're still unsure of. He was then moved to the street, where he was shot in the middle of the forehead: 9mm, silencer. Time of death is estimated at 6.00 a.m."

"That is some effort to go to, dragging a man – especially a big, strong guy like Rufus – just for the kick of shooting him in the right place," Capestan said. "What could justify such an effort? The killer puts him underneath the street sign to perfect his gruesome crime scene. For his own enjoyment? To send a message? To frighten other possible victims? Maybe that's what it was. Which brings us to our little newcomer: Jacques Maire." The commissaire tapped the photograph with her marker pen. "He was the first to be shot, was he not?"

Even though his research had barely begun, Orsini took the floor.

"Yes, two days before, on November 25. Our colleagues in Avignon are heading up the inquiry and, since we are not supposed to make an official link between the cases, I haven't been able to reach out to them for information. But I do know the *La Provence* crime reporter well. It was him who wrote the article," he said to Capestan. "To all intents and purposes, we've got the same staging at the crime scene. Maire was struck on the face, but not as badly as Rufus. Maybe he talked sooner. Then he was killed with a bullet to the forehead, also in the small hours. It was the night after his name appeared on the war memorial."

"Well, he was no coward, this guy. If it'd been my name on a memorial to the dead, I'd have hopped onto the nearest scooter and made off like the clappers!" Rosière said.

"True. But he was firmly rooted in the town – he will have had arrangements to make before running."

"What's it like, this place?" Rosière asked, her patron saint medals jangling as she crossed her arms over her chest. Pilote, sleeping at her feet, cocked an ear in expectation, but lowered it immediately. False alarm.

"L'Isle-sur-la-Sorgue is a tiny town in the Luberon, just east of Avignon. There's an antiques shop for practically every man, woman and child, and it gets very busy from April onwards. Most people touring the pretty towns of Provence will pass by L'Isle, Fontaine-de-Vaucluse, Gordes, Roussillon, and a few others. In short, a small town, but heaving with tourists. Jacques Maire was something of a pillar of the community. He owned one of the last big businesses in the area, selling bespoke Provençal furniture, handmade, quality wood, and all the rest of it. He sponsored most of the local sports clubs and societies. He also put money into the crèche and the library. He was an extremely courteous man with no apparent issues, and very popular, even though he wasn't born and bred, which he took a bit of flak for, as in most small-town parts of the country. After all, he had 'only' moved there twenty years ago."

"Yup, nothing like injecting a load of wonga to soften up the local diehards. Those sorts of loudmouths are always long on opinions and short on loyalties," Rosière said. "Anyway, what else do we know about old Jackie Boy?"

"Seventy years old, relatively handsome, married to the same woman, Yvonne, for fifty years. She's been living at a home called Les Lavandes ever since being diagnosed with Alzheimer's. The couple have two children, aged forty-two and forty-seven. The daughter lives in the north of England, whereas the son owns a house four hundred metres from the family home."

"Was the war memorial engraved or just painted?" Lebreton asked.

Orsini bent down towards the coffee table, where a bulging paper bag of clementines had pride of place, a present to the team from Dax, who was busy tearing into his third. The familiar scent of citrus fruit filled the air, lending the meeting a fragrant, comforting feel that jarred with all the talk of murder.

"Both," Orsini said, helping himself to one. "According to a local craftsman I called, the engraving was fairly rudimentary, done with some sort of amateur artist's tool. And the paint was applied pretty sloppily too. That said, we all know what craftsmen are like when it comes to other people's work . . ."

"But the person still went to the effort to do the engraving. Is there a C.C.T.V. camera we can pull any footage from?"

"No, that's not something I can glean without contacting the police," Orsini said, peeling his clementine with the precision of a cellist.

"Of course," Lebreton said, snaffling a bright orange one for himself. "So is all this pomp the killer's way of terrorising another victim, or as we were just saying, is he doing it for kicks? Sadistic pleasure?"

"Yes. He's a psychopath, even if the crimes aren't completely ritual – he used a different medium for each announcement," Capestan said. "We'll need to compare the victims and try to guess who'll be next. Dax, can you look into Jacques Maire's records too and see if there's any crossover with Rufus? Start with the most recent. Maybe they called each other or spoke to the same people."

Dax carried on staring into the emptiness for a brief eternity before jolting into action, taking out his notebook from the inside pocket of his trusty leather jacket, then carefully writing down his instructions.

"Has the funeral already taken place?" Lebreton asked, uncrossing his legs.

Orsini shook his head before tucking in to another gleaming segment.

"The autopsy has delayed the burial. It's happening on Friday."

"Do you reckon it's worth our while getting down there, capitaine?" Capestan asked.

She knew the answer already, but she wanted it to be Orsini's initiative, since he had discovered the case and launched the investigation.

"Yes. And en masse, I would suggest."

Capestan glanced at the team. In addition to Orsini, Rosière and Pilou were squirming in their seats, itching to get going. Lebreton would join them, for sure. Looking into the victim's business and friends, circulating Rufus's photograph and the e-fit . . . all this research would require two further reinforcements.

"Any other volunteers?"

The rat's nose emerged from Merlot's sleeve before leaping onto Évrard's knee.

That settled it, then.

11

The South was grubby and cold and far. Rosière, her derrière wedged into the luxury leather seat of the Lexus, admired the lack of Provençal charm parading past her rain-spattered window as Lebreton drove them down the Pontet road. Their eagerness to get going seemed perfectly idiotic now that they had travelled pretty much through the night. Duped by a bogus mental image of meridional France, Rosière had expected to be met by sun-washed terracotta tiles bathing in turquoise skies, with a chorus of cicadas working their thoraxes off in the heat. Fat chance.

Provence in winter provided a masterclass in dreariness. The houses' whitewashed façades were not designed with drizzle in mind. Like dusty bits of blotting paper, they absorbed the rain-water, producing hazy grey blobs that gave an overbearing sense of rubble. In summer, it was the enchanting hillside villages that drew people's attention; December, however, was there to empha-sise the hellish succession of retail parks, fields covered in flapping tarpaulins, forlorn warehouses and outlying mega-discount stores that joined the dots between the tourist landmarks. All along the dual carriageway, the bare trees drooped under the weight of carrier bags impaled on the branches by the furious mistral. The ghostlike white plastic, covered in holes, appeared to have been stuck there for an eternity, wretched tokens of widespread indifference. Rosière was deeply pissed off.

"Just say if you're nodding off, O.K.?" she said to Lebreton. "It's not like the beautiful views are going to keep us awake."

"Don't worry, I never sleep anyway. We'll be there soon."

"Yup. Let's hope the hotel is at least bearable, otherwise I'm straight back to investigating in Paris. Jeez, I'm telling you, the next murder better involve a trip to Venice or Acapulco, if not I'm staying put. Fed up of this crap."

Lebreton, somewhat taken aback, glanced at his colleague for a moment.

"What exactly were you expecting? It is December, after all – can't be picture-perfect all year round."

"Well, no danger of that."

The commandant, despite his amusement, had to voice his disagreement:

"We're in the most beautiful region in the world. It's both wild and gently quaint; as pretty as it is impressive. It's ugly for two months of the year, albeit an ugliness that plenty of people would yearn for. We're on a bypass – if you were to judge Paris by the Périphérique then it would hardly fare any better. Leave Provence alone, Eva," he said with a smile. "I love it with all my heart."

"That's enough, don't you start, too!"

Provence, Tahiti . . . What was it with these sun-seekers and their two-bit paradises?

"Yep!" Pilou yapped, ever quick to defend the interests of his beloved mistress.

"Yes, absolutely! I'll even prove it to you," Lebreton said. "When we get there we'll go for a coffee, somewhere quiet in a pretty part of town. And a biscuit," he added for Pilote's sake, who sat down immediately on his blanket, content with that bargain.

"Well it's not like there'll be anything else to do," Rosière moaned, aware that she might have gone over the top. "It'll be on me, my good chauffeur. What time's the funeral?"

"Eleven o'clock. Orsini came down on the train last night. Évrard and Merlot took one this morning."

"Yes, Orsini sent me a text. Said he had popped into the funeral parlour to get all the info. Not hard with that mug of his . . . All it would take is a tie and hey presto, he's a fully paid-up under-cover undertaker! I bet they chucked him the keys to the hearse before he could say 'good morning'. Prize-winning misery guts, that one."

This time, Lebreton did not rise to Rosière's one-woman slanging match. Did Sir Pure-of-Heart just turn a deaf ear? she wondered, at once slightly hurt and delighted to be able to shoot her mouth off without fear of one-upmanship or consequence. Lebreton was an escape valve with no risk involved and no limits. Very relaxing. The perfect colleague. The perfect friend, if she dared go that far. On the subject of colleagues and slanging, she was yet to bring up D'Artagnan.

"What do you reckon – the new guy, he's pretty nuts, right?"

This time Lebreton obliged with a raise of the eyebrow. It was hard to deny.

"Surely old man Buron can't go sending us every head-case from the greater Paris area? We're a scrapheap, fine, but we've still got standards. I'm a bloody author, for Christ's sake! Capestan used to be the golden girl; you were a top dog at R.A.I.D.; Orsini's a pain in the arse, but he's a bright spark; Évrard, sure she's got a bit of a gambling problem, but she's still pretty normal. Almost too normal. Even Merlot . . . he's a bullshitting booze-hound, but he knows what he's doing. Dax and Lewitz are loveable idiots, but they can still surprise us. But this guy, he thinks he was born in 1593! He seems a dead cert for a gold medal in the Wackolympics!"

"Aside from that, he seems perfectly rational."

"Yes, aside from that, like you say . . . If you overlook the fact that he talks about Richelieu as if he bumped into him yesterday, or that he chucks his glove at you the second you tease him, aside from that he seems perfectly rational . . ."

This time Lebreton could not hold back his laughter. The day before, Dax, with his customary tact, had pointed out to Saint-Lô that he was unusually short for an ex-musketeer. Saint-Lô took great offence, telling the "lieutenant" that he could hardly have visited many medieval villages, and that if he wanted to base his views on the proportions of men from centuries past against Disney movies, then he had only himself to blame. Not to mention the fact that many illustrious characters throughout history have proved, if proof were needed, that there is no link between size and vigour. Thereafter, he had thrown his glove into the face of a quite baffled Dax, demanding a duel. The lieutenant picked up the glove and declared in all seriousness:

"I don't think this needs any jewels, it's perfectly nice as it is. If you insist, though, I'm sure we can find something in Les Halles?"

Dax's innocence had completely disarmed Saint-Lô, who was unable to come up with a fitting response. He took back his glove, murmuring something about it being fine as it was, and two hours later Rosière was still chuckling about it on the terrace.

After a roundabout and what looked like a breeze-block whole-saler, a sign welcomed them to L'Isle-sur-la-Sorgue.

Having dropped their bags at their genuinely charming hotel, Rosière and Lebreton enjoyed their coffee at a table overlooking the river with their coats unbuttoned. The rain had stopped and the sun was reasserting itself. Bit by bit, the mellow colours were waking up: the yellows of the façades, the orange rooftops, and the reddish terracotta tiles began to unfurl in the new-found brightness. At their feet, the limpid Sorgue flowed past, rustling the green water-parsnip as it went. Rosière's groans began to subside, and she had to admit that the criss-crossing canals, the languid water wheels, the succession of little bridges and pergolas, shady courtyards and white stone, did in fact merit some attention. Although she could not resist a sneer when Lebreton had read out from the hotel brochure that the town was nicknamed "the Venice of Provence".

A text message flashed up on the capitaine's iPhone. Orsini: *Ceremony starts in 30 minutes. Meet in front of church, town centre.*

"Right, fun's over. Drink up your coffee, it's funeral time," Rosière said, finishing hers off in one gulp. "Let's see if our local hero really was as popular as all that."

Beneath a blue sky that was finally doing this magnificent part of the world justice, a respectful bustle reigned in the place de l'Église. The occasional outburst of jolliness was quickly suppressed, the culprits resuming their reverential hush straight away. A few people had dressed up, but sombre clothes were not well suited to the southern climate, so they had clearly had to scratch around the back of the wardrobe. The men tugged at their cuffs as their jacket buttons struggled to contain them. Most of the women had opted for a black stole over an everyday dress. The boys, who had relented to wearing black trousers and wedged into brand-new shoes, looked like waiters. One of them, who was chunkier than his friends and half-throttled by his tie, looked completely inconsolable. He could not have been more than twenty years old and, red-eyed and nose running, was doing everything in his power to contain his sorrow.

"He's the apprentice at the furniture shop," Orsini said, sidling up to his colleagues.

"Seems to have hit him hard," Rosière said.

"Yes, Maire was his first boss, a real role model too. The guy helped make the coffin. He and the other craftsmen chose the best bits of the finest oak. Three days it took them. They'll carry it up to the altar as well."

Orsini paused as a faint squeak of tyres indicated that a car was drawing to a halt.

"Look, here comes the hearse."

The widow, who was in a real fluster, appealed to the two people standing alongside her.

"Where on earth is Jacques? He must be dawdling at home."

Her dismayed friends had run out of ways to remind this woman, whose brain was gradually being eroded by the implacable effects of Alzheimer's, that her husband was right there, in the coffin emerging from the long black hatchback.

"I'm saying it for his sake! All his friends are here . . . What a shame for him to miss a party like this."

The children and their partners were keeping their distance, unable to bear having to tell their mother, yet again, every minute, that her husband was dead. They left the disease to its own devices and hid themselves away behind their own grief.

Carried by the employees from the furniture workshop, the coffin passed through the high doors to the sound of the bells tolling. Behind the dry-eyed widow still busily upbraiding her husband, oblivious to the fact he was gone for ever, the embarrassed funeral procession made its way into the church. "A very fine example of the Provençal baroque style, famed for its cherubs," if Lebreton's research in another leaflet from the hotel was anything to go by. The church was indeed lavish, bright and strangely joyful given the occasion, even if the congregation did remain thoroughly despondent. The three police officers scanned the crowd, looking for any striking details or out-of-place attendees. Orsini was with his pal from the local newspaper, a svelte old fellow sporting a pocketed vest that made him look like a war correspondent and a toothy grin worthy of Fernandel. He was bombarding the capitaine with information that he was passing on to his colleagues in a murmur:

"All those present in the church are from the region. No strangers."

"That's odd, bearing in mind Jacques Maire only lived here for twenty years. Didn't he have any friends from before? No other family?" Lebreton said.

"None who are here, anyway."

"That's not normal," Rosière said. "You don't suddenly start afresh at the age of fifty. His previous life can't have had any overlap with his life here. Smacks of a change of identity. Even the widow doesn't have any family, does she?"

"She has an older brother and two nieces, but they live in Arizona. That's a big trip at his age."

As she sat up straight, Rosière bashed her knees against the chair in front of her. They had packed the rows in tight. Lucky thing Pilou had stayed at the hotel. She was thinking. Two nieces . . . A plan was forming in her mind.

The ceremony was about to finish. From his spot in the middle of the row, Lebreton could see the widow asking inappropriate questions amid the sobbing of the children and various employees. The apprentice, with his companions in the front row, was fidgeting as he gazed with pride at the coffin he had polished with such skill and toil. When the sermon was over, the priest dipped the aspergillum in the holy water and held it aloft before sprinkling the gleaming oak casket in the shape of a cross. As the first droplets fell, the apprentice, driven by a professional fastidiousness that he could not control, leaped towards the coffin, quickly wiping the wood with his handkerchief to avoid it staining. Once the last bit of water had been rubbed away, he sat back down, only to behold the priest's horrified expression as he stood there frozen, sprinkler in mid-air. The apprentice, as red as a beetroot, muttered something and looked aside to avoid seeing any more. The whole congregation, shrouded in such a serious atmosphere, did their best not to burst out laughing.

While Rosière was chewing the inside of her cheeks, Orsini and Lebreton continued scrutinising the faces around them. In the second to last row at the back left of the church, a thin man in a grey suit seemed to have missed the kerfuffle. He was scoping out the room too, his eyes darting back and forth. Without thinking, he pulled at the ends of a shiny green wrapper to release a Quality Street. He wolfed down the chocolate before his line of sight crossed Lebreton's, causing him to look away hurriedly.

There was a big surge as the coffin and funeral-goers, heads bowed, made their way outside, momentarily preventing Lebreton from seeing the man, despite his height. When he eventually extracted himself from the row to peer through the assembly, the man had disappeared.

Outside the church, the children received condolences in a trancelike state. A few metres away, their mother seemed rather surprised by all the handshakes and outpourings, her good manners compelling her to accept them despite their being so misplaced.

"Wait, stay put, I'm going to try something," Rosière said to an alarmed Lebreton.

Slaloming through the crowd, Rosière reached the widow and clutched her in a consoling embrace.

"Oh, Auntie!"

After complying with this impromptu cuddle, the lady smiled at her with that glimmer of anxiety you often detect in Alzheimer's patients, unable as they are sometimes to recognise even their closest family. But the name "Auntie" did not seem to register at all. The capitaine had been wide of the mark. Not remotely proud but determined nonetheless, she withdrew into the throng.

Rosière's much-loved grandmother had suffered from Alzheimer's. She stopped recognising people when they spoke to her, starting with her children's husbands and wives, then her grandchildren, and eventually her own children. Her memory fell apart, but for the most part her intelligence remained intact, and she was determined to conceal her condition. During pauses in conversation, her grandmother would watch out for a sign, a detail that might shed light on the other person's identity, something to help her tell whether she was talking to her son-in-law or the postman. So that she did not have to swim around in doubt, Rosière would kick off every conversation with the word "Granny", then wait for her grandma to break into a broad smile and say "Sweetheart!", as she did with all of her six granddaughters. Perhaps she was not sure which one exactly, but that was not the point – it worked for any of them. Rosière had often wondered what would have happened had a Jehovah's Witness rung her bell and said "Granny" for some reason or other. She might well have answered "Sweetheart" before handing over all her dosh.

"What are you doing, Eva?" Lebreton asked when she was back by his side.

"Don't panic. Unfortunately she won't be affected and will have already forgotten about it. We've only got two days to fish for information, there's no point beating about the bush."

Before Lebreton could restrain her, Rosière had slipped into the crowd and was back in the widow's arms.

"Oh, Poppet!"

"Darling!"

Poppet. Bullseye.

"How are you, Poppet? It's been an age since we last saw Uncle Jacques. I was thinking about him the other day. What was he called again when we were little?"

"Yes, an age, you're right. It feels like yesterday, though," the lady said, suddenly all misty-eyed. "He was Jacques Melonne back when you were tiny. I preferred him then too. So handsome back in those days, with those broad shoulders . . ."

"Was that when you knew Serge Rufus? Or he did?" she said, flashing her the e-fit, now shorn of its green fur.

It was the oldest memories that stuck, so it had to be worth a try.

"Hmm, no, never heard of him, my darling . . ."

Rosière put the image away and carried on her questioning. Behind her, other well-wishers were growing restless.

"Tell me again why you changed your name?"

"Aha, darling, you're really trying to worm something out of me, aren't you! Tut tut! The thing is, I never actually knew. One day he came home and said: 'Pack your bags, the kids' too, we're leaving. It'll be tricky to adjust at the start, but we'll be fine, you'll see. I promise.' And he was right – we're very happy . . ."

"Right, but – "

"Why don't you ask him yourself! You're talking about him like he's dead. Jacques! Jacques!"

The widow was off again, pursued by an endless wave of commiserations and blurry faces. Rosière was pushed aside so she gave up, her heart heavy.

She was sure that one day she was likely to end up surrounded by strangers who knew more of her life story than she did, and that it would drive her mad with vulnerability. She had a fresh pang as she saw the mass of people swallow up the widow she had just conned, even if she would remember nothing of it. All that to find the killer of a husband she thought was still alive and whose presence she still felt.

Lebreton watched his colleague come back, sashaying along as she plumped up her fiery barnet. As outraged as he was, he had to admit that the discovery of the victim's true identity marked a giant leap forward.

12

The café was in the outskirts of the town and looked like an abandoned roadside diner. Its broad terrace, which probably came alive
in the summer months, was now just a crude stretch of concrete
covered in murky puddles and strewn with litter. In one corner,
a stack of white plastic chairs was gathering rainwater, bird droppings and dead leaves. The pergola, devoid of vines, resembled a
rotary clothes airer. Even the surrounding landscape, fashioned
with warmth and languor in mind, showed the wintry side of a
coin that usually faced the other way. Évrard and Merlot exchanged
a glance before pushing open the door.

A vast room with a tiled floor and walls clad in a suspect white
render was cut in half by a long bar – one side for the restaurant,
the other for the café and its weekly belote tournament. All eyes
centred on the new arrivals as the conversation died out and playing cards were laid flat on the tables. It was like walking into a
Western.

With all the humility of Richard the Lionheart addressing a
vanquished people, Merlot proclaimed in his customary baritone:

"Oh, I love happening on little bistros like this – the provinces
do them so well! No doubt they'll have the finest pastis on tap."

He swaggered straight to the counter and addressed the

barmaid, who looked like she was only too familiar with braggarts of his sort.

"Two Ricards, please . . ." he said, before nudging the man next to him, turning to his colleague and adding: "And for Madame?"

It turned out "Madame" wanted a Ricard too. She wondered how many billion years it would be before banter of this sort would cease to generate solidarity among the men propping up the bar.

"Any chance of signing up for the tournament?" Évrard asked as she poured a centimetre of water into her pastis, causing it to go cloudy and take on its pretty yellow hue.

The pre-dinner cards tournament was more a formality than anything else. Now that the first few rounds were over, the losers were still playing other games at other tables, and would carry on until closing time. Among the most fervent competitors were the staff members from Jacques Maire's furniture workshop. The bookkeeper, in particular, who, according to the guy at *La Provence*, was a competent employee but a mediocre card-player and an even worse drinker. He would have plenty of info., and Évrard and Merlot had been charged with extracting it, even if it meant giving him "several skinfuls", as Rosière had so delicately recommended.

To this end, the best strategy involved losing game after game, because traditionally in belote the defeated player must do the honourable thing and buy a drink for the others. A fight to the defeat. Évrard felt a cold sweat on her back at the prospect of downswings and busted hands. In the casino, losing was almost as addictive as winning – like the adrenaline rush you get when you peer into an abyss. Not for money . . . Never again would she play for money.

Focus on the cards. When there are no stakes, the sheer

enjoyment of playing takes over. Whipping out the right trump at the right moment, forcing someone to up their bid, getting a four-card trick, discarding your tens or banking ten points off the final trick. The sensation that comes with gathering your cards, scraping them across the baize, and placing them in a perfect rectangle in front of you. The cheeky glance at the empty space in front of your opponents where their chips ought to be.

Yes, in those circumstances, winning was good, important even. Évrard was going to have to force herself to hold back.

"Got to ask Monsieur," the barmaid said, ramming open the cash register to insert Merlot's crumpled note.

The so-called Monsieur had a large moustache and a small envelope in which participants were placing a tariff of eight euros per pair, after which he noted down the players' names on a big piece of squared paper, arranging the games as and when people arrived. He ushered them to a table in the corner, next to a grubby window that almost entirely obscured the dark sky outside, casting a perfect reflection of the room with its strip lighting.

As she sat down, Évrard wondered how such a gloomy place could give off such a comforting atmosphere. Was it the green felt on the tables, or the full glasses placed in the corners? Perhaps it was simply the presence of a good twenty or so people, chatting happily, in the centre of this complete wasteland where only cars had seemed to pass, without a single pedestrian troubling the pavements.

Merlot had to push his chair as far back as possible to accommodate his prominent belly. His arms needed to be at full stretch for his hands to reach the table. He stroked his bald pate with a satisfied motion before swivelling his entire body round, the stiffness of his neck suggesting that for some time his only exercise had been restricted to the elbow department.

"Come come, my friend, some opponents, for heaven's sake!" he blared at the organiser.

There would be a succession of challengers over the course of the tournament. Their objective was to keep an eye on the book-keeper's team and stay in as long as they did so they would be eliminated at the same time. Then they could, as naturally as anything, offer to keep them company until closing time, a feat they managed in spite of Merlot's apparent determination to sabotage the games. He was an extraordinarily bad player. He had assured Évrard that he had a command of basic tactics, but once again, in his inimitable way, he had vastly overestimated his abilities.

Waving his cards around for all to admire, Merlot chatted gaily with Jean-Marc, the bookkeeper, having already plied him with four rounds, the effects of which meant he was beginning to confuse his clubs and diamonds himself. If her opponent started playing as badly as her partner, Évrard was going to find it all the more difficult to let him win.

"Remind me what's trumps again?"

"Spades," Évrard said.

As it was ten seconds ago, she thought to herself. The book-keeper was asking for updates with the regularity of a Swiss cuckoo clock. It gave her an urge to bash his beak the next time it popped out.

"Who bid?"

"You did."

"How much?"

"A hundred and thirty."

How could this guy have been in charge of anyone's accounts? He was incapable of concentrating for more than four seconds at a time. Not after all this Ricard, at least.

"A great man left us this morning," Merlot said, with the authority of one well qualified to hand out such praise. "He will be a huge loss. It is rare to encounter men of his calibre, real captains of industry, these days."

Évrard thought "captains of industry" was perhaps overstating it, what with the furniture workshop probably not nudging the C.A.C. 40 index, but for now she was looking at her third ace of spades – perfect for sinking the other team – and she felt torn.

"We'll miss him, good old Jacques," said Karim, the book-keeper's partner, with heavy eyes and a grave expression.

"What's trumps again? Hearts?" Jean-Marc asked before paying his own tribute. "A saintly man! We'll be signing on by the end of the week, but still, a saintly man!"

"No, spades are trumps. You're rambling, Jean-Marc, that's the Ricard talking. Don't bore our friends with all that."

"Come on, Karim, you know as well as I do – the workshop'll be shut in a month without the boss. Who pulled a spade?"

There was no aggression in Jean-Marc's tone, he was simply speaking his mind, but his partner was wriggling in his seat. The showing-off struck him as inappropriate. Both men spoke with a strong Provençal accent, drawing out the syllables and pronouncing the "e" sounds, even the silent ones. Évrard's instinct for mimicry had meant that she was now singing the end of each word, too. She spoke up before Karim could divert the bookkeeper away from any further indiscretions.

"Anyone else going to bid again? Have you had any visits?"

"Hmm . . . No. What's trumps again?" the bookkeeper said, looking around the table for clarification.

How was it possible to be so bad, Évrard lamented. During the tournament, the level had been fine, but these two . . . No wonder they had progressed so far: none of the others had persevered long enough to defeat them. They were so rubbish that it stopped being fun. For once, though, the pair seemed to be putting the tourists in their place. This was their chance to be local heroes, and the thought was giving the bookkeeper a big head and the urge to show off. For the police officers, that presented a great opportunity.

"Nice finesse!" Évrard said approvingly, even though the man had just forgotten that the ace of clubs was down and that he now led with his ten. "Don't they say that if you want to know the future of a business, you should ask the bookkeeper?"

"Damn right, young lady! And let me tell you, if the boss hadn't come along every month with his own money, we'd have filed for bankruptcy long ago!"

Own money. To what tune? Where from? Was the workshop a front for money-laundering? Évrard felt they had struck on a crucial piece of information.

"Substantial sums?"

"Jean-Marc, it's spades, concentrate, will you, instead of banging on. You're holding everyone up with all this talk," Karim said, growing all the more irritated by these direct questions.

"C'mon, Karim, you telling me we wouldn't be underwater without the boss's bucks? When a shop sells fewer pieces than it has employees, it's simple maths. Let's be frank – big Jacques, God rest his soul, was clueless when it came to spending his lucre! That workshop's a public service, not a business."

"Yet it seemed to be flourishing."

"A bottomless pit. But the boss was a man of means, so . . . The kids don't want to take it on, and the widow, well, she's running on empty. As for us . . ."

So at least his employees had no interest in killing Jacques Maire. But why did he go chucking money away like that? Was it some sort of mafia racket?

"Wasn't there a Serge Rufus who was supposed to be taking over the business? Or ensure it stayed afloat? I'm sure I heard some mention of that . . . Help me out, friends, you know the chap I mean!"

No, Merlot's friends did not know the chap in question. They raised their eyebrows, and Jean-Marc took the chance to ask for another look at the last trick, which had already slipped his mind. Merlot took out the crumpled e-fit, half-nibbled by the rat, from his inside pocket and flattened it out on the table for his opponents to see.

"And him? He might look a little outlandish in this picture, but perhaps this fellow was in line to take it on? Ever spot him lurking about?"

The two players shook their heads. It was starting to smell policey; they would struggle to glean anything more. Time to call it a night. Évrard, free at last, cut Jean-Marc's ace with the last trump that he had forgotten to count, and played her hand, which defeated anything her opponents might have.

"You're inside," she said with a sigh of relief.

"Are you sure it was your turn?"

13

In his new capacity as inter-service liaison officer, Lieutenant Basile Diament, Varappe Division, had been given a minuscule, window-less office at the end of a corridor one floor beneath the attic at number 36. Once the lieutenant had managed to manoeuvre his two metres and 120 kilos behind the desk, the room only seemed smaller. He was like Gulliver in the land of the Smurfs. Only no-one wanted to have lunch with this particular Gulliver, who had gone three weeks now without a banquet.

He would be back soon. A friendly colleague had reassured him that it was just to make a point. No big deal. It would not be for ever. Just do this job and rejoin the fold.

The guy better be right.

Basile Diament had not spent years busting his balls only to wash up in an office narrower than his shoulders. He had put up with too much crap, grinding out each promotion with gritted teeth so he could fold up his uniform, to crack now. Not now he had reached the B.R.I., the holy grail, the elite squad he had trained for day and night, including weekends, always thinking that every extra second of graft would help him stand out from the next person. Having landed grants for his studies and made his mother so proud, Lieutenant Basile Diament was not about to give up because of this minor speed bump. It was only a warning. Nothing but a warning. He would have to toe the line and bounce back, just like at the start.

The start. He thought back to his first day on patrol, when he had pulled on his uniform, fastened his buttons, buckled his belt and straightened his cap. An outfit that confirmed him as a soldier of the Republic, an embodiment of law, order and security, for everyone. He had walked down the street, shoulders back, with the sense that he was part of something greater than himself: in these clothes, he represented the nation; an offence against him was an offence against the whole of France. And if he himself was at fault, then the entire nation would suffer from his dereliction. Basile Diament was keenly aware of what he stood for and the faith people placed in him. He was there to defend them.

In the armoury, along with all his colleagues in blue, he had grinned from ear to ear when he was handed his service weapon. His weapon. He had tested its weight in his fingers, ejecting and replacing the clip, checking the safety catch before sliding it into his holster. Each motion guided by the thousands of images he had gobbled up from T.V. He was mimicking the pros, even though officially he was becoming one. The officer in charge of the armoury handed him a piece of paper to sign.

"Just don't go selling it to your pals in the banlieues," he had said with a sneer as he stowed away his clipboard.

What pals? What banlieues? His mother had worked all hours of the day to keep them within the Périphérique, and luckily enough she managed it. Basile had grown up on rue de Belleville in Paris's twentieth arrondissement. His mother, a white woman from the Ardèche, had married his father, a West Indian, and the two of them had had a son together, a good Parisian half-blood.

First posting: border police.

His ranking from his examinations meant he had little choice in the matter, but it was nearby and he was happy. The young Diament had taken up his post. In uniform and in an airport to boot, life seemed limitless, as expansive as Roissy-Charles-de-Gaulle itself.

Before long, thin men with glazed looks started arriving. Hoping for asylum, they presented their poorly forged documents that did not stand up to Diament's scrutiny. He had to tell them no, to try to explain. As if they were not tired enough already. He would point them towards an area on the far side where they could wait, before they were told no again.

Diament did not go in for politics. He had no opinions and knew that decisions were made on high because the people at the top were aware of the bigger picture. Diament just said no. But he often got the feeling that he was the only person not to derive pleasure from it.

At times, the young policeman wondered whether his skin colour had played a part in this posting. Whether it might have been deemed the safest way to judge how far his loyalty stretched. Whether the powers-that-be were afraid that his half-caste status inevitably made him into a brother, an accomplice, as if gangs formed with the help of a Pantone colour chart. In his team, there were a couple of second-generation guys of North African origin. Were they going through some kind of initiation ceremony too? That said, the police now recruited from a far wider range of backgrounds. Things had changed.

Some things. Perhaps not his white working-class pals.

Every morning, Diament ignored the mocking looks as he

opened his locker. The disparaging remarks and the jokes – of course you've got to be able to take a joke. We're all on the same side, right? Right, guys? These men – just a handful of loudmouths, really – were scraping the barrel in terms of intelligence, leaning hard on the one quality that afforded them any importance whatsoever. They were white – that was all they had going for them, so they wore it on their sleeves, buffing it up, massaging it to make up for their piddly frames. Basile Diament's height spared him any direct confrontation, not to mention the need to talk back. He would shut his locker, check the final button on his uniform, and leave the changing room. He kept to his path.

His mother had warned him about this from an early age: "Until you're thirty, don't react to anything, my boy. No-one makes wise decisions until they're at least that age. Play the game until you're thirty, then take the time to think and speak. Before that, it's just too tedious."

Diament had put up a defence made of steel and concrete. The structure was sound, albeit with a bit of flexibility. Enough to weather strong winds or withstand the odd tremor. But one day the first bolt would come loose and the whole thing would come crashing down. Not anytime soon, he hoped.

He returned to his booth, with its bulletproof window, and sat on his stool.

Instinctively, the thin man came towards him. A flicker appeared in his eyes when he saw the officer; not a roaring fire, more like the last gasp of a match. No. No, Diament begged inside. Don't let hope creep up on you. My colour means nothing. Not to you, at least. Only to them.

In his bedroom at night, Basile cried often, to release the pressure, to wash away the memory of those faces that had reached the end of the road, but were still so far from arriving. They would have left again already. In the space of a few hours, they would remake a journey that had taken them so many months and so much grief. For a moment or two, Basile would let his tears flow with theirs. He had been a traitor to both factions.

He had stuck at it, passing his exams and earning his stripes. He played the game, waiting patiently to turn thirty. He was still going, and soon he would be back in action.

The month before, it had taken just one second for him to stray off-course. One fleeting moment at the police fair and here he was in this tiny office.

It was recoverable. Open dossiers, maintain communications and soon he would be back in the Varappe Division.

Commissaire Serge Rufus's murder.

Their instructions: only hand over files that are of no interest; forget to include important sheets in their reports. We don't want those loose cannons investigating anything of substance. Don't let them snap at our heels. The case was practically sewn up anyway. A guy had confessed that very morning.

So, which files would he send next?

Diament smiled. This pile here seemed just the ticket.

14

Capestan crossed the room with the latest bundle in her hand. Lieutenant Diament had also sent across the video footage from the surveillance cameras at the cemetery.

Dax, wearing one of those headsets with a built-in microphone, was typing away like his life depended on it. Capestan glanced at the screen on her way past, which was dominated by a moorland covered in an army of dwarves. In the foreground, a troll with green fur was leaping up and down and swiping at the air with a sword.

"Dax! Surely you're not playing games with the suspect?"

The wild-eyed lieutenant replied with nose still glued to the monitor, and the troll still butchering the enemy:

"Actually, I am – is it bugging you? He was so slick the way I made him that he's become my avatar . . . Anyway, it's no biggie, we don't even know who he is! Until we know his name, it's – "

"This is an online game, isn't it? Anyone can see this . . ."

"Yeah, so it works as an appeal for witnesses too!"

"But we don't want to make an appeal for witnesses! We're not even sure this guy has anything to do with the murder. For the moment, no-one's identified him – we're basing it purely on the shopkeeper's memories. It might turn out he was mistaken or got the day wrong, and that this man was just picking up some mugs for his little sister. Dax, you've got to . . ."

Capestan suddenly leaned in to see the corner of the screen:

"You've even named him 'The Killer'!"

Dax quit his game. He was starting to get the feeling he was in trouble. He lowered his voice to answer:

"Well, yeah . . . 'Cause we still don't know his name . . ."

The lieutenant seemed so contrite, without being sure why, that the commissaire did not have the heart to nag him, settling instead to summarise the matter:

"Listen, for a whole heap of reasons that I don't have time to explain, I'd really prefer it if you picked a different avatar and leave this hidden at the back of your P.C. Can I count on you?"

Grudgingly, his frown gave way to a dutiful nod.

"Noted."

Then, as if to confirm his agreement, he wrote "Do not play with suspect" in capital letters on a Post-it and stuck it on the side of his monitor, beneath the previous one.

Anyone popping in from head office was going to have a field day.

Capestan went into the snooker room, where Rosière was pinning tinsel to the window frames. Lebreton, Merlot, Évrard and Torrez were deep into another game of three-on-one. The rat squeaked as Merlot nearly flattened him during an attempt to pot the black. Rosière let out a shudder of disgust.

"What did you call him in the end?" she asked, no doubt trying to face her fear.

"Ratafia, like the animated film."

"Don't you mean *Ratatouille*?"

"No, no, Ratafia – it's a play on words."

"Yes, but *Ratatouille* would be the right play on words. It's a children's film, so they chose to pun on a vegetable dish rather than a fortified wine . . ."

"Well, his name is Ratafia," Merlot said, displeased at being contradicted about so trivial a matter.

As the conversation appeared to have reached a close, Capestan shook the chunky brown envelope she was holding.

"A present from number 36!"

"Is it the video from the camera at the cemetery?" Rosière asked straight away.

"Yes."

The capitaine made a flouncy about-turn, clamped a drawing pin between her teeth, then carried on putting up the thick red tinsel.

"Well, we all know there won't be anything on it . . ."

"Eva – "

"Anne, you know as well as I do, come on!" Rosière huffed over her shoulder. "Those files you've got there, what are they? Are they dated this month, or last month?"

Capestan quickly checked the spines.

"1998, 2002, 1999 . . ." she said.

"And let me guess – they've not managed to find the latest bank records?"

"Correct."

Capestan was beginning to get to know Rosière. Right now she was just having a bad day and letting off some steam.

"Basically, the only reason we landed the Rufus case is because you knew the victim and are likely to get exclusive info. from the son. As far as the boss men are concerned, it wouldn't make a fat load of difference if we sat around on our butts playing marbles."

She was absolutely right. In essence, if not in tone.

"No doubt, Eva. But is that stopping you? If so, since when? Your work on Maire's double identity was tip-top, yet here you are in your slippers stringing up tinsel as though the job's done and dusted. Already got your sights set on retirement? I know you don't, so quit with the whinging because it's driving us down even further. Also," Capestan said, unleashing her finest smile, "don't forget we're in the middle of an investigation and that we're ahead of the game. That other lot are playing tough guys, flipping every Mafioso mattress in town without finding a thing. Whoever they've got in custody won't get them anywhere, whereas we've got a hundred leads."

"Fair enough, Anne, you win. My bad . . ."

To give Rosière her due, she was pretty quick to admit when she was wrong and could curb her moods.

"Plus, we didn't stop at nattering with the widow or enjoying a game of belote – we did some extra digging," Rosière said.

Capestan sat down in one of the big leather armchairs around the coffee table. Her colleagues went to fetch some files, notebooks and stools before joining her, with the exception of Torrez, who hitched a buttock on the edge of the snooker table. The commissaire put a pad of A4 paper on her armrest and clicked the top of her biro.

"What have we got and what have we not got? Jacques Melonne, for example – do we know who he is?"

"Not yet. He's been called Jacques Maire since the Internet

became a thing, so the name Jacques Melonne doesn't appear when you Google it. Orsini has tucked into the newspaper archive, but with just a name and nothing else to go on, he doesn't stand much chance. Yes, yes," Rosière added, before Capestan could look up, "of course he's cross-referencing with Rufus. But in terms of links with organised crime, Central Archives – "

"I know, we don't have access," Capestan said with a wince.

"No, we do," Rosière said, "so long as we provide three hand-written copies of the request and wait until *Star Wars 22* comes out."

Henri Saint-Lô had drawn up a stool. The others widened the circle to let him in. With the precision of an acrobat, he twirled the stool into position, then settled atop it with a soft leap, making the lowly folk to his side seem like they had concrete blocks for shoes. But he did not appear to be playing to the gallery with his displays of deftness – rather he was possessed of a genuine love of finesse. He had a wide-angled approach to life, occupying a space that juxtaposed the real world. He was so close, yet so alone. With a frown, he signalled that he was listening. Capestan resumed.

"We can't compare the firearms, either," she said with an air of regret. "Shame, but we'll have to do without. What about the money at the furniture workshop – any luck tracing where it came from?"

"Switzerland," Évrard replied. "He had a company car with a subscription to the *péage* and a Total card. We managed to persuade the bookkeeper to copy the documents for us. Same movements every month. That doesn't tell us the provenance of the dosh, of course – but a monthly drive to and from Geneva sounds like money laundering."

"Dodgy provenance, though, I imagine."

"Stranger things have happened."

Pilote made the most of the short silence to let loose a powerful yawn, which he rounded off with a squeak of contentment. He hoisted himself up one leg at a time, stretched the length of his body, then trotted off to his bowl, not without a quick sniff at Torrez's shoe on the way past. The rat leapt out of Merlot's pocket and scampered up to his shoulder.

"Though this does all furnish us with a date," Saint-Lô said, twizzling his moustache pensively.

"Meaning?"

"Surely Maire did not expose himself to the perils that led to his slaying during his latter days as Seigneur de L'Isle-sur-la-Sorgue – no, this must have happened in his shadow years. Hence the change of name. As such, the link with the victims dates from before. Twenty years past, or perchance in their even greener days."

Capestan had arrived at the same conclusion. And she knew where Serge Rufus had been working twenty years ago.

"We need to find out when Rufus crossed paths with Jacques Melonne prior to his change of identity. Twenty years ago was when he was posted in Paris, just after Lyon. Because we don't yet have precise dates, I think we should look into both regions. In any event, we should probably dig around some of the old stuff too," Capestan said, waving the dog-eared papers from number 36, a knowing smile forming on her lips.

"So the bigwigs have shot themselves in the foot!" Rosière said.

"Exactly!" Capestan said, her smile broadening as the realisation slowly dawned on the rest of the team. "Old stuff is all we've got! Old and irrelevant . . ."

"The twats!"

"Steady on, Eva, these are our colleagues . . ." Lebreton said, trying to be responsible despite his gleeful expression.

While the five of them leafed through the documents, annotating them and compiling lists of questions as they went, Lebreton went back to the street sign and the war memorial.

"What about Rufus, and Melonne's dates of birth . . . are they easily accessible?"

"While you were in Provence, we all looked online, sticking to legal methods, and didn't find anything. According to Dax, you've got to get around a couple of barriers on official websites to get them. Nothing particularly complex, but you'd still need a vague idea of how to hack."

"So our killer's a hacker? A young person, maybe? Our victims are quite old, though."

"No, most likely the killer knew their dates of birth because he was close to them," Torrez said, piping up from his perch.

Without thinking, he released the cue ball with his left hand, sending it round the cushions until it rolled back straight into his palm.

"Right, so we're back to a killer of the same age with a link somewhere in the past. Torrez," Capestan said, "we don't have Maire's backstory, but we do know Rufus's – where he studied, schools, etc. Don't we have his file from H.R. somewhere?"

"Yes. Do you want to look on his class lists or at his uni. records to see if there are any Jacques?"

"Worth a try."

Lewitz tiptoed into the room clutching a stack of wooden planks, discreetly gesturing at them not to pay him any attention.

He laid them along the foot of the back wall and crept out even more quietly.

"Have we had any matches on the phone records?" Rosière asked.

"No, we checked with Dax. Nothing special. But Orsini is examining the company accounts and their Orange records, which the bookkeeper kindly photocopied for us too. Maybe they'll throw something up. Let's see tomorrow," Torrez said, hopping down from the table.

Six p.m. That was him off home. His departure planted an idea in Merlot's mind, who suddenly leaped to his feet:

"Aha, this evening there's a rerun of the Miss France competition on television!"

"Ah yes, excellent," Rosière said, as if the information was of particular value. "Choosing Miss France – let's make an evening of it."

"I don't know what you think, dearest, but I wasn't much taken by the president – Geneviève Something, isn't it? – and her rules – "

"Come off it! Sure, she's a stickler, but she runs a tight show for the girls ..."

There was no point whatsoever trying to intervene in the tide of debate between Merlot and Rosière who, without the least concern for their comrades still at work, headed to the sitting room and its vast flat-screen. Saint-Lô pursued them with his self-assured, man-of-action stride. Lebreton and Évrard looked at their watches, shrugged and, with a glance at the commissaire, got to their feet as well. She thought about it, then extracted herself from the deep leather armchair. She checked her mobile and saw a missed call from Buron. Before reaching the sitting room herself, she decided to phone him back.

"Good evening, Monsieur le Directeur. You tried me earlier?"

"Yes, Capestan, good evening. I just wanted to keep you abreast of the situation . . . One of the B.R.I. suspects has been referred to the public prosecutor. He's confessed that the weapon was his, or at least 'had been' his. He's got no alibi for the night of the murder, a criminal record the length of my arm, and bruising on his knuckles . . . In short, it's over."

"'Had been'?"

"Yes, he claims he had sold it."

"To who?"

"Some bloke with a beard and glasses, apparently! Quite frankly, these sorts of piss-takers could at least try to be a bit subtle."

There it was – they had a lead on the weapon. It wasn't over at all.

"No, no, that corresponds with our e-fit. And you're forgetting the stiff in L'Isle – you can't possibly close the case without factoring him in . . ."

"I'm not forgetting anything, Capestan, thank you very much. The suspect's just spent three years in Carpentras, twenty kilometres away from L'Isle-sur-la-Sorgue. I think it's sewn up, commissaire. I'm sorry. Let's compile all the elements and – "

"No! No, no. Give us a few more days on our own, otherwise our findings will come to nothing. The guy they have in custody, I've read his file, he's of no interest whatsoever. He would never have come up with any sort of theatrics like the – "

"The suspect's file . . . Unabridged, was it?"

Capestan paused, her teeth clenched. Buron had found his

target. All the same, she was not about to back down, not when they had got this far in their investigation.

". . . No, probably not. But it's not him. Call it what you like, pride, inner conviction, but – "

"Permission granted, Capestan. If you want to carry on, go ahead. I'll only inform H.Q. about the bare minimum. But don't be under any illusions . . ."

Buron might be quick to disagree with her, but he very rarely let her down. Capestan was hoping she could be the exact opposite.

"Thank you, Monsieur le Directeur."

The team had reassembled and were now absorbed in fresh objectives: finding the channel, opening some red or white, etc. They seemed determined to hit the sofa to see who had been crowned the new Miss France. Évrard had taken it upon herself to lay a fire: a few scrunched-up bits of newspaper, some twigs and kindling, and three enormous logs – clearly the lieutenant was in it for the long haul.

"Fires are forbidden in Paris, aren't they?" Dax said.

"What are you, Fireplace Police?" Évrard replied with a grin, not straying from her task.

Dax smiled back, before appearing to wonder whether such a force actually existed.

"D'you reckon they would monitor the chimneys, or rely on informants?"

Évrard did her best to ignore him as she wiped her sooty hands on her jeans.

Sitting on the window sill, Saint-Lô contemplated the darkness outside. His eyes darted from the tiles to a flurry of pigeons, then settled on the orange glow of the street lamps. With his longish hair, powerful nose, trimmed beard and jaunty moustache, his profile was like something off an old coin.

"Pizza, anyone?" Capestan said, glancing at Lebreton who, like her, was sticking around more for the atmosphere than the programme.

"No! Spag. bol.!" Lewitz declared, gesticulating in a flamboyant manner that must have signified Italy in his mind. "A Lewitz speciality, children, just you wait!"

From the kitchen, which was spattered with sauce marks up to the ceiling, Capestan heard Merlot's booming voice:

"And still they insist on wearing those wretched frilly numbers! When will they move onto swimsuits, for the love of God?"

"They're already in swimsuits . . ." came Évrard's response.

"Yes, but with gowns on top!"

Rosière was scraping the plates into the bin before loading them into the dishwasher.

"We're not having much joy with those files from Diament, are we. Same with Melonne," she said, without breaking her rhythm.

"No, we're wasting time. We'll need to put the whole of Rufus's career under the microscope. That would settle the organised crime matter, not to mention the possibility of collusion. I will ask Buron for more files, as well as the archives in Lyon. I'm not sure why, but I feel like my compass is pointing more to the south."

"Do you reckon he'll give them to you?"

"No, I don't think so," Capestan said, thinking back to her last call and the near conclusion of the case. "But there's no harm trying."

Rosière was using a knife to dislodge some melted cheese from one of the plates, before turning back to the dishwasher.

"And when are you going to question the son?" she asked.

Fair point, and one that Capestan did not want to answer. She had been appended to this investigation because of a link that she was stubbornly refusing to exploit. Her private life would not be subjected to the schemes and hopes of her superiors or her colleagues.

She did not want to "question" Paul. And she was too keen to see him again to hold out for a chance encounter.

The silence from the direction of the dishwasher reminded her that Rosière was there.

"When I'm ready, Eva. Not before."

15

Alexis Velowski set down his tray and the still-folded newspaper on the bedside table. He plumped his two big pillows before meticulously laying them against his headboard. He kicked off his slippers and lifted the corner of his duvet before sliding back into bed to indulge in his favourite morning pastime – breakfast in bed. He loved this moment of peace and quiet in his bedroom, with its exposed beams and small window tunnelled into the thick walls that looked out on a patch of sky and the tip of a bell-tower. A thin layer of condensation served as a reminder that it was nicer to be inside than out. After years of trauma and bitter struggle, he had finally managed to salvage a degree of serenity, however fragile.

Alexis took a glug of tea and bit into his tartine before returning his cup to the saucer in the middle of the tray. Then he slowly unfolded his broadsheet, the Lyon daily *Le Progrès*.

He started by flipping through the national and international sections, made a brief foray into the T.V. listings, then glanced at the death notices as he took another bite. The third one down made him freeze.

"The Nagging Memory Association regrets to announce the cruel death of Alexis Velowski. The funeral will take place at the

Église Saint-Paul on December 8. No flowers, no wreaths and no friends."

A cold sweat chilled him to the core of his pyjamas. December 8 was today. Velowski turned to his alarm clock. Six twenty-seven.

He had to react, quickly. Forget the fear that was pinning him to his bed and move. Fast.

He leaped up, spurred by an adrenaline rush that sent his muscles into overdrive and set his brain alight.

Be methodical. A bag.

In the bottom of the wardrobe, he found his ultra-lightweight black nylon rucksack. He slid in two T-shirts, two sets of boxer shorts, the key and his manuscript.

He darted into the bathroom and haphazardly gathered up some toiletries that he shoved into a sponge bag. If he survived until his next shower, he would buy anything that was missing. He put on a pair of black trousers, some socks and his trainers, then pulled a jumper directly over his pyjama top, all as quickly as possible.

Holding the bag in his left hand, he grabbed his parka from the coat rack. More out of instinct than anything else, he stuck a fistful of Quality Street into his pocket and opened the front door, shutting it behind him. It was only after taking a few steps downstairs that he realised he had not even given his Vieux-Lyon apartment a farewell glance.

Église Saint-Paul. The address suddenly struck him.

His building was opposite it. Right opposite.

He was still two floors from the main entrance. His heart pounding, Velowski stopped for a quick moment on the landing. He could feel each beat pulsating in his ears, marking the passing seconds. He could not stay – too dangerous. He could not leave, either – also too dangerous.

What was his least risky option?

His instinct for survival was pointing towards leaving. Flight. But that was his inner caveman, the same way a reptile would react. That was not a decision.

Alexis was boiling hot. In Lyon, in winter. December 8. The Festival of Lights. The Holy Virgin Mary would only have eyes for those thousands of candles today; the beacons celebrating her would be commanding all her affection. All she would hear would be the vast, collective prayer of the city's dwellers – the voice of a wretched sinner begging her for mercy with his dying breath would never receive her unending compassion. He would die without forgiveness.

Not today. He could not die today. Not yet. The timer on the light ran out. He stared at the dark hole of the staircase. Go for it, hurtle down it, make your move.

After a brief hesitation, he gathered himself, listened intently, then made his descent.

At the last turning, he leaned over the banister and peered into the entrance hall below. The bins had been taken out and the area by the mailboxes was clear. There was no blind spot from where he was standing – it was safe for him to go down the final few steps. Six forty-three.

Do people murder this early?

Maybe his killer would still be in bed.

He had to take his chance. He had to leave now.

Velowski clenched the handle of his rucksack again and again. By squeezing the strap in that way, his hand seemed to be thinking on his behalf, as if his arm was rejecting the bag. Should he hide it? Yes. Yes, hiding it was the best option. In the cupboard with the electricity meter would work – that would be quick and safe for a while, because the E.D.F. guy came round to take the reading only last week. Not the cupboard in the downstairs hall – too obvious, the first in line. Also a bit too big – it used to be a set of toilets. Alexis ran back up the stairs, opened the bag, took out the key, then closed it, stashing it to the left of the meter. He listened. Nothing.

He went back down and gently opened the heavy door of his Renaissance building. Alexis scanned the peaceful place Gerson. Cars parked under bare trees, wobbly flagstones, and the walls of the squat church plonked on the broad pavement. A few metres below to his left was the fence protecting the railway that linked the old-fashioned Gare Saint-Paul to the leafy suburbs of western Lyon. Few trains, no noise. The only nod to commerce in the square – a part-café, part-theatre – perched at the top of some stairs, would not be waking up before evening. Alexis was alone in this forgotten space. He could not see anyone. He stepped forward.

The door slammed heavily behind him.

"Hello, Alexis."

Velowski jumped and wondered if the pain he felt was a heart attack. Or just fear. He tried to pull himself together, to force his face into something resembling composure.

"I've been waiting for you. I kept it all. I'll give you everything."

"I know, Alexis."

16

At this early hour, out of the dead of night but before the start of the day's bustle, the flagship that was number 36 was steering through calm waters. With just a few people on the bridge, silence reigned supreme, enjoying the few short minutes it had left. The only activity came from the coffee machine as it delivered plastic cups into tired, pre-programmed hands that bore them away down deserted corridors. Capestan had already drained hers before knocking on Buron's door. She knew it would not be easy to get the archive material from him, especially the stuff from Lyon. The directeur was not about to burn a favour for the sake of her squad, especially not on a case that was supposedly closed. From their base on rue des Innocents, they were not meant to cause trouble. Their job was to do their duty as and when, as discreetly as possible.

Nevertheless, Buron welcomed her with his door wide open, offering her a dry smile and his usual patriarchal bearing. After the customary greetings, he invited her to sit down, before installing himself behind his desk.

"So how's the latest arrival getting on, that little D'Artagnan? As immortal as ever?"

"No, remember he's not immortal, he's more of a time-traveller..."

"Yes, of course, completely different!" Buron said with a guffaw, picking up a few papers.

"It is actually, because it means he arrived directly from the seventeenth century, without sticking around for the intervening four hundred years. He just woke up again in 1982."

"Right," Buron said, giving up his research and crossing his hands on his desk, "I can see he's much better."

Capestan just shrugged. At times, Henri had the nostalgic look in his eyes of the permanent exile, one who cannot feel at home in any land. Even though he was not really from the seventeenth century, he still displayed the symptoms – he was alone, out of kilter, out of place, with no friends or family to anchor him in the now. He had made his own reality.

For a police officer, Capestan attached little importance to the notion of truth. If a man told her he was a woman, she believed them. When a compulsive liar tried to improve their lot with a burst of delirium, she would listen. And if someone wanted their former glory to well up in the present, she saw it as cause for admiration. Establishing the truth held no interest if it simply meant turning up as the rational party and clodhopping through people's dreams and imagined selves, before leaving with perfect, boorish indifference.

"After all, maybe he really has travelled through time," Capestan said.

An expression of surprise that bordered on disgust passed over Buron. He pulled himself together, however, and contemplated the commissaire with resignation. He still did not follow her logic, and this he found distracting.

"Typical," he said, swatting the unimportant issue to one side.

"On to more serious matters, Capestan. What brings you here? I don't have all day."

This was Buron's way of saying no. Systematically no.

"The link between Melonne and Rufus must date back to the start of the 1990s. You may not remember, but before joining the B.R.I., Rufus spent some time in Lyon, teaching at Saint-Cyr . . ."

"Yes, vaguely. What of it?"

"I would love to have access to the Lyon archives from that time, to look at the cases he was in charge of. I imagine there's a whole load of them, but if we find Melonne's name in one of them – "

"Really? Really, Capestan? I'm going to have to call up Lyon, ask for a favour and become indebted to the entire local brass, just so you can have a random gander at several thousand files in the hope that a name jumps out."

"Yes, really, Monsieur le Directeur. I would really appreciate it."

"You're winding me up, commissaire."

"Why would I want to do that?"

Buron suppressed a smile and brought his notepad closer. He unscrewed his pen lid and noted down the request.

"Fine. I'll see where my mood takes me. Anything else?"

"Without wanting to take the mick . . ."

"Naturally . . ."

"Since Crim. and the B.R.I. have wrapped up the case, I would be more than keen to take receipt of everything they have kept for their sole usage: recent financial records, that sort of thing. And Rufus's Antigang file; all his files, in fact. That way we can close all the doors."

"Hmmmyes . . ." Buron murmured, still writing.

"And finally, thinking in terms of the street sign and war

memorial. If you come across any other peculiar murders from now on, here or elsewhere, perhaps you could let us know?"

Buron nodded.

"I came up with all this by myself, would you believe. But for now, nothing to report," he said by way of conclusion, pushing down on his desk with his huge hands to stand up.

Capestan got to her feet as well. As he accompanied her to the door, she returned to the subject of Henri Saint-Lô.

"You know his employment start date is 1612?"

"Yes, his file went missing during a transfer in the 1980s. Whenever we asked him about his first post, he replied 'Musketeer to the King'. One day, some joker had the bright idea of making it official."

Buron pouted in irritation, then pushed his glasses up onto the top of his head before continuing:

"The mystifying powers of bureaucracy took care of the rest..."

"He must be in line for a major bonus for long service."

The directeur smiled as he considered the sum. Ever the good manager, he thought the funniest jokes were the free ones. As for Capestan, she was not overly worried about Saint-Lô's salary – there were certain levers in the H.R. engine room that not even the mighty Buron could pull.

A flashing light on the directeur's enormous desk indicated that he had an incoming call. Buron stepped towards it, picked up the telephone and pressed a button.

"Yes?"

He listened for a few seconds, still looking at Capestan.

"It's just been found? . . . Right. Get the Rhône préfet on the line, please. He's a friend. I have a favour to ask him. Thank you, see you shortly."

The directeur hung up and turned to Capestan, arching his eyebrow like someone about to play a winning hand.

"You asked for something weird and something from Lyon, commissaire. Consider this two for the price of one."

The red velvet of the banquette was almost fraying in the spot where Saint-Lô came for breakfast every morning to partake as discreetly as possible of his piece of bread and half saucisson. In the lavish old mansion that now housed the Musée Carnavalet, he loved nothing more than admiring the "Procession of the Catholic League", a painting by François Bunel the Younger. Even though he was little enamoured of the League, the crowd on the paving stones of Paris stirred his emotions.

On the canvas to the right, a paunchy monk reminded him of his mucker Capitaine Merlot. He was friendly with Merlot. A lively camaraderie was developing between the two, what with their shared appreciation for hearty chinwags and unsophisticated wines. The apartment at rue des Innocents was warm enough, and the troops less prone to bickering than usual. In place of ambushes and scandalmongering, there was action and fraternity.

Soon it would be ten o'clock. Saint-Lô could tarry no longer – he had to honour his monthly meeting with Professor Stein. Yet again he would spout freely about his childhood: the stud farm, the fencing, the hours of reading, the threshing, the death. And the constant sensation that the man of science was trying to corner him.

"Such a fine work," he sighed, standing up and fitting his broad-rimmed hat to his head.

17

A new murder, this time in Lyon. The compass really was pointing south. Buron had secured them a "friendly visit". They had needed to act fast. Capestan and Torrez had left on the first T.G.V., leaving Lebreton in charge of the subsequent departures. The team only had two days to carry out their research and discover any overlaps between the three cases. They would need all hands on deck to get everything done.

In the area between the carriages, Capestan and Torrez took it in turns to call hotels, each of which laughed in their face. A room? On December 8? They'd have to pray for a miracle. Millions of visitors were descending on the city for the Festival of Lights. In the end, they managed to find four. Lebreton would have to deal with the rest.

The taxi they had hailed at Gare de la Part-Dieu dropped them at the entrance to place Gerson, next to Église Saint-Paul. Capestan felt a sharp pang of nostalgia digging into her stomach. She took a deep breath and gazed at the familiar façades to calm herself. She settled the fare. Torrez, who was getting nervous now they were about to encounter a new set of colleagues, potential victims of his unbridled bad luck, stood next to his commissaire. She buttoned up her black coat and hitched the strap of her big leather bag over her shoulder. With his hands thrust into the pockets of his sheepskin jacket and his walking boots firmly planted on the ground, the lieutenant seemed adamant that he would not move an inch before she did. She looked at him and smiled.

"Let's go. He was right about it being weird."

They ducked under the police tape without anyone coming up to check their I.D. As they approached the officers hard at work around the body, the group appeared to swell, subside, then gradually reform, like a shoal of anchovies before the jaws of a shark. Torrez's shadow filled them with terror.

"You're a national celebrity, José," Capestan said to her partner.

"I worked hard to make it this far," the lieutenant said, his voice struggling to disguise the dejection beneath the joke.

"Don't worry. At least we'll have plenty of space to make our observations."

Before reaching the corpse, Capestan went over to one side to greet her opposite number from the Lyon police. Torrez stayed put, as upright as a flagpole in the middle of his temporary wilderness.

"Good morning. I'm Commissaire Capestan, we – "

"Yes, hello, we were told. Commissaire Pharamond," the man said. He was about fifty, his greying hair in good need of a brush, but there was a spark in his eyes despite the rude awakening of the fanfare and flashing lights.

They exchanged a cordial handshake. Pharamond pointed at the body lying in an empty parking space.

"Strangulation, according to our preliminary findings. My view is it happened early this morning, because it's impossible to get a space here before the nightclubs along the waterfront close."

Capestan smiled.

"Now that's what you call on-the-ground knowledge."

Pharamond agreed with a modest smile.

"We found his wallet on him, with money inside. Alexis Velowski. He lived in the building just above. Neighbours told us which floor. No keys in his pocket. We called up a locksmith, and that's how we found the newspaper announcing his death."

Capestan nodded.

"He didn't have his keys?"

"No, no keys, and the door was simply slammed shut with a set inside . . . Either he forgot them on his way out, or he had another set that the killer ran off with."

"If he read the newspaper, he must have been distracted and rushing."

"Yes. Although as you'll see, he took the time to pocket some chocolates," Pharamond said with a teasing tone.

Her curiosity piqued, Capestan turned to Torrez and asked him to join them, before they both headed over to the corpse, which the rest of the officers abandoned quicker than a croupier burning a card.

The man lying there must have been about sixty, with a thin frame and nothing particularly remarkable about him. His black trousers were well cut, expensive no doubt, as were his cashmere jumper and parka. Under his jumper he appeared to be wearing a pyjama top. Evidently he had been in a hurry when he chose his outfit.

His flushed face had gone blue, his left ear was bleeding and his eyes were flecked with red spots. His mouth, wide open in a desperate bid for air, had been stuffed to the brim with Quality Street. In their macabre makeshift bowl, the shiny pink, green, blue and orange wrappers burst forth in an explosion of colour that was incongruous in its jolliness.

As ever, the brutal, irreversible spectacle of death demanded a moment of silence. After a long minute, Torrez squirmed slightly in his sheepskin jacket:

"They're awful, those pink ones – they've got a sort of sugary, white cream inside . . . I prefer the coconut ones, but I can never remember which colour they are."

"Blue. The blue ones are coconut," Capestan said as she observed this strange feature of the crime scene.

It looked as if the man had been literally choked to death on sweeties. If they were dealing with the same murderer as Rufus and Melonne, he had done away with the pistol and the silencer. Maybe he had a special hatred of this victim and wanted to kill him with his bare hands? Or did this humiliating display give him particular pleasure?

This man had not been beaten. No need to get him to talk. Either he did not know anything, or he had spilled the beans without offering any resistance.

Commissaire Pharamond came towards them, causing Torrez to move instinctively to the alley to the side. Capestan waited for him.

"They're about to take the body away if you're done. We're still checking out the apartment, doing photos, talking to neighbours and all the usual stuff. But if you want, tomorrow I can give you the keys and grant you access to the sealed evidence. You can form your own opinion."

"Ah, thank you, that would be handy. As for talking to neighbours, you're bound to bump into some of my officers – they have some photographs to show around."

Pharamond paused to think for a moment.

"Remind me which squad you're part of again?"

"A branch of number 36," Capestan said, shamelessly skirting round the issue.

"Number 36. The famous number 36. If you had to spell it out, it would definitely be in capitals, wouldn't it? Number Thirty-Six!"

Capestan prepared herself for the usual sniping comment about Parisians. Perhaps she had not been profuse enough in her thanks. With the B.R.I. and Crim. stonewalling her at every turn, she had greeted her colleague's complete cooperation with a naturalness that, looking back, had bordered on a sense of superiority. A wave of guilt swept over her and she changed tack immediately.

"Yes, it takes a lot of people to keep the myth alive," she said with a smile. "My guess is that no-one has explained why we're here?"

"Not really, no. It sounded like it had something to do with another case, but there was 'nothing conclusive enough to merit burdening us with information that was almost certainly irrelevant'. They wouldn't want to distract us from our petty little concerns, now would they."

"Indeed not."

Capestan had to choose between continuing in this manner, just with a frank apology, or breaking away from the party line and offering to return the trust that the commissaire had thus far given them. The second option struck her as both the most decent and the most sensible: if she shared the names of the other victims, the officers in Lyon would be able to link their cases as quick as a flash if she was right in thinking that this bloodbath stemmed from some old local grievance.

An impassive Pharamond waited as she thought it through, clearly not holding out hope. He did not try to force her hand or wrangle in any way. Capestan opened her bag and brought out an envelope that contained the notes for the Rufus and Melonne cases, along with the photographs they wanted to distribute around the neighbourhood. She handed it to the commissaire, who accepted it with a pleasantly surprised raise of the eyebrow.

"Unofficially and very much on the sly, if possible, here's a summary of the two cases that are in a similar vein to the death notice in *Le Progrès*. Serge Rufus, a retired commissaire, in Paris, and a furniture manufacturer who went by the name of Jacques Maire, born Jacques Melonne, in L'Isle-sur-la-Sorgue."

"Were their deaths announced in the newspaper as well?"

"No. On a street sign and a war memorial respectively. The killer is sadistic, he enjoys frightening his victims, and painstakingly plans the murders in advance. But he's no maniac. He's not on a rampage that he won't deviate from; he's having fun, more than anything else. Our preferred theory is that he has a desire for vengeance that has been left to fester too long. He beat Rufus badly, but not Melonne, and it would appear this guy not at all."

"They talked quicker than the policeman."

"Yes, that was our thinking," Capestan said. "But maybe our sense of professional pride is blinding us . . ."

"Maybe. Thank you for this information, commissaire. We'll waste less time, I reckon. Can I assume that if these names turn up in any files, you wouldn't be averse to seeing them?"

"I would never dare ask, but since you put it so politely . . ."

The commissaire nodded. He held out his hand again for Capestan to shake, then the forensics team reassumed control of the scene and the curious victim. Torrez emerged from his alley and the two officers left the square on the side that led onto the Saône embankment.

Quai de Bondy. Another swoosh of nostalgia pinned Capestan to the spot. Buildings with colourful façades stretched the length of the riverside. Every hue of Florentine ochre lit up the Lyonnais architecture. To the left climbed the Croix-Rousse hill, its base girdled by the mighty river; while to the right, on the opposite bank, the Fourvière hill rose in the Renaissance quarter, culminating in the basilica that touched the heavens, the city's highest point.

Capestan had spent her happiest years as a twenty-something on this charming, wonky stretch. She trained at the École Nationale Supérieure de la Police in Saint-Cyr-au-Mont-d'Or, living in one of the old town's classic buildings: thick walls, crooked doors, no lift, flights of stairs worn by six centuries' worth of inhabitants, huge wooden-slatted blinds that left you with a simple either-or decision (up or down), and a view of the Saône that made it impossible to leave the window.

Anne Capestan could spend hours at a time there, day and night, never quite getting over the beauty of it. Especially on December 8, when the window sills of the city glinted with the dancing flames of a thousand tealights. A night when families went out to visit their own town, the children – overexcited at the late bedtime – always running two or three metres ahead, testing to see how far they were allowed, and cutting through people waiting in line at the food vans for a piping-hot merguez. And all the while, every building bathed in the glow of centuries past. Well before they grew into a major tourist attraction, the lights were the most striking signal that winter was underway.

It was during one of those countless nights with her face pressed against the window that she had had a revelation. Down on the pavement below, she had seen Paul armed with a pot of paint, and she knew that for the rest of her life, it would only be him.

18

Sitting in a soft, misshapen IKEA sofa, Paul gazed at the neck of his beer bottle wondering what had driven him to act in such a way. In the director's chair opposite him, Denis, one of his fellow Donkeys, was agreeing that yes, he had indeed behaved like a donkey, a proper one at that, and that no amount of moping around would change the fact that he had got exactly what he deserved.

Paul was a show-off, pure and simple. Although perhaps without the pure. And he was an idiot. Even though he never took himself seriously, he loved the adrenaline that came with performing, the sense of glory and power that went to his head and sent his limbs into overdrive, making him feel like the lord of all he surveyed. He had always been the head of the gang, matey but macho, the pack-leader at whose feet people fell. Although they were still local, their on-stage success was already red hot, and the siren call of Paris was the absolute focus of Paul's burning ambition. Whether in Factory's or Marquise, he was one of those nightlife kings who would enter a club like a conquering hero, oozing supremacy as he fired out nods, grins and finger-guns like alms to the dazzled masses. He was handsome and smiley, content with basking in the glow of his condescension.

He had never been a Don Juan. Notches in the bedpost were

not his style. His fickle heart was more disposed to passionate, exclusive, albeit short-lived, love affairs. But this girl was different.

He was madly in love, with eyes for her and her alone. Her presence eclipsed anyone else near her, reducing them to mere interlopers. But Paul had this need, no doubt galvanised by his success, to push his ego ever further forward, to puff his chest to the point of bursting, to play the "you don't know how lucky you are" card, trying to make her realise how many girls would dream of being in her shoes, or that somehow he was doing her a favour, and that she should be grateful.

Now he was afraid he had blown it. What a moron. Worse still, she seemed resigned to his aloofness. God, he was besotted by her, yet he had wounded her with his self-importance. She had flashed him a half-smile and nodded slightly, then gone home to sleep, letting him return to his club and his vanity.

And he had carried on, like the 23-year-old oaf he was. He was already pretty pissed, arms in the air, a conqueror's smile, surrounded by his pals. "Hey, guys, I'm nailing a future commissaire!" he said in triumph. "A commissaire! And she's pretty hot, too! Right? She's a fucking bomb!" He was happy, chuffed with himself. None of this would have done his street cred. any harm at all, especially with the lads. He gave some high-fives, clinked some glasses, and from that moment on he wasn't nailing anyone. His voice had carried as far as Anne. With a girl like her, whose pride was explosive to say the least, offending her meant playing with fire.

For three days he called her to say he was sorry, trying every tone, using every trick in the actor's book, despite meaning all the words he said. "Yes, yes, I understand," she would reply before hanging up. He had run out of solutions, reduced to staring at his beer bottle in despair, his stomach in knots from missing her so much, in the company of a friend who was running out of patience. He had ruined the best thing that had ever happened to him, all on his own. He had taken aim at his foot and emptied the clip. He had destroyed his life, the real part, the bit that is meant to last for ever.

"Right, Bébert, you can't wallow here like this."

His two fellow Donkeys called him Bébert. A nod to Robert Redford. Their way of acknowledging the resemblance without massaging his ego. Clearly it had been effective enough.

"Hey? I said you can't wallow here like this. Drop it or try to do the impossible, don't just sit there not eating, refusing to leave the house, letting your beers go warm for hours on end. What do you want to do? I mean, what do you *really* want to do?"

Paul tore his eyes away from the bottle and started thinking, listening. What was his instinct telling him to do? Was he still in with any sort of chance? How far was he willing to go to win back Anne? Nothing remotely clever came to him. Nothing spectacular or inventive. He just wanted to grab the big pot of paint that was sitting in his corridor and daub "I LOVE YOU" in giant letters on the pavement beneath her apartment. That was what he wanted to do. He was still a teenager at heart.

"In another life, I'd have gone and painted something under her window. But I'm too old for that now."

Denis hauled himself out of the director's chair, kicked the bottom of his jeans down towards his biker boots, stubbed out his cigarette in the full ashtray on the table and said:

"Perfect – that's what you're going to do. Come with me."

And without even looking back at Paul, he slid on his Schott bomber jacket, checked he had his car keys, and grasped the pot by its steel handle. Paul jumped to his feet and picked up a paint-brush. Action time.

The Volkswagen pulled up on the quai de Bondy beneath Anne's building.

"Double-park," Paul said. "I won't need long."

His wits a little dulled by the flat Carlsberg and his heart pounding at a hundred thousand beats per minute, he got out of the car with the three-litre pot of white acrylic paint swinging from his hand. It was desperate, ridiculous, but it was his last throw of the dice.

"You keep watch, hey, Denis? If I get seen by the police my father will tear me a new one."

Denis nodded, got out of the car too, then stood close by, scanning the surrounding area with a vigilant eye. At 4.00 a.m., even this part of town was quiet. Paul spent a few minutes fighting with his keys to get the lid off. It had not occurred to him to bring a screwdriver. Eventually he managed to lever it off, plunge the brush into the pot and remove it covered in a ring of bright white paint.

He glanced at the building. Her apartment was on the third floor. All the lights were off, which was hardly surprising given the time. Anne was asleep. He turned his back to her dark window, feeling stupid, but charged and feverish too. Maybe she would be moved by this. He felt so guilty – why not cancel out one childish act with another? An eye for an eye and all that. His stomach was churning, telling him to do it.

He started writing in capitals on the pavement. The concrete was dirty and dusty, and the acrylic was not sticking; the brush just came back covered in grubby bits that stained the paint in the pot.

Beads of sweat were blinding Paul, forcing him to wipe his brow with his sleeve. He was boiling. It was not working, so he tried again, putting so much paint on the brush that he might as well have poured it straight onto the ground. Sure enough, the letters started to form. He had managed her first name and made it as far as the "V" when the first drops of rain began to fall, setting him back once again.

Acrylic. Water-soluble.

It was not going to hold. The shower suddenly intensified, reducing his effort to a watercolour. Paul tried to fix it, correct it, fill in the blurs, catch the letters, but the rain carried on falling mercilessly on the pavement, bouncing up and forming rivulets that carried the white away. Paul tried and tried again, like a stubborn fool, but he knew he had been defeated. Before him stretched a vast, runny, off-white puddle that was rapidly heading for the gutter. The sewers would be oblivious to the hope they were gulping down. On his knees on the pavement, the paintbrush clenched in his fist, Paul heard his friend calling to him. A car was coming – time to hit the road. He stood up, recovered the pot and went back to the Volkswagen, his shoulders slumped and his hair sopping wet. Without so much as a flash of lightning or the hint of a flood, Paul had been defeated by a measly downpour.

He collapsed into the passenger seat in silence. Denis said nothing either as he turned the key in the engine and slid the car into first, only for the other car to stop alongside them. As the driver's window wound down, Paul recognised his father. He lowered his window too. He was not really in the mood for jokes that evening.

His father was never in the mood for them. For once, they were on the same page.

"Everything alright?" Rufus asked, his voice suspicious. "What are you doing here at this time? Still spilling out of the clubs?"

It was impossible for words to be uttered with greater disdain. Serge Rufus shook his head contemptuously. When his father sat back blankly to start his engine, Paul could make out a man in the passenger seat nervously sucking on a sweet.

19

In this city, on this investigation, Capestan thought about Paul constantly. She had struggled so much these last months to tear his image away, and now that he was back in full Technicolor, all resistance was futile. Try as she might, she could not free herself from his broad smile, his tawny eyes, all his golden glory, and any effort she made to draw a veil over him depleted her ability to think straight.

More than in any other inquiry, she was relying on the rest of her team to deduce on her behalf, even if – more than in any other inquiry – the rest of her team was relying on her for the eureka moment. With her head and her heart wedged between two breeze blocks, Capestan was losing her most basic reflexes. She was too preoccupied to keep her defences even a little secure. The spate of traumatic cases she experienced with the Brigade des Mineurs – the ones that caused her own downfall before destroying her marriage – took advantage of her lowered guard to come back to haunt her.

As a young woman, her cheerful, carefree soul had propelled her towards a handsome, funny man. His company had let her bob along the surface of a resplendent sea with the summer sun on her face, but her tenure at the quai des Gesvres had changed that, the darkness rushing up from the shadowy depths to grab her ankles and pull her down, down, down. She had swallowed her fair share of water as her arms spun round like the vanes of a windmill. All in silence.

He had left her, then she had left the Brigade des Mineurs. Ever since, she had been on an even keel, her new squad serving as a breakwater. The unhappy endings and grim news flashes had become a distant memory. But mental health is not something to be toyed with. Paul's return was stirring up turbulent waters that would either spit her back onto terra firma or upend her for good. Capestan had no idea which it would be.

The rest of the troops managed to join them in the afternoon. Lebreton, Rosière, Lewitz, Dax, Merlot, Évrard and Saint-Lô were bunched at the foot of Velowski's building. The dry, bracing cold had taken them by surprise. With the exception of Lebreton and Orsini, they were stamping their feet on the pavement to warm up. Rosière had equipped Pilou with a scarf. As the officers chatted, a cloud of condensation mixed with their cigarette smoke, cloaking the delegation.

Capestan joined the group while Torrez lurked at the mandatory distance. After a brief catch-up and a summary of the morning's events, roles were divvied up. Merlot, Évrard, Dax and Saint-Lô were to cover every inch of the area, showing people the e-fit and the photos of Rufus and Melonne. Saint-Lô was delighted by the prospect of roaming the Renaissance quarter, which he had known back in the day when it was "a month's horse ride from the capital". The others would take care of the neighbours in the building after examining the apartment. Off they set.

Up on the landing, Capestan lifted the yellow tape and invited her officers to step inside.

"Don't touch a thing! We have a look, take some notes and then we leave. Let's hand it back to our local colleagues in the condition we found it, please."

They did a painstaking lap of the expansive apartment. Old waxed-oak parquet floor, whitewashed walls, exposed wooden beams . . . there was no mistaking that they were in Vieux-Lyon, but it had been renovated to a high spec. too. The elegant furniture seemed to have come straight from the finest antiques dealers. No books or magazines anywhere, just a pile of daily newspapers. Capestan went over to a row of frames hanging on the wall. A black-and-white wedding photograph that must have dated from the 1930s – the victim's parents, surely. A group of students on a stone bench in front of the buildings of the Université Lyon III. A few other pictures of friends and one of a woman, all from the eighties or nineties. Not one of them featured Alexis. Capestan turned around and quickly glanced across the room. No mirrors either. Velowski could not bear to look at himself. And for the last twenty years, he had not had any regular visitors. A clean break with the past, just like Melonne.

In the big sitting room, a deep, beige, velvet L-shaped sofa faced a flat-screen that belonged in a multiplex. The guy had money, lots of it, but he had not spent it on a flashy villa. Quite the opposite, Capestan thought. Here, all his spending could be done discreetly, reasonable sums or things that could be paid for in cash. The apartment owed its considerable size to the fact it had been merged with the one next door. The commissaire thought back to Jacques Maire, his spendthrift ways and the murky origins of his wealth. The money issue was key.

Only Rufus did not seem to have a hint of a fortune, concealed or not, and he was the only one who was beaten up. Maybe the aim had not been to make him talk, but just to punish him. Maybe his role in the story was different to the other two victims. What was the story here?

A rugged policeman, a generous patron and a tormented sophisticate.

Where had this mishmash of characters met? Who was killing them off? How many more of them were there? Were there others to come, or was this guy the last on the list?

They did not have a serial killer on their hands. There was a *numerus clausus*, the commissaire was sure of it. But there was every chance that the *numerus* was seven thousand, and that the killer was wreaking vengeance on the Yellow Pages.

"Oh, blimey!" Rosière said with a whistle.

She had just opened a double-door cupboard in the sitting room to reveal an entire shelf's worth of boxes of Quality Street, all stacked on top of each other.

"If this guy was after a hit, he should have gone straight for heroin – would've saved him some space. Come and have a look!"

Rosière grabbed a box at random and gave it a shake. A faint noise issued from the white tin. Rosière whipped off the lid.

"Wow, the old boy really did not like the reds! Check it out, he didn't throw them away either. If you ask me, he's gone and filled this box with the leftovers from the others."

She opened up a few more that no longer had the plastic wrapper round the top.

"Jackpot. I tell you what, you'd need some serious gnashers to munch through all this lot, not to mention a decent bit of wonga. What a waste!"

"In terms of 'wonga', the man was hardly short of means," Orsini said, making no attempt to disguise the bitterness in his voice. "But in terms of taste, his shortcomings are patent. He might have gone to Voisin, Bernachon or any number of fine chocolateries in town. Anything to avoid this mass-produced garbage. Perhaps the man was deprived as a child and chose to heap these forbidden sweets on himself later in life. An urge for revenge, albeit a rather mediocre one."

"There's nothing wrong with Quality Street!" Rosière said indignantly. "It's what my son gets me every year for Mother's Day."

Orsini shrugged indifferently. He was too busy opening drawers, rummaging around the man's desk, searching for documents and looking for clues to worry about his freewheeling colleague. He stopped and turned round slowly to survey the room. Everything was sleek, clean, empty, regular. Nothing gave them a glimpse of the owner's true being; the officers were bashing their heads against a brick wall. Even his admin. seemed to have been hoovered up – the victim must have stored everything digitally. According to Capestan, Lyon police had gathered up some tax returns and a few old payslips, but nothing particularly revealing. No accounts. They had also set to work on his computer and tablet, which they had taken in for analysis. The printer was the only thing left, its wires dangling off the side of the desk. Orsini's expression became even more closed. None of the victims were giving them a handhold. They would not learn anything. Another closed door.

The culprit was all they had. He could explain. If they ever found him.

"Your son gives you Quality Street for Mother's Day, does he?" Lewitz asked.

"Yes. Flowers, too. And he never forgets," she said defiantly, "so it's better than perfume once a decade. And let me tell you, when he brings them round, I'm quicker to unwrap the sweets than I am to fetch the vase."

Lebreton, one hand in the pocket of his jeans, the other massaging his neck, was standing in front of the shelving unit, suddenly alert to a memory that had come rushing back.

L'Isle-sur-la-Sorgue. The funeral. The man scanning the congregation who disappeared as soon as he made eye contact with Lebreton.

The commandant headed towards Capestan, who was examining a frame on a side table as she tied up her hair.

"Do you have a photo. of the victim?" he asked.

"Yes, the pictures of the body and a copy of his I.D.," she said, pulling them out of her bag.

Lebreton glanced over them before handing them back.

"The victim knew Melonne. He was at his funeral."

Spot on, Capestan thought. The strands were getting tighter, even if their material was still unclear.

"Did he know any of the family or friends?"

"No. He was watching, I think, like we were. He didn't mix with anyone."

"O.K.," the commissaire said. "I don't feel we're going to find much in the apartment, unless there's anything linked to Provence . . . I'll check the bedroom and bathroom."

Lebreton nodded and made for the kitchen.

Capestan opened the cupboard above the basin, which represented the only mirror in the apartment. No sponge bag, razor or hairbrush. On the flat surface that supported the bowl, there was a glass with a tube of toothpaste and a toothbrush. Capestan visualised the body. The man was clean-shaven and his hair was tidy. He must have taken a bag. He may have forgotten his toothbrush, but he must have taken a bag. No two ways about it.

The contents of his chest of drawers seemed to be in order, as did the shelves in his wardrobe, with their neat piles of boxer shorts, shirts, T-shirts and jumpers. He had taken a bag, but he had packed light. And no-one had found it yet.

The breakfast tray and the copy of *Le Progrès* were still lying on the unmade bed. Bearing in mind how shipshape the whole place was, these signs of a hasty departure spoke volumes about how frightened he was.

Standing in the middle of the corridor, arms crossed over his buttoned-up sheepskin jacket, Torrez was gazing at a painting. The abstract work appeared to be bugging him. Capestan shared her theory with the lieutenant, who nodded back at her, before shaking his head at the canvas and walking off.

"Let's try by the front door. Maybe he left the bag and slammed the door shut, then realised he was locked out. Either that or the killer swiped it."

"Yes, that's the most likely scenario. I don't know why I'm obsessing over this. It's just so weird that we can't find anything personal in this apartment! Five photos, some sweets and a couple of remote controls. Hardly a life story!"

"Have you had a look through the boxes?"

"Yes, Rosière thought of that. Lewitz did it. Nothing."

Torrez stared at his watch and, in true fashion, jabbed his finger against the face.

"Six p.m. Hungry o'clock," he said as he opened the door. "See you tomorrow."

Fine. Always easier to book a restaurant for nine people rather than ten. So long as they accepted dogs. And rats.

The members of the squad were wedged side by side at a long table near a window that was partially covered by a small, red-and-white chequered flag. By some miracle they had got lucky with a reservation at one of Lyon's best-known *bouchons* thanks to a last-minute cancellation from a group of businesspeople. As with all the famous ones, the owner treated you as though you owed her a massive favour, all the while making you feel like a pain in her backside. The place was tiny, hot, and full of wonky shelves that just about managed to support an array of copper cooking vessels, local boules trophies and small picture frames with lofty philosophical quotations about credit, patrons and the benefits of wine. The restaurant's main room looked directly onto the kitchen and straight through into the office, beyond the chaos of the pots and pans being thrashed about on the stoves which added to the already considerable noise.

Capestan was keen to play the local-girl card, warning everyone that the food here was the real deal, proper Lyonnais fare, and that they would need their game faces and plenty of stamina. If any of them did not feel up to the mark, they might as well head home straight away. Merlot had brayed approvingly and ordered three carafes of Côtes-de-Rhône to get things underway, before turning his attention to the menu.

"Ah! The poultry hails from Bresse, dear friends! Now that'll be a plump bit of chicken, just how we like it," he said with a wink at Rosière, whose green-eyed glare seemed less than impressed with the compliment.

"What's tickling your fancy?" he said, turning to Évrard.

"I'm wondering about the magret de canard . . ."

"Prepare to be hoist by your own canard!" he said, puffing out his cheeks and leaning towards his neighbours. "That'll be one heck of a plateful."

The capitaine was in his element. This was the sort of place where he could jostle for space, eye up other people's dishes and stain his shirt with complete impunity. He was a happy man, as he often was.

He alone had come away with anything resembling a result on the e-fit. The baker on rue Saint-Paul had sold three croissants to a similar-looking man, albeit with shorter hair. Instead of adding to his wig collection from one crime to the next, he was taking them off. Or maybe he just let his hair grow long beforehand, showing a true sense of anticipation.

The owner, still in yesterday's apron, appeared at the end of their table. In her sixties, with short silver hair, she stood there impatiently, pencil and notepad at the ready, jabbing her chin at the diners in a bid to make them hurry up and order. She then spotted Merlot staring at her with an arched eyebrow worthy of the Arc de Triomphe, and realised she had forgotten the third carafe. With a quick sorry, she took a step back to retrieve it from the bar.

Soon after, a succession of platters arrived that the officers passed round the table. Lentils with vinaigrette, pig's trotters, rosette de Lyon saucisson and cornichons. When the next course arrived – fish quenelles, sausage in brioche and andouillettes – everyone was already stuffed, but they still managed to force it down, with Merlot ordering a fresh round of carafes.

A single street-lamp was lighting this narrow street in the Presqu'Île, the heart of Lyon, and through the fogged-up window the night sky was pitch black. Outside, Rosière and Lebreton smoked a cigarette as they waited for the procession of crèmes caramel and pears poached in wine. Capestan watched the rest of her squad as their chairs groaned under the weight of their charcuterie-laden bodies. The more boisterous members were still talking loudly, while Évrard and Lewitz, who had the absent-minded look of people still busy digesting, were simply soaking up the atmosphere. A text message flashed up on Capestan's mobile. It was Torrez: *I've found the bag.*

Capestan met Torrez outside the building where he was waiting patiently beneath the misty halo of a street lamp. He punched in the door code as he explained how it had dawned on him:

"My son used to smoke on the sly and to keep his cigarettes hidden from his parents and sisters, he always stashed them in the cupboard with the E.D.F. meter. Yes, I know, like some horrid little dealer. Anyway, I said to myself, imagine our guy sees his name in the paper, does a runner with something important, then thinks the killer might be waiting outside. So he puts the bag to one side and goes for a look-see downstairs, then comes back to scoop it up. Only he gets killed. So I came to check," he said, hitting the lights and leaping up the first flight of stairs. Capestan followed him.

He opened the cupboard and pointed at the black canvas bag at the back.

"Tadaaa!"

Capestan stooped down to remove the bag from under the meter. As she had suspected, it contained very few clothes and a half-empty sponge bag. And an enormous manuscript. Velowski had not bothered with the computer – he had a printout.

"That's quite a find, José," the commissaire said, weighing up the thick document. "I wonder what on earth this is going to tell us."

Capestan woke with a start from a nightmare dominated by children with sunken eyes. She sat up straight and took a slow, deep breath to calm down her heart, which felt ready to burst out of her chest. In her head, she sang the first Joe Dassin track that came to mind, as loud as she could, to chase away the images. Then she took in the white walls, the beige curtains, the impersonal decor. Capestan succumbed to the strange loneliness that you often get from hotel rooms, then started thinking of her own children, the ones she did not have.

When she was younger, like all her contemporaries she had teased other people about having to go on holiday with noisy, tiresome children ... Then bit by bit, the jokes had worn thin. Now, her silent concerns had given way to all-out anxiety. Capestan was not keeping an eye on the clock, but every time she tore a page from her calendar, it did remind her that her best chances might be behind her.

After taking a shower and slinging on some clothes, the commissaire sat on the edge of her bed and turned on the T.V. She flicked through the channels and stopped on "Friends", an episode from a season she knew by heart. This would do the job. She watched, leaning towards the screen, giving it her full attention, until the grey fug subsided and her brain could function normally. By the third episode, she was ready to go down and join Torrez at the buffet.

The lieutenant was already working his way through the groaning plate of croissants and cold cuts in front of him. He was negotiating it methodically, keeping his poise. As his mouth was full, he had to lift up his butter knife to greet his colleague.

"Sleep well?" she asked him.

The lieutenant attempted to swallow his mouthful so he could respond, but the task was impossible in the time available, so he settled for an affirmative "Hum hum", followed by an interrogative "Hum?" back at her.

"Very well too, thank you. I'm going to find myself a coffee and some grub. Can I bring you back anything?"

Torrez was too busy with his croissant to answer, and a moment later Capestan set down her plate of bread, butter, jam and fruit, as well as a cup of coffee, before taking her seat and unfolding her napkin.

"At home, I never eat in the morning," she said, "but as soon as I see a hotel buffet I can't help filling my boots."

"Same here. You know I'm happy I came," Torrez said. "The kids have been taking it in turns playing with a stomach bug. I don't even know how my wife managed to pick up the phone when I called this morning."

There was definitely a hint of compassion, but there was a stronger hint of glee that he had escaped the madhouse. Torrez tried to cover his tracks.

"No, I'm only joking. It's over now anyway. Those bugs are worrying as hell. When my eldest ended up in hospital, I tell you, I wasn't laughing then. It lasted four days. Changed my life," he said, deep in thought, albeit still chewing. "Suddenly the earth shifts beneath you and you realise that it's constantly moving. Your whole existence, everything you've spent years building up, now hinges solely on the health of a single being. Makes your head spin. After, you're shaking all the time. In fact, until you've had a child, you don't know what fear is."

"What about the fear of not having one?" Capestan said into her plate.

Torrez did not react for a fraction of a second, then looked down.

"Yes, yes, of course," he said.

He sliced some ham and laid down his cutlery.

"Actually no," he said. "In that case, the despair can be real. But fear . . . fear is abstract. The thought of losing them – that's real terror."

Capestan looked into the lieutenant's kind eyes set in the midst of his shaggy beard and hair. The one time she lets out an iota of weakness, she ends up being put straight. Had she given in to self-pity? Possibly. She would have done well to boot the matter into touch and fire back a comment about not being allowed a little whinge, but she could see Torrez was already squirming, embarrassed by his lack of tact. He was unsure what to say next, fidgeting with his knife and fork in his bearlike mitts. Just as he was about to chow down the last of his ham, he said:

"You know, my kids, they're not mine. I can't. Came from a donor. Doesn't mean they're not mine, though."

"Of course, I wouldn't doubt it for a second," Capestan said with a gentle smile.

The room with its floral curtains hummed with conversation, morning greetings and the clinking of cutlery on plates. Every time the waitress opened the door to replenish the buffet with fresh fruit juice, yoghurt or thermoses of boiling tea, the thrum of the dishwashers and the water urns escaped the kitchen. The smell of coffee and toast dominated the others. Torrez lined up the crumbs lying on the tablecloth. As was often the case, despite his cursed aura and taciturn nature, he was in a chatty mood in the presence of his partner.

"And I'm in no doubt about you," he said. "But there's still one thing, you know . . . It's like that guy in L'Isle-sur-la-Sorgue . . . You can do all the about-turns you like, but in the end, nothing changes. You can't help where you're from. Same way you can only be a father if you produced the seed, even if you take off when the baby's three months old. It all boils down to your D.N.A. and where you were born – these are the only two things that can't be contravened. People treat the rest as though it doesn't matter, and you've got to prove yourself in a way you'd never expect anyone else to."

Maybe Torrez was right. Not definitely, but Capestan still smiled as she handed him a tartine, which he accepted with extreme gratitude.

The commissaire saw things differently – she only believed in merit.

One hour later, Capestan was waiting for Commissaire Pharamond underneath the clock at Gare de la Part-Dieu, where the team were about to board the train back to Paris. She saw him hurrying towards her from the other side of the station. He stopped in front of her to catch his breath and handed her a thick, yellow, cardboard envelope.

"Here, I ran off a copy of an interesting case for you. You'll find at least two of the victims in there – Commissaire Rufus and Velowski. The third must be in there too, but you never know."

Capestan looked at the file, resisting the powerful urge to pop open the elastic bands there and then in front of her opposite number. So there were two, maybe three of her men lurking in the same case. Lyon, 1992. The link they had been waiting for.

"Thank you, commissaire. And we can return the favour straight away. We found a bag. This bag. It contains a manuscript. Hope you don't mind, but I made a copy of it."

Pharamond stared at the bag, his eyes bulging out of his skull.

"What on earth? Where did you find it?"

"In the E.D.F. cupboard at Velowski's building."

"Wow, that's amazing!"

He unzipped it and grabbed the thick wodge of paper, which he flicked through with his hairy hands.

"Let's not get carried away," Pharamond said. "We still don't know who's got jurisdiction. There's every chance the case will be taken away from us . . ."

"Yes, we might well be taken out of contention in favour of the B.R.I. or Crim. Let's see how things pan out. In the meantime, thanks for your valuable cooperation," Capestan said.

"Likewise, commissaire. Delighted to have worked alongside you."

Capestan smiled and held out her hand, then went to join her colleagues who were huddled on the platform. Without uttering a word, she flicked open the envelope so she could at least read the heading of the case.

"Lyon – August 4, 1992 – Armed robbery at Minerva Bank – Two dead, three wounded."

Heavy stuff. No doubt whatsoever now that the case would be taken away from them.

Just as they were starting to get some answers.

Torrez filled the kettle, returned it to its base, and clicked the button. While it came to the boil, he positioned the butter right next to it so it would soften, looked out six bowls and laid them on the kitchen table, which was already equipped with a box of cereal, a bottle of milk, knives, spoons and serviettes rolled up in a personalised napkin ring for each family member. He slid three slices of *pain de mie* into the toaster and popped a teabag into his wife's bowl. The water was now ready and he poured it in immediately, since his wife liked it when it had had a little time to cool down so she could drink it straight away.

Then he filled a baby bottle with 240cl of water and counted out eight scoops of milk formula. He gave it a shake, ran it under the cold tap for a moment, and placed it on the highchair. Next he took out the three slices of bread and replaced them with three others. After that, he grabbed the packet of kibble for the rabbit and went over to Casillas's cage. It was still open. Torrez let out a sigh. Either the animal had been especially cunning, or his children had been especially disobedient. He called out in his booming voice so the whole apartment could hear:

"Where's Casillas?"

"Real Madrid!" his eldest son called out, barely suppressing his laughter.

Torrez sighed again and watched as his brood flooded into the kitchen, planting kisses on his cheek and tipping back their chairs. He sat the youngest in her highchair, got her started on her bottle, then made sure everyone had enough milk, toast and hot chocolate. As ever, his coffee would have to wait.

First he checked that the children had brushed their teeth properly after wolfing their breakfast. All this time, his wife had been finishing getting herself ready between sips of tea. Now she kissed him goodbye and ushered the flock into her car before depositing them at their various schools and nurseries.

This left Torrez to tidy the kitchen, bedrooms and bathroom, sorting everything out and airing the whole house. Then at last he could savour his coffee in a moment of peace and quiet. Inevitably, he thought back to that scene in the film "A Special Day" where Sophia Loren, wearing some ghastly blouse and pleated stockings, gathers up the laundry her family had so carelessly discarded. The only difference being that he, unlike Sophia, was blissfully happy.

Once his coffee was down the hatch, Torrez unfolded the ironing board, pulled up the laundry basket, filled the iron with water and plugged it in, then cracked his knuckles. He set down the chess clock he had located in a specialist shop and waited for the iron to heat up before making a start. When the light came on, he grabbed a shirt. Practice makes perfect.

20

Curled up on her white leather sofa in her swanky rue de Seine pad, Rosière was gazing at the transparent cover of the manuscript from Lyon. She scratched behind Pilou's ears. The dog relished any opportunity to lie up beside her. She steadied herself for a moment before diving into what promised to be a decisive piece of evidence in what she had nicknamed the Three Chaps Inquiry.

As the resident seasoned novelist, Rosière had been designated the task of combing through this 650-page clue. She was Capestan's secret trump card. The commissaire knew they had precious little time to work on the Velowski case before it was palmed off to Crim., no matter how much progress they made. With the means number 36 had at their disposal, if they got their scalpels into the file about the armed robbery in Lyon, they would leave the squad at rue des Innocents flailing in their wake.

Capestan had therefore concluded that if no-one came knocking for the manuscript, then there was no reason to give it to them. And if no-one divulged the existence of the manuscript, then no-one would come knocking. The now-dismissed team in Lyon would not provide all the information, full in the knowledge that Capestan already had it and no doubt believing that departments in one area of jurisdiction would cooperate seamlessly.

Rosière took a breath and set to work. The heat-sealed cover, no doubt courtesy of some high-street printing shop, resisted a little. What did Alexis Velowski have to say that required such a doorstop? Would she come across the other victims in there? Would it be any good?

Rosière was on page 102 when the opening notes of Vivaldi's "Spring" resounded through the house. With a furrowed brow and her eyes more narrowed than ever, the capitaine was trying to decipher the meaning of the words in front of her. It was not very clear.

The melodic tones were quickly followed by the yapping of the dog, who had leapt towards the door like a bullet to make it known that there were people inside, and fierce ones at that. The capitaine was starting to tire of the Vivaldi doorbell, not least because the dog now barked at all four of the seasons whenever she took him to a shopping centre. It must be Lebreton coming to fetch her. Rosière stood up with an effortful "humpf".

The commandant was waiting patiently at the front door with his hands in his trouser pockets. They had time for a coffee, after which they would go straight to a meeting where they hoped to find out what these men had in common.

Rosière, swathed in a fuchsia wrap dress and a long-sleeved white cashmere cardie, with golden mules on her feet, opened the door, letting the dog pounce headfirst into Lebreton's knees.

"Hi, Louis-Baptiste, I'm almost ready. Will you have a coffee while I get my stuff together?"

"Hi, Eva. Sounds perfect."

He followed her into the vast hallway, through the sitting

room, then the dining room, finally arriving in the kitchen, where Lebreton perched on a chrome barstool as Rosière talked him through an endless array of capsules in a smart wooden box. The commandant picked one out at random and a few seconds later Rosière was placing a steaming cup on the marble counter in front of him.

"Stay there and give it your best George Clooney for a couple of mins. I'm going to get my bag and his lead. One second."

Something struck Lebreton about the house, but he could not put his finger on it. He glanced around the decor. Everything seemed to be in order. What was it then?

Rosière came back down and, accompanied by Pilote, who was running in circles ahead of them, they went outside. It was only when they were on rue de Seine, garlanded with its bright arches of lights, where a few notes of "Jingle Bells" spilled out of every shop, that Lebreton realised what had been bothering him: Rosière, the queen of Christmas decorations at rue des Innocents, had not hung up a single one in her own house.

No-one was coming home this year.

The whole commissariat was abuzz with a curiosity worthy of a screening of "Maya the Bee". Lewitz was walking around with his arms full of photocopies of the dossier. Évrard was cleaning the whiteboards and humming to herself. Dax, Lebreton and Saint-Lô were arranging the chairs, while Rosière carried on reading the manuscript and Merlot helped himself to a glass of something or other. Orsini, sitting with his legs crossed, hands folded on the pad of paper in his lap, was already staring blankly at the boards. Torrez, who would not emerge until the very start of the meeting, was still ringing round to find out where the golden paint from the war memorial had been bought.

As for Capestan, she was standing pensively at the window, which was criss-crossed with the contents of a snow can that left a sort of shooting-star effect. They now had the background and the link, there was no doubt about that. A story about a gang, which meant that the B.R.I. or the B.R.B. would definitely be interested. Capestan had no intention of sharing the case with anyone herself. They were in open competition and she was personally involved, so she had every reason to keep shtum. An important decision needed to be taken and the commissaire wanted to buy herself enough time to think things through. One page in the dossier had flipped her view of the investigation on its head. She had removed it from the version that Lewitz had photocopied for the team.

Consider all the possibilities. Do not shatter everything until you're sure.

Capestan gazed at the Fontaine des Innocents sparkling with frost. The people outside were mere bundles of wool and fur flitting hurriedly from shop to shop, their shoulders hunched up to their ears. Out they came with presents that for now seemed indispensable, but which in two months would be entirely forgotten. Logos embossed on paper bags paraded past the noses of the homeless onlookers. The trees at McDonald's with their white lights were making the biggest contribution to the square's fairytale feel. Soon the Christmas market would set up shop, with its uniform seasonal specialities displayed in a myriad of tiny, fleetingly charming huts. Where did they spend the rest of the year? Is there some Christmas-market-hut park, where the feckless reindeers drink to Santa Claus's health while he's chilling out back in Lapland?

There was nothing for it. Capestan could not mention this page to the team. Not yet. Even if the missing sheet would be noticed in a second flat.

At her back, the silence that so often accompanies impatience made her aware that the squad was in position and that the time had come to talk about this armed robbery. Évrard had even muted the music she usually left playing under her breath.

From his stool in the corridor, Torrez waved at her discreetly. First things first:

"Have you found something, José?"

"Yes. I've got a buyer for the paint, three days before in an arts and crafts shop in Avignon. Matches the e-fit that I scanned and sent over to them. As for the death notice in *Le Progrès*, that was done over the telephone – no joy there."

"Payment?"

"Prepaid card. Honestly, let's not get bogged down – it's clearly the same killer."

"Agreed," Capestan said, picking up the black marker pen and writing a heading in block capitals. *Lyon – August 4, 1992 – Armed robbery at Minerva Bank – Two dead, three wounded.*

Lewitz was caught off-guard by a sneeze, before blowing his nose with all the subtlety of the lead trombonist in a village brass band. He wiped the offending area with a tissue before saying:

"Nice choice doing it in the middle of the summer holidays – good for a getaway!"

"Same in terms of police numbers, too," Capestan bounced back. "Which brings us back to our first stiff: Serge Rufus. He was first on the scene, with a new recruit and two interns in tow. Pretty much zero experience, then. But he did a decent job, since he arrested one of the two gunmen, the dangerous one who had shot the victims."

Capestan replaced the lid on the marker.

"Let's go back to the robbery, though: in the middle of the morning, two men in ski masks carrying automatic pistols burst into the Minerva Bank by the waterfront in Lyon's sixth arrondissement. The first runs behind the counter and stuffs money into a bag, while the second holds the two bank clerks at gunpoint, along with the four customers present at the time. Once they've loaded up the cash, the first guy goes to find the manager, probably to get him to open the vault. That's where we meet Alexis Velowski: in his office, the crook kills two people right in front of him. Velowski was completely traumatised. He went on to stand as a witness in the trial before spending six months in a care home with depression. The killer then went back into the bank lobby, but the alarm had been sounded, which is why Rufus is there with his measly back-up. The second gunman, the one who just kept watch, managed to get away."

"Jacques Melonne?" Rosière said.

"You may well ask. The description doesn't fit: build, voice, height, eye colour. The witness statements from the customers and the staff don't really pair up with the police officers' version. There was the ski mask, plus the tension, and of course the speed – it can't have been more than fifteen minutes from the moment it started to the time of arrest. Jacques Melonne's name appeared in the list of possible accomplices because he was a vague acquaintance of the gunman from before, but he wasn't their favourite candidate."

"The likelihood looks a little different now," Lebreton said, his Roman nose red and swollen with a winter cold.

A good half of the team was lugging the virus around and the bins were overflowing with scrunched-up tissues. Sniffing could be heard at regular intervals, with varying levels of restraint.

"Absolutely. Here we have our three cases rolled into one: Rufus the policeman, Velowski the witness, Melonne the runaway."

"In a game of 'Happy Families', the missing member has to be the . . ." Évrard said, before trailing off.

". . . the killer. Precisely. We can assume we're looking for the gunman who fired the shots. He's taken out the person who arrested him, the person whose testimony sent him to the clink, and the person who fled never to return. He came back for revenge . . ."

". . . or maybe in Melonne's case, to recover the money too," Évrard said, tugging at a strand of her wavy blonde hair. "Have we had any info. on transfers from the Swiss bank accounts since the murder?"

"No, no info. The vaults of Geneva do not open easily," Orsini said. "Especially when we don't have a motive or any authority, of course."

"Of course," Capestan said with a nod, looking the capitaine in the eye.

She thought back to the absence of any pictures at Velowski's apartment. He felt guilty. About what? Cowardice? Complicity?

In the sitting room, their words were in sync. with the flashing of the Christmas lights. The crackling fire punctuated their sentences now and then, lending them a depth that had not been intended.

"Our killer could well be the driver too, no?" Lewitz said in his nasal voice. "Who's the driver?"

"There wasn't one."

"Are you kidding? No driver in a hold-up like this? Were they planning on getting away on their children's scooters?"

"No, in a car – it was parked down the road."

"Parked? Not turning around? These guys were confident, weren't they."

"Maybe they couldn't find a driver or didn't want to split the loot with another member. There weren't any drivers in the list of their frequent associates," Capestan said.

Lewitz's point was not completely irrelevant. The commissaire made a mental note to look into it after lunch.

She was still hesitant about revealing what she had read. Not there in the middle of a meeting. That said, she did not like keeping secrets from her colleagues. Who would she talk to? Who would hold their tongue? Could she rely on the team? Could they stick together if they didn't trust each other?

Capestan looked at her officers' faces. Dax somehow both in deep concentration and completely uninterested; Rosière still in a bait; Orsini seemingly trying to challenge her, without any luck; and Merlot with an empty plastic cup in one hand and in the other, the rat he had narrowly avoided squashing. Next to him, standing up and gripping the back of his chair, Saint-Lô was fizzing, desperate for action:

"So then, our rogue is unmasked! What are we waiting for? What is his name? Where is his base?"

Yes, these were the pressing questions. The others could wait.

"His name is Max Ramier. And our job today is to flush him out."

Lewitz cast his spirit level to one side and went to fetch the plumb line from his toolbox. He held it up to the top corner of the bookcase that he had just finished for the games room.

Good. The spirit level and the plumb line were in agreement: it was leaning to the right, rather dramatically, in fact. Or perhaps it was the floor. Yes, that was it, the floor was not straight. And anyway, from a distance you could hardly tell, and once the unit was full, no-one would know any different.

The lieutenant scooped up the board games and books that everyone had brought for the communal stash. When he put the Scrabble box on the middle shelf, it stuck a bit on the fresh paint. That would make a nice souvenir.

21

"Is there one person in the entire prison service willing to take my call, or am I going to have to show up in person? I'm warning you, this is Lieutenant Torrez on the line. You don't want me face-to-face. Yes, I'll hold. Again."

An exasperated Torrez chucked his hands-free kit to one side and gripped his iron even tighter. He pressed the steamy tip onto the shirt collar with such force that the board quaked on its aluminium legs. They had been pinballing him from one department to the next for over an hour and, for one usually so calm and dogged in his research, his patience was wearing thin. He was not making much progress on the shirts either, which worried him with the deadline looming.

Max Ramier had not been released for good conduct. He had served the whole of his sentence and, in the process, sown a healthy amount of terror in the prison yard. Few people had called him a friend, and he had confided in fewer still. He was an aggressive man prone to furious outbursts that were as sudden as they were inexplicable. Other than him never speaking about any hidden loot, there was not much more on the prison grapevine. He never spent anything and did not harp on about any grudges or unfinished business. This set him apart from other armed robbers, who often ranted about settling scores, baying for blood and blaming anyone and everyone outside the clink for the bad luck that had landed them there. Ramier was all action and no talk, which was rare.

Once that avenue had run dry, Torrez was focusing his efforts on official channels. He needed Ramier's address. The one from the armed robbery case notes had not been in use for years, the slammer taking its place by default: when the rent stopped coming in, the administration had resolved matters. But Ramier could not have left Lyon-Corbas prison without stating an address, even if it was only temporary. He must have been assigned a probation officer too. This was the information Torrez was still waiting on.

One more tricky crease at the end of the sleeve and Torrez put down the iron with a sigh. He would never make it.

Three sharp knocks at the door announced Capestan's arrival.

"Come in!"

She opened the door and flashed him her customary smile.

"Any excitement from the cells?"

Torrez gave her a quick lowdown.

"Great. Will you text me if you hear any more?"

The lieutenant nodded. His commissaire had not even seemed to notice that he was ironing in his office. She was so unintrusive that at times it verged on indifference. Torrez knew that was not the case – she just kept her questions and concerns, her hurt and her anger, to herself. She was quick to share her joy, her enthusiasm, but revealed nothing else. She maintained a sunny front and appeared completely open, all the while letting no-one learn a thing about her. But as hard as he had found it to decipher her fully, Torrez was beginning to understand her. He could tell she was anxious. A problem was fluttering around her head; the lieutenant could almost see it through the windowpanes of her eyes. He would know what it was when she was ready to tell him. If she wanted to keep quiet, then surely she had her reasons. Torrez did not doubt the commissaire for a second. After she pulled the door shut behind her, the lieutenant's mobile sprang back into action. Finally. His threat of a personal visit had come good.

Capestan went back to the sitting room. She had been planning on telling Torrez, but he already had his hands full, so no point interfering. She was drifting around the commissariat, turning but not settling, as if running away from an inevitable brush with the top brass, the telephone call that would take the case away from them. Or a question that would force her to take action.

Dax had copied the name "Max Ramier" and pasted it into every online search box imaginable. Every time he looked up to see his "Delete illegal hacks always" Post-it, he would grunt an "Oh yeah" and return to his keyboard. In four hours of searching, he had already found three people with the same name, all quite useless but nonetheless duly noted.

The commissaire sat at her desk and switched on her lamp. Early afternoon and the light from outside was already too dim. As Capestan focused all her thoughts on the warm ring cast by her orange lampshade, Lebreton gave her desk a gentle tap.

"Was Diament given the file about the armed robbery?"

"No. The information still hasn't made it up from Lyon. And I was too busy to phone them myself this morning . . ."

"We've got to tell them, Anne. It'll look like we're withholding information, which is exactly what we are doing. It's dishonest. It's downright foul play."

Capestan plucked a tissue from the box on her desk and used it to mop up a tea stain from her mug.

"It's fine, it's not like their intel. has reached us at supersonic speed either."

"We've got to obey the rules, Anne. What are we gaining by doing this? A day, maybe two? They've got a guy on remand, let's not forget. That gives him the perfect alibi for the murder in Lyon. And since all the crimes are linked, they'll have to let him out."

He was right, of course. Anyhow, at some point the file would land at number 36. Except Lebreton did not know the full story. He had not read the sheet. Capestan dropped the tissue into the bin at her feet.

"No."

"Anne, please . . ."

Capestan hesitated. Her instinctive misgivings about him from their clash in the past had not completely gone away. Which was a pity. If anyone in the team was capable of making well-considered, wise and balanced decisions, it was the commandant. She had to bring him up to speed. He would understand and his opinion would be valuable.

The commissaire cautiously pulled the sheet of paper from the top drawer of her desk.

It was not just the three victims in the Minerva case. Another name was lurking in there.

"Here, read this. It was in the file. I'm not giving it to them, although they might find it out for themselves. And I think that every moment we extract from them will count. Just tell me what you think. It's at the bottom of the page. The victims' name."

The woman and the boy killed in Velowski's office were called Orsini.

"Shit, shit, shit," Lebreton said under his breath, staring at the document.

The idea of vengeance, their findings in the inquiry, everything appeared in a new light. A new darkness, if truth be told.

Why had Orsini not said anything? He must have known that his name would come up eventually.

Why was he playing for time?

And most pressing of all: was he simply an investigator, or was he a murderer?

The sound of the doorbell rang through the commissariat. Lebreton looked up and eyed Capestan. They both knew it was Lieutenant Diament at the door. They had to react fast. Now was the time to decide. Lebreton handed the sheet back to her:

"It was fine in your drawer. Shall I let Diament in?"

Capestan shook her head. No. Any dirty deeds were her call. She picked up the abridged file and headed for the door.

The towering Lieutenant Diament was standing in the doorway looking extremely irritated. Contact had been broken and there was a sense that he harboured a deep disdain for the officer responsible.

"You have something for us, I hope."

"Absolutely, I was about to call."

"No you weren't."

Something about Diament's reserve and lack of enthusiasm made him impossible to play. His huge paw seized the dossier and he flicked through it with his thumb.

"All there?"

"Of course. Why do you ask? You wouldn't ever send us incomplete documents, would you?"

Capestan loved to play.

No smile or expression of regret from Diament whatsoever. Just the faintest glimmer of a "fair enough".

"Goodbye, commissaire," he said in a cursory manner, but only after spinning on his heel.

"Don't forget to release that poor suspect of yours," Capestan said as he was getting into the lift.

She could not resist a little sideways dig from her starting block to his. The inter-departmental race was on. And this time, she could not afford to lose. A colleague was at stake.

Soon she would have to confront the colleague in question, but first she needed to run a few small checks.

Nestled in the leather armchair under the window in the snooker room, Rosière was close to finishing the manuscript. She had read it in a oner to get a feel for the story. A sort of Victorian comedy of manners in the mould of Jane Austen. The plot and characters had nothing to do with the armed robbery in Lyon or the trauma it had caused. Yet something, a vague, subliminal sensation, was nagging Rosière. In and of itself, the novel was not worth the paper it was printed on. The situations were out of kilter and the reactions muddled. She might have written this off as amateurism but, curiously, every page, every sentence, seemed to have been mulled over and carefully constructed. Velowski was trying to say something without wanting to say it outright, all the while hoping people would know what he meant without fully understanding.

He had typed with one hand at the keyboard and a can of worms in the other. He needed people to take time to get to know him. This manuscript had been his only means of escape. It was not entirely trivial, even if authors do cling on to their texts as if they were their youngest child. Rosière intended to get going, ignore the story and click into writer mode. On a piece of A3 card, she drew up a grid and filled in the boxes along the top and down the side: names, objectives, methods, interactions and characteristics.

As she was straightening her glasses, Lewitz popped his head round the corner.

"Torrez has found something for Capestan. Come and have a listen," he said.

"Coming," she said with a grumble.

Pilou took off like a pilot fish.

"Twenty years in prison, not a single visit," the commissaire said in summary. "Ramier killed Melonne for the money, but resentment must have pulled hard on the trigger too."

She clapped her hands together before carrying on:

"So, we have an address, that's great – 25, avenue Montaigne. Let's go."

"Avenue Montaigne?" Rosière asked.

"Yes."

"That's the address of the Hôtel Plaza Athénée, that is. Seems our guy couldn't resist a bit of a splurge."

22

They had had to organise a stakeout on the hoof because Ramier was not at the hotel when Capestan and Lebreton showed up. The need to improvise brought about two further problems. Firstly the squad, cut off from the public prosecutor's office, had no search warrant relating to this brand-new suspect. Unless they caught him red-handed or he did a runner, they would not be able to arrest Ramier. And second, after reading the file, the B.R.I. would arrive at exactly the same conclusions as their rue des Innocents friends and rush to the scene twice as fast and with a warrant to boot. Perhaps they were already on their way.

If the B.R.I. swooped in ahead of them and nicked Ramier, the case would be closed in a second. They would have their man, leaving the squad to walk away feeling even more deflated and humiliated than before. From her post on a bench just up from the palace beneath a line of horse chestnuts, Capestan was watching the far end of the lavish avenue Montaigne, praying for something to happen. She needed Ramier to arrive now.

The withered husks of the bare trees had been replaced by electric lights that weighed down the flimsy branches. The lack of foliage meant the hotel was fully visible, complete with its immaculate stone façade and miniature balconies draped in scarlet geraniums.

Endless window boxes combining with the red of the blinds put the finishing touch to this landmark site.

Gaggles of young girls had virtually chained themselves to the railings that protected the box hedges lining the hotel's terrace, smartphones at the ready, apparently praying for something to happen too. Surely they were not waiting for Ramier. As yet more of them gathered from the surrounding streets, Capestan wondered which other star had pulled such a crowd.

Parked a few metres downstream of the Athénée, Saint-Lô and Lewitz were using their wing mirrors to keep a close eye on the broad avenue, as well as making the most of their height advantage in the chunky seats of their 4x4.

Lewitz could not believe his luck. He caressed the black leather racing steering wheel, letting his fingertips graze the gearstick with a tenderness and admiration that he would not have been able to muster had it been Rihanna's booty. His only regret was the tinted windows. He had said so earlier to the car-hire people:

"Hey, wait, I want clear windows, you hear me. If I'm riding a Porsche, I want people to gawk at me when we hit a red light! And I'm not rolling the windows down in the middle of December . . ."

"No, no, ignore him," Rosière had said, holding out her Platinum card. "These windows are just fine."

Just as the man behind the desk thought to himself that the millionaire should let her toyboy live a little, Rosière turned to Lewitz and reminded him of the purpose of the luxury model:

"It's for a stakeout, Lewitz, a STAKE-OUT. Undercover. And outside the Plaza, a Cayenne happens to be the most discreet option, O.K.? But if you're sat in the front looking like a dog with two tails, it won't be low-key for long, will it."

Lewitz caved. More because of her bankcard than her reasoning, but still he caved. There were several things he did not regret: the sleekness, the comfort, the hundreds of buttons and the beast of an engine. Obsessed with his Porsche, he did his best to convey his enthusiasm to a partner who could not have been less interested in the finer details of the automobile. Saint-Lô turned to him briefly and gave an appreciative nod out of simple courtesy. In his days as a guardsman, he had endured hours of conversation in taverns with toothless wenches, learning to listen without hearing in a manner befitting his inner poet. Suckled on the work of François Villon, Du Bellay, Ronsard and Clément Marot, he knew how to remove himself from the world, especially a world that no longer acknowledged him.

As a child, Saint-Lô had envisioned a whole other destiny for himself, one built on battles and derring-do. He had dreamed so often of finding his own Excalibur to pull forth, or saddling up to seek fresh conquests and glory. But his heart, soul and flair were trapped here, in a century where everyone sneered.

Yet Saint-Lô now felt a different breeze on his face. His moustache detected the gust of adventure. It had been an age since anyone had entrusted him with even the most minor mission, and keeping an eye on this palace of the vanities was captivating him just as much as guarding the king's encampment ever had in days gone by. So while Lewitz was babbling, Saint-Lô was being reborn. He felt the lifeblood of the musketeers coursing through his veins and awakening the ardour of his spirit. He knew he was ready to strike down the enemy and fight to the bitter end. His love of poetry and his hunger for battle were taking him over like ivy scaling a virgin wall. The finest swordsman in all the land had reported back for duty.

If Max Ramier were to wend his way through the crowd of screaming young girls swarming round the hotel entrance, Saint-Lô would spot him and rouse Lewitz from his blissed-out state.

Meanwhile, Rosière was busy trying to harpoon her plateful of salade italienne with a piece of elegant silverware.

"Bloody rocket, always takes at least five goes with your fork to get anywhere."

Sitting alongside her, Lebreton was stirring his coffee in a delicate china cup. Rosière threw down the implement in defeat and tore off a piece of bread to mop up the dressing. They had been holed up in the hotel's bar for two hours now, where they had seen no end of crystal, jewellery and snobbery, but no Ramier, nor any other celebs. Waste of bloody time and now she was fed up. Her stiletto tapped along to the frantic rhythm of her impatience.

"These stakeouts are a pain in the arse. I hate waiting about."

"No-one likes waiting, Eva," Lebreton said, crossing his long, slender legs.

The blend of his thoroughbred physique and his dandy style meant he fitted in perfectly with these made-to-measure surroundings, not that he seemed to care.

"Erm, you do! Look at you there, all calm . . . It's like a hobby to you."

Lebreton gave a crooked smile that emphasised his thin scar. His eyes followed a tray of cocktails elegantly swaying beneath a velvet-clad waiter. The e-fit with the green fur and scabbard came back to him.

"It's weird that a crook seeking to keep a low profile would choose a palace hotel," he said.

"Not really. First off, maybe he's not bothered about keeping a low profile. He's not shy of theatrics, as we saw with the street sign. Like all armed robbers, he must have an ego the size of a ram-raider's car. Plus, the thought of guffing into some silk sheets must have got him very excited in prison. He can afford a taste of the high life now that he's gone to the effort of swiping back that lucre. And these so-called 'palace' hotels are all the same – discreet to the point of turning a blind eye to their guests' activities. Until a scandal comes along to disturb their peace and impunity, I bet many a puffed-up prince has paraded around the capital's connecting suites with a bevy of slaves. No-one bats an eyelid at reception when they hand over the keys to anyone who can afford it: monsieur has made an excellent choice; we very much hope to see you again soon; blah, blah. Anyway, old Ramier's small fry compared to most of this lot."

"Yes, you're right. He must have enjoyed giving the address to his probation officer, too," Lebreton said.

"Tell me about it. Like a rat who's moved in to a grain store."

"Speaking of rats, where's Merlot?"

"Training up Ratafia for active police work."

"Is it having any effect?" Lebreton asked with surprise.

"Well, the little critter certainly knows his Côtes-de-Rhône from his Beaujolais, that's for sure. When it comes to cocaine and explosives, I think progress has been somewhat slower. But Ratafia is already managing to follow Merlot around without getting flattened, so his survival instincts are intact. Perhaps one day he will indeed serve his country! He'll never be as useful as a dog, but then I suppose we all have our pet causes . . ."

A man with a beard swanned down the corridor, his reflection appearing in a hundred mirrors. The two officers froze and followed his path, reflected ad infinitum. No – too thickset, hair too white. False alarm.

"Damn, that was Santa Claus," Rosière said, slapping her fist into her palm. "Or some hipster – those beardy ones are a dime a dozen on set nowadays."

The capitaine shook her head with a wry smile. Lebreton tapped the rim of his coffee cup with his fingernail.

"Speaking of Santa, you don't fancy coming for Christmas Eve dinner with my family, do you? It'll be my first without Vincent and . . . it would be great to have a friend there."

Rosière looked away to disguise her relief. A great lump dislodged itself in her chest and vanished under the influence of companionship. She was well aware of how sensitive Louis-Baptiste was being in pretending that she would be doing him a favour, when it was her that needed comfort too. She reached out her bejewelled, multicoloured hand and squeezed Lebreton's forearm:

"Oh, thank you, dear Loulou, I'd be so, so happy to chaperone you. Really, thank you. We'll need to go shopping."

Évrard, an enormous Nikon hanging against her stomach, had melted into the crowd. The girls, just like the sales assistants in the surrounding boutiques, albeit more noisily, were keeping a keen eye out for the appearance of Kim Kardashian and Kanye West. They did not react, therefore, when Évrard tensed up at the sight of a brown-haired man of average build, now without a beard or glasses.

"I've got a visual. He's going past the Canadian Embassy," she said into her mobile, which was set up for a conference call.

After a quick glance towards the embassy, Capestan replied to all mobile units.

"O.K., Évrard, we'll let him go ahead and the two of us will bring up the rear. Lebreton and Rosière, you come towards us but stay out of sight, in case he tries to take off. When we're close enough, Évrard, we'll nab him. My guess is he'll run, in which case you guys in front can take him. If he manages to slip away from you, Lewitz and Saint-Lô, we're counting on you. Warm up the engine."

The commissaire fell in next to Évrard and the two of them approached Ramier in tandem. Just as Lebreton and Rosière came into view and took up position, an enormous S.U.V. whistled past them and screeched to a halt right in line with Ramier. The armed robber, whose reflexes had not been dulled by captivity, took off remarkably rapidly for a man of his age. Six burly officers dressed in black and wedged into bulletproof vests erupted from the vehicle, only to stop in shock for a moment. This second was all it took for the girls to assume that the gleaming S.U.V. was holding their idols and that these men were their bodyguards. Straight away they clattered into the rapid response unit and pressed against the bodywork, sprawling themselves across the bonnet and plastering themselves onto the windscreen, sweeping Lebreton and Rosière along with them. There was no way past. Deafening the officers with their piercing screams, the teenage girls were flipping their phones into selfie mode and immortalising the livid expressions of the helpless B.R.I. While number 36 lit up Instagram, Kim and Kanye made the most of the diversion to reach their suite incognito.

Capestan could not believe it. The second her squad was poised to arrest their lead suspect, Antigang appeared in their pimped-up wheels to try and pinch the guy from under their noses. Their cover was blown and Max Ramier would not be hurrying back to the Golden Triangle anytime soon. The commissaire was fuming until she spotted Lewitz and Saint-Lô pulling out in their Porsche and setting off down the avenue in the same direction as the runaway.

"Faster!" Saint-Lô bellowed as he caught sight of their fugitive flying down the pavement like a dart.

Lewitz was being pigheaded and refusing to step on it, driving along with all the urgency of an arthritic granny. He had eased her into second and seemed to think that was sufficient. His boy-racer, petrol-head reputation today seemed entirely unfounded.

"Forward!"

"No, no, no, we don't want to ruin it. It's fine, we'll get Ramier, it's fine, it's fine."

"Hell's teeth!" Saint-Lô said, his hand twitching towards the driver.

"No, don't you touch the steering wheel! That's mine!" Lewitz shouted, spitting cold fury.

Saint-Lô stared at his colleague in astonishment. He had once had a similar attachment to Alezane, his first mare, and all of a sudden he understood: Lewitz was utterly petrified at the thought of destroying this car. He loved it. In giving him the most powerful engine of all, the team had put his car-killing curse into neutral.

When the time came to give the vehicle back to the hire company, the brigadier would burst into tears.

Meanwhile, Ramier had already made it to the Seine embankment. He seemed to be running towards the Eiffel Tower itself. They needed to start from scratch – the stakeout had descended into a downright fiasco.

Merlot intended to make the most of this brief moment of calm to take a closer look at the Advent calendar that Rosière had been so gushy about, but a sharp squeak diverted him from his plan. He peered beyond his stomach at his feet. The cry had issued from Ratafia, whose tail he had just stepped on. Merlot leaned down perilously on his straight legs and scooped up the rat, allowing it to scamper into the sleeve of his jacket. When the rodent had snuggled up on his shoulder, Merlot flattened his head and body with a long, comforting caress.

"There there, little Rata, it's alright."

Once the rat had calmed down, the capitaine was able to return to the initial object of his attention, namely the Advent calendar presiding on the table. Merlot prodded open today's window with a chubby index finger. Empty. Next one. Also empty. Boring into them with less and less patience, the capitaine reached the box for Christmas Eve, where he was met by a little tube of paper. Merlot unrolled it and read the note: *Ha ha! Got you!*

So Rosière had had the temerity to assume he would steal the chocolates. Such little trust. Merlot was outraged.

23

"That's why we have elite units – so that the nearest bunch of clowns don't come crashing in and bungle the arrests! As we speak, Ramier should be behind bars, not out for a jog!"

"Which would be the case if your knuckleheads hadn't shown up all guns blazing. The only thing missing was the 'Texas Ranger' theme on some loudspeakers."

Appearances mattered, and Capestan was trying to look calm in her armchair. She was battling her desire to revolt and the pangs of indignation that pumped through her limbs with every sound uttered by Commandant Frost, the head of the B.R.I. With his scorpionfish face, chainsaw smile and sinkhole eyes, he oozed self-satisfaction. The man was entirely bereft of manners or even-handedness. His every interjection hammered home the fact that they were the experts on the ground. No chance of an apology, then.

The two of them had been summoned to Buron's office, and Capestan was struggling to share the same air as him. Duperry, the Crim. divisionnaire, was there too and seemed to reserve a similar revulsion towards him, although this extended to both Lieutenant Diament (insignificant pawn) and Capestan (head of the official dregs squad). No-one here had the least respect for anyone else, with the exception of Patron Saint Buron, who was leaning over his desk, arms wide apart, like Zeus on Mount Olympus. In such company, Capestan had no choice but to take the blows.

"No," Frost said, baring his fangs, "it's just that the sight of officers with the right to bear arms – and a warrant from the public prosecutor – caught you off-guard, didn't it? What were you banking on arresting him for, anyway, out there all alone? When you don't have the wherewithal to act on a file, it's best to hand it to those that do. Amateurs."

"Can I remind you that these 'amateurs' tracked down this file, while you 'pros' have spent a week patting yourselves on the back for putting an innocent man in custody."

"Ah, women. One look at this guy's mug will tell how 'innocent' he is," Frost said to Duperry and Buron.

These two were clearly not about to bite on this bit of locker-room banter. Buron, for reasons that were perhaps more political than genuine, knew it was best to spurn such comments. He was playing the role of the table-tennis referee who would soon be confiscating the ball. As for Duperry, he just wasn't listening. He was looking at his mobile with a barely veiled disdain, punctuating every lost quarter of an hour with a weary sigh. In the line-up of armchairs facing Buron's desk, Duperry was in the furthest to the right, nearest the door. His impeccable suit, sky-blue shirt and Windsor-knotted tie contrasted with Frost's scruffy clothes and unkempt white hair.

At the very left was Diament. His upper body too broad to fit between the armrests, he had been obliged to sit at an angle and only seemed interested in following his boss, albeit a boss who made a show of ignoring him and, on the rare occasion he said anything at all, cut him short with a curt click of the tongue.

Capestan ignored the deliberately sexist provocation, but after thirty minutes of enduring the scorn of this short-sighted windbag, her desire to lash out was starting to intensify. Not content with screwing up their inquiry, he was now trying to teach them a lesson.

"Of course he's guilty, just of a different crime. Now, if the B.R.I. have taken to plucking people at random and seeing which case they can link them to, like pairing up socks, then that's your business. Ultimately, the fact is that your elite squad were miles wide of the mark. We may well be clowns, but you've hardly showered yourselves in glory either."

"That'll do, Capestan," Buron said calmly.

Frost turned to the directeur with an air of satisfaction.

"You are – "

"Same for you, Frost. Both your squads have behaved in an irresponsible manner. Your subterfuge and guesswork have let our main suspect in a triple-murder investigation get away. With a colleague of ours numbering among the victims, let me remind you. You have made a mockery of the Maison de Police. Luckily you've both obsessively kept things on the down-low, so this shambles hasn't got out of control. But I didn't summon you here to listen to you squabble. This is the Police Judiciaire, pull yourselves together. I expect you to work together in a way that befits this institution. No more childish turf wars. Duperry, you haven't said a word. Is your department in charge now or not?"

Duperry tore his eyes from the device and put it back in the inner pocket of his mouse-grey suit jacket. He offered the hint of an apology for the directeur's benefit only:

"We have another ongoing investigation, so I needed to check our progress . . ." he whispered confidentially before raising his voice for the others. "Indeed, our people are officially leading this triple-murder inquiry. However, out of respect for the late Commissaire Rufus and to honour the B.R.I.'s determination to solve this case, we do not want to encroach on their turf. Coordinating efforts can often be complicated, and as such we are placing our trust in any decisions made by the B.R.I., to whom we have delegated all investigative powers. We will only intervene at the very end, allowing them, it goes without saying," he said, ramping up his unctuous tone, "full credit for its successful conclusion."

Then, turning to Buron with a look of concerted malice, he added:

"If the conclusion is successful, of course."

Duperry was revelling in the opportunity to wash his hands of the failures that had bedevilled this inquiry from the start. Crim. had never been enamoured of the B.R.I. and had no intention now of blotting its immaculate copybook in such mediocre company. As for Capestan's paltry Brigade des Innocents, the divisionnaire had quite simply omitted to mention them.

Frost, who was sufficiently unsubtle a character to have only retained the words "honour" and "delegated", nodded in Buron's direction too. He was hell-bent on confirming the eviction of Capestan's squad as explicitly as possible.

"Right. I suppose we'll come and collect all the paperwork . . ."

Buron folded his glasses and sat back in his chair. He appeared to be giving this outcome serious consideration, which sent a shiver of anxiety and incredulity down Capestan's spine. He would not dare. The directeur twisted the stem of his glasses between his thumb and forefinger, then addressed the commissaire directly:

"You should have handed the Lyon file to Lieutenant Diament as soon as you got back. Same for your previous findings about Jacques Melonne. I shouldn't have to repeat myself, Capestan."

The irritated commissaire resisted the urge to argue that this was the first time he had said anything of the sort, and that as it happened, he had specifically granted her permission to keep quiet about it. Capestan knew that her survival this far had Buron's fingerprints all over it. He was a master of double standards. Now he was giving the two birds of prey circling over her head enough of a titbit to satisfy them, so she nodded.

"Understood, Monsieur le Directeur."

"Good. In that case, the terms of your collaboration remain unchanged. However, you are not to obstruct any squads from number 36 – that's an order."

One thing followed by its opposite. Communicating without giving anything away. The commissaire could read Buron like a book. Frost could not.

"With respect, Monsieur le Directeur, you must be joking. I realise you were hoping the son's girlfriend would bring something big to the table, but we've seen where that's got us . . . There's a conflict of interest; it'll never work. And their risky decisions are threatening the success of our investigation."

Without raising his tone, Buron stared straight into Frost's eyes to remind him who made the decisions. The directeur did not need to justify himself.

"I'm in charge of ensuring that the Police Judiciaire uses the full range of talent and personnel at its disposal. I'm not asking for synergy, I'm asking for cordial relations. And I expect to be kept updated on a daily basis. Lieutenant Diament, I'm counting on you as well."

The lieutenant, surprised to be spoken to in a meeting where Frost had so far denied him any involvement whatsoever, stammered for a moment before recovering his natural impassiveness.

"Affirmative, Monsieur le Directeur."

Before Frost had a chance to utter another word, and with Duperry having already extracted a buttock from his armchair, Buron called the meeting to a close by replacing his glasses and opening a fresh file.

"Madame, messieurs, you may leave. Goodbye."

24

Rosière, with the manuscript under her arm and Pilote at her heel, was heading straight for Capestan, who was drinking a cup of tea on the deserted, freezing terrace.

"I've got some bad news for you, Anne."

Bad news. Capestan was taking a bashing from all sides: one of her colleagues, Orsini, was likely to be implicated in a triple-murder case; and their main suspect had taken off quicker than a bat out of hell. Now more bad news. Capestan was struggling to imagine what could possibly make things worse.

Rosière chucked the manuscript onto a deckchair and took out one of her long, thin cigarettes. She sparked it up with her gold lighter and took a short drag before elaborating:

"It's about your father-in-law . . ."

Ah. Anything involving her husband could possibly make things worse. Of course, there was another chink in the armour of this inquiry. What message would she have to deliver to Paul now? For a short while, her father-in-law had been cast as the man of the hour in this case. Was Rosière about to smear his newly polished name? "Bad news" hardly sounded like she was going to be buffing up his medals. When she was done with her dirty rag, nothing would be left shining. Capestan carried on swirling her tea, then eventually looked up at the capitaine, her way of saying: *Go on, shoot, I'm listening.*

"O.K. So I've read and reread the manuscript. It's coded. I began by switching round the places, jobs, names, ages and initials, then I went deeper by deconstructing the characters' motivations. That way I managed to isolate the protagonists of the armed robbery. I cross-referenced each of them with the stuff from the file to flesh out their C.V.s and figure out their real-life stories. And it fitted. Alexis Velowski was not just a witness – he was an accomplice. I think he might have even been the brains behind the operation. But he hadn't planned on it going tits-up, and he crumbled. Rufus was an accomplice too. In the text, the man who represents 'justice' needs money to kick-start his son's trendy career. And the guy who plays the 'patron' in the story could correspond with the producer of your ex-husband's trio."

"Sorry, what?"

"The dough from the bank job organised by your father-in-law enabled your husband to become a comic."

The commissaire fell silent.

Capestan nodded and picked up the papers from the chair, before sitting down and placing her mug on the painted-metal table. Rosière took a perch opposite her, with the dog lying underneath.

So Rufus was a bent cop. No great surprise there. Professional misconduct was just the icing on the cake of an abject life. Although he had done it for the sake of his son, who became a star on the back of a stolen ticket.

Capestan was not sure what impact this news would have on Paul. Blame or regret? A fresh wave of affection, or an outright rejection of such backhanded meddling? The commissaire was not even sure she wanted to tell him. She would think about it later when things had cooled down.

First there was the inquiry. Rufus's involvement made it easier to understand why he brought such a lightweight unit to an operation as serious as a hold-up. These officers were meant to let the perps get away. But Rufus surely had not expected blood to flow.

"Who sought out who to arrange the hit?" Capestan said, tracing her thumb around the rim of her mug. "Who introduced them? Who had the contacts?"

"Melonne. He and Velowski grew up in the same neighbourhood. The manuscript doesn't say where; neither do the police files. When Velowski became a banker, Melonne, who already had a string of petty crimes on his record, got back in touch. Melonne was an armed robber, but he was no psycho. He'd never fired at anyone. And he was an informant to Rufus. The three of them must have harboured dreams of money and grandeur without any of the consequences. Their mistake was hiring Ramier, an unknown entity. There again, Melonne was the middle-man. He met him in prison as a young man and did not know how dangerous the guy was. Same for Rufus. Before then, Ramier had got away with his bigger misdemeanours, so his record made him seem like your average young shitbag."

"Any other participants?"

"Perhaps, but no guarantees. My analysis leaned on the details we already had locked down."

Two cooing pigeons swished their wings on the far corner of the terrace. The presence of two humans sitting calmly, slowed by the winter chill, had little effect on these feathered Parisians. They were happy to occupy the meagre stretch of ivy on the wall, which was a welcome distraction from the square's stony landscape. Pilote sighed – he would have to get to his paws and restore some order.

Melonne had got his hands on a huge fortune, as evidenced by his round-trips to Switzerland. He had also spent it in prodigious fashion, atoning for the two corpses that no doubt haunted his nights. It had eaten away at Velowski too, who had chosen to make himself disappear, the money letting him retire from the world. But Rufus? Capestan could see no sign of it in the last twenty years. In his gossip-gathering, Merlot had not struck on any major changes in lifestyle.

"When they put that bloke in custody and thought the case was closed, the cowboys sent us those files. Did they contain Rufus's bank statements?"

"Yes, I think so. But a policeman was never going to fall for the trick of sticking his ill-gotten treasure in a good old high-street bank. We could always check for cash withdrawals . . . if there aren't any, then maybe he had a hidden stash."

"Yes," Capestan said. "We need to find out if he hid the money somewhere, and whether Ramier had to torture him to discover its whereabouts."

"Or maybe he invested the whole lot in his son's career."

Rosière rolled the tip of her cigarette round the ashtray, then aimed a maternal smile at her colleague.

"This time, you do need to go and see him, my darling."

Capestan nodded. She had no choice. Two shudders – one of impatience, the other of reluctance – collided head-on, fusing then fading into nothing.

There would also be the matter of whether or not to divulge

the information. As with Orsini, maybe silence would be the best option.

"Have you said anything to the others?"

"No. This is your shit-sandwich, not ours. Your call."

Capestan, who hated keeping any secrets from her squad, now had a second crisis of conscience to deal with. On this case, she was making them all work their arses off, prodding them every which way, only to keep all the findings to herself. She was not too keen on that image of herself.

Rufus's corruption also meant she would be tarnishing the reputation of another police officer. Setting one more in her sights and turning her back on the rest. Maybe two, if she counted Orsini. They had been right to baulk at the start of the Rufus case – they were bound to crash even further down the pecking order.

On the other hand, Crim. and the B.R.I. had not seen this manuscript. And if they did see it, they did not have a Rosière to decode it. If she wanted, this information could stay within the four walls of the Commissariat des Innocents.

Whose reputation would she tarnish? Who would she lie to? Her squad? Number 36? The Palais de Justice? Paul? What should she say, and who to?

Capestan turned these questions over and over in her head, twisting them like a vase to check for defects. One false move and the whole thing would shatter.

She had to confront Paul and disfigure the version of his father that she had promised, without really thinking, to leave untouched when she told him about the murder.

Or she could keep this quiet too and hope a chance downpour would wash it all away.

But she had to see her husband again, that much was for sure. Desire, fear and guilt were closing ranks for a new battle that Capestan was doing her best to avoid.

The commissaire searched for an apology in Rosière's eyes, which were full of compassion but devoid of doubt. She let out a deep, slow sigh and picked up her mobile from beside her cold tea.

25

The rows of empty seats in the Italian-style theatre disappeared into the darkness. At the front on the spotlit stage stood an energetic, cocky young man. As he paced the boards, he seemed to be asking God himself what He thought of his stand-up and whether it wasn't all too clever. He was demanding more light, more sound, more laughter. He had talent, but not as much as he had ambition. Capestan recognised in his expression the same false modesty affected by most of Paris's funny-men.

God did not answer, leaving the job to the producer sitting in the middle of the auditorium, who was firing out instructions in a majestic voice that immediately turned Capestan's spine into a tuning fork. The commissaire stayed in the shadows at the back and admired the thick hair that was made even blonder by the lights. Over the years, his profile had thickened without ever getting fat. Paul kept an eye on it. He was vain, after all, something his father had always mocked him for. The son had inherited Serge's manly beauty but left the ruggedness behind. A comedian and a show-off. A loyal, kind man, just one who ran away from hardship with almost childish predictability. When Capestan started unravelling, he had not lasted a year. She had stopped laughing; he had stopped staying. His punishment came with no deadline and no chance of an appeal.

Anne knew that she had not been very accommodating, or even particularly pleasant. At the time, she had put up a hard, cold, abrupt front. All her strength was focused elsewhere, on the investigations and the need to stay afloat. She had nothing left with which to make herself bearable. Living alongside the nocturnal king of glitz almost made her into a full-blown schizophrenic, prone to bouts of real bitterness. Her love for Paul was like a high-wire act that left her nauseous. She had tried to keep her balance amid the brilliance, the joy, the intelligence, but what she experienced in her job suddenly made all this seem improper. She had tried, but she had not tried hard enough.

And neither had Paul.

Capestan breathed out. She resented the figure calmly issuing stage directions from his seat. But at the same time, her legs were jittering with excitement, urging her forward as fast as possible to sit next to him, to breathe with him, alone in the dark theatre. Except she had questions to ask him.

Spotting her as she approached, Paul eagerly waved her over. He stood up, bearing those show-stopping good looks of his, but caught his knee on the bottom of the neighbouring seat. She walked up the row and wondered whether to leave a gap between him and her, eventually opting to sit right next to him. He held her shoulder and gave her a quick peck on the cheek. They sat down and watched the guy on the stage reel off his routine, holding back any mention of murder or suspicion. They enjoyed this short moment where their auras could meet again. It felt calming. The material-to-material contact of Paul's cotton shirt and her cashmere sweater transmitted a sensual warmth between them, as if the threads were momentarily intertwined. Allowing this thrill to register but not letting it dull her determination, the commissaire spoke to him in hushed tones:

"We're making progress. We're sure we have identified your father's killer. Max Ramier, if that name rings a bell at all. Here's his photo," she said, showing him a police mugshot on her mobile.

"No . . . Not so far as I remember, anyway."

"And these men?" she said, bringing up Melonne and Velowski.

"Yes, maybe these ones, but it's hazy. I can't really say. And . . . do you know why he killed him?"

"Settling scores, it seems."

Capestan hesitated. Either she told him now or she didn't.

"It's to do with an armed robber, who's also a murderer. Your father arrested him and sent him down. He took his revenge when he was released."

Paul nodded, taking in the news that he had no doubt been hoping to hear. What did he know about his father's corruption? Was he already aware? Capestan could not tell, and this uncertainty, which had not occurred to her before, suddenly worried her.

All the same, she was now committed to a course – lying through omission – and she would have to stick to it, even if that made the follow-up questions harder. Capestan decided to change tack.

"How's the new guy?" she asked, nodding at the comic.

"Very good. He's pretty pushy, but he's starting to make a name for himself. Plenty of hits on YouTube, the odd thing on T.V. He's popular with the Friday night games shows. He's got his head down and working his way up."

"And you? Still not keen to get back into it yourself?"

"Sometimes . . ."

Paul patted his hair with mock arrogance.

"I found out yesterday that I'm no longer a total has-been."

"Something new?"

"No, no. Vintage. It's early days, but the idea of a comeback has done the rounds at a few production companies. Film, this time. Feature-length, a sort of throwback thing."

"Great . . ."

Paul made a face as if to say that it was nothing to get too excited about.

"If the script's any good then yeah, it could be great."

"Needs some funding, I imagine."

"Yes, that's part of it. Of course. In fact that's all of it," he said, stroking his stubble.

"How did that all work out when you first came to Paris?"

Paul let out a short laugh.

"Seriously? I haven't got the faintest clue . . ."

"Are you kidding?"

"No, I know, it must sound crazy, but you need to cast your mind back. Remember what I was like then – a blowhard. Denis was in charge of the business side of things, I was just the pretty boy."

"Nonsense, Paul, stop that."

Doing himself down again. This tendency followed him everywhere, as if it had been chiselled into his pedestal. No-one had ever managed to sand it down. Paul had written every single sketch, each one making millions laugh. His humour was close to the bone but never hurtful. It united people. And all this thanks to a work-rate and rigour that no blowhard could have managed. When it came to money, it was true, he paid less attention. She would have to follow up on these practical matters with Denis.

Maybe he knew details that Paul did not, namely the cost involved in putting their show together.

"Come on, I was hardly outstanding back then. And I wasn't looking very far ahead," he said modestly. "All I was interested in was moving forward and living my life. No inkling about fans, success, causes or consequences."

"You were looking for an escape route. And you were young at heart."

He gave a slight shrug, causing his shirt to rub against the velvet of the seat.

"You were too, weren't you?" he asked, the question sincere.

"Kind of. Less so," she said with a smile.

"Ah."

Except around you, she thought to herself. In those days, Paul made her ten years younger (and several I.Q. points stupider). He just had to turn up and she would lose her focus completely. That was when their love was starting to take root, turning her brain to mush and the rest of her body into tumult.

"Does this have anything to do with the investigation?"

"No, nothing," she said.

The seats meant they did not have to face each other, which made it easier to lie.

"The armed robbery happened when you were still in Lyon. Do you remember your father having any unusual visitors or any major shifts to his work patterns? Threats, blackmail, anything like that?"

She hesitated, out of habit more than anything, before adding:

"Changes to his mood?"

"His mood," Paul said, letting out a heavy sigh. "Yes, the last few years in Lyon were odd, but I can't put my finger on why. I was setting out on a new life, with new people, a new desire to defend myself, too. I had moved out of their apartment. I'm not sure if it was because his grown-up son was flying the nest, or if it was something at work, but he did behave differently. Back then, outside of you and my career, I wasn't really aware of anything. I'd had enough of my father."

"Yes, of course. Had you seen him more recently? Did you notice anything, any nervousness?"

"No."

Paul stared at a phantom piece of fluff on his jeans, brushed it away, then turned to Capestan.

"I never saw him again after the wedding, you know that."

Capestan knew.

26

In the small bedroom of the country hotel, Paul was fumbling with his tie, his hands trembling with rage. He could see his father's disapproving, fixed grin in the wardrobe mirror. From his superior height and with his muscles threatening to burst the seams of his suit, he was haranguing his son, pushing him to give up, to walk away.

"You'll never measure up to a policewoman; you don't have the stature. You're just a joker. Look at you with your matching tie. Spend hours picking it, did you? How much did you blow on that playboy suit, anyway? Unbelievable, all pampered, smooth-faced and stinking of perfume – "

"Shut it," Paul snapped.

Now Serge's smile turned nasty. He walked up to his son with a poisonous look in his eye.

"You can't afford to take that tone with your father. Listen to me, you shitbag. You can't afford to take on Capestan, either. She'll come up against things you don't even want to know about. While you're sipping cocktails in the evening, she'll be swimming in filth you can't imagine. And when she gets home needing a guy with strong shoulders, someone who can handle it, what'll she find? Look at you, for fuck's sake. What'll she find?"

"A man who talks to her, listens to her. A man who won't lay into his son. Maybe that's what maman would have wanted."

Paul held back the "you bastard" that was coming next. He felt tears pricking at his eyes, but he did not want to give him the satisfaction. Shit, he finally had something good, something beautiful, something great in his life, something that lit up the darkness he had known, but no: his father's shadow was still lurking, still growing, still threatening it all.

"Your mother could always rely on me, she – "

"Rely on who? Old Billy Big Balls here? You're the worst husband she could have had. She's had a shitty life and she's been crushed by sadness."

The fist struck him on the arch of his eyebrow, which burst open under the shock. Blinded and almost out cold, Paul smashed into the mirror, shattering it and sending splinters of glass across the floorboards. He managed to stay upright by hooking his fingers onto the frame, but a stray shard nicked his palm. He wiped his brow with the sleeve of his starched shirt, spattering the bright white fabric with red droplets as his suit and tie soaked up the blood gushing from his head. Paul looked up to see his father standing there triumphantly, ready to land another blow just to show him who was boss. A familiar, deep-rooted terror rose up inside him, coming from before he could remember, etched into his body from when he was small. Far worse than the pain itself, it froze his limbs, his thoughts and any instincts that might have let him fight back against this man, the very embodiment of domination.

But Paul was bigger now. Rugby, boxing, hockey, martial arts and late-night scuffles had all given him a taste of violence. He had been getting ready for years now, waiting for that chance, that flicker that would overcome his fear.

"Today is my wedding, papa. You should have thought twice before playing with symbols. Today is going to be different."

Paul stood up straight, his eye puffy and half-closed. He realised he was as tall as his father – perhaps even taller – and just as broad. A rush of strength came from deep within him, seizing control of his arms and filling his rib cage. He grabbed his father's suit and delivered a furious uppercut.

He knocked him out with a single blow. Then he slapped him to bring him round.

"Go back to your room, clean yourself up and change your clothes. I'm getting married in fifteen minutes."

The registrar's gaze alternated between the bride's sublime face and the swollen features of her husband-to-be. Paul felt sorry for the poor man having to stumble and stammer, endlessly referring to his notes and finding it impossible to concentrate.

The twenty-year-old Anne was wearing a somewhat understated cream dress, her hair tied into a quietly elegant bun. Paul had opted for the jeans and green polo shirt that he had hoped to wear the following day. Even more puzzling for the town official must have been the complete absence of stress or resentment in the bride's demeanour, not to mention the fact that the beaming groom with the pulped face seemed as happy as could be.

After the confrontation, Paul had taken a shower to calm his fury. He then rolled his bloodied clothes into a ball, chucked them in his bag and changed. Bit by bit his hatred subsided, leaving room for the only thing that mattered – he had fought back. On his command, his father had left the room. For the first time, he had made the enemy fall back. Never again would his old foe try his hand, not now that he knew the sound of the knockout bell. That day, he had thrown off the shackles; finally his life could intertwine with Anne's. The fear would stay for a few more years, carved into his heart, but his will was striding ahead.

When he had stepped into Capestan's room to prepare her, her face became distorted. The moment he started explaining she had lurched for the door, but he held her back. They spoke. This was his battle. He told her about his rage, his peace, even his joy. He felt boosted by a new sense of being. A ceremony awaited. She had unleashed that smile of hers, the one that should have showed up on the weather forecast. They had gone downstairs and headed to the town hall, together.

Having officiated, with difficulty, in front of a roomful of rather perplexed people, the registrar pronounced them man and wife. They exchanged thin rings and kissed quickly, because their guests were looking, and because Paul's cheek was still extremely sore.

The newly-weds turned to face the crowd. Their families forced a smile, though there were some stony glances from one side of the aisle to the other. Paul's father, visibly injured himself, was standing tight-lipped and straight as a gallows, with a menacing look. Aunts, uncles and cousins, embarrassed but hardly surprised, pretended not to see him, all the while avoiding eye contact with the Capestan family. It made for a tense atmosphere.

As for Anne's parents and close family, they managed to remain perfectly dignified and seemed oblivious to any controversy. They must have wondered whether or not their disappointment ought to run deeper, to challenge the very root of the view they had of this mischievous yet kind little girl, who had chosen an unorthodox path as an adult.

Her decision to join the police had been curious enough. Even though her many successes at the École de Saint-Cyr had flung open the door to the most prestigious positions in the field, rather than staying in criminal investigation, a career in the law seemed far more natural for a young woman of her circumstances. But as her grandfather always used to say, more out of regret than admiration: "Anne has her own way of doing things – she's a free spirit." By going ahead with this marriage, she was flirting with pariah status. No-one wanted to judge, of course, but such uneven unions rarely worked out. When it came to bringing up children, these differences – which intensity and passion can mask in your twenties – would come flooding back and cause chaos for the couple.

Paul was aware that his outfit, his face and his father were feeding into his in-laws' already firmly embedded and no doubt natural concerns. He felt bad for Anne and was doing his absolute best to limit the fallout.

Beside him, Anne was not in the least worried, smiling from ear to ear and ignoring everything else.

As for the friends and witnesses, once they had been reassured and made each other's acquaintance, they got on like a house on fire. The ceremony had rolled out the pink carpet as far as flirtatious conversation was concerned.

It was time to get back to the hotel for dinner and dancing. Anne and Paul had chosen to keep it simple, partly to avoid accentuating the disparity, but mainly because Paul had insisted on footing the bill himself. The place was warm and rustic, perfect for the sixty or so people they had invited.

All the guests sat down either side of two long trestle tables, a little surprised that the sparkling wine had already been poured out, the last few bubbles dying at the surface. Everyone raised a warm glass to toast the couple, taking care not to mention the rather ominous circumstances of the celebration. Then they waited for the food, which took an absolute age.

Finally, the owner emerged in his white chef's apron, with red eyes and a surly expression, carrying a few starters. His young commis, who looked ill at ease in his checked trousers, handed out plates too. When he was in range of Paul, the groom leaned across the table and said in a lowered voice:

"What's going on?"

The boy squirmed and glanced over his shoulder to see if the boss could hear.

"It's the owner's wife. She took off this morning. Left him. So, he's not really in the mood for a wedding banquet . . . It's quite a job, you see, plus all the happiness here is bringing him down."

Paul and Anne shared a look of pity.

"Poor man . . ."

"Yup, and the problem is the food's all getting cold, 'cause she always did front-of-house."

"Hold on . . . Isn't there anyone else you can call up for some extra help?" Paul asked, still whispering.

"Well, round here, last-minute on a Saturday . . . can't really see it happening. Plus he's in no state to get on the phone . . ."

The commis stared Paul straight in the eye. He had one more piece of news to put the icing on the cake:

"Also, I'm really sorry for your bash and that, but it's just . . . the boss's wife, she took off with the sound system, too. To piss him off."

He shook his head, genuinely sad for them.

"Which is a bit of a bummer for the music later."

After a long silence, Paul and Anne felt a mad, nervous laughter creeping up on them. The day was descending into a shambles and the absurdity of the situation was starting to test people's understanding.

The owner's deathly voice was suddenly heard next to the junior, who took it as his cue to disappear.

"Don't worry, we shook on it, we shook on it – you will have your wedding feast."

"Yes, great, I'm not worried, not at all," Paul said in an attempt at reconciliation. "Maybe we could give you a little hand with the service?"

"If you think that'll be necessary . . ."

"Yes. Yes, I think it will."

Family and friends nobly took it in turns to help throughout the evening, forming an unconventional but effective team of waiters. The guests turned a blind eye to fingermarks on plates, and the cutlery seldom knew right from left, but nobody wanted for anything.

Denis must have done fifty round-trips on his scooter to fetch enough kit to sort out the music situation. Sitting side by side at a table where people were constantly standing up – themselves included, from time to time – to retrieve dishes from the kitchen, Paul and Anne held hands for a moment.

"Going well, wouldn't you say?" Paul asked.

"It's wonderful."

She stared straight into his eyes in the way she knew would pin him to the wall.

"Really wonderful."

Paul puffed his chest with so much pride it looked like a zeppelin. He was happy. He felt barely a pang when he saw his father leave, even though he knew full well he would never see him again.

When Paul found the owner at 5.00 a.m. to settle the bill, the bereft man told him that Serge Rufus had already paid the full amount.

Paul never knew if it was a way of asking for forgiveness, or one last attempt to humiliate him. He never had the courage to tell Anne.

27

Sitting in front of "The Snake Charmer" in the Musée d'Orsay, Capestan wondered, as she did every time she saw one of Douanier Rousseau's sombre, poetic masterpieces, what the artist – and more broadly the France people – had done to deserve the tribute from the 1980s pop group Compagnie Créole. *Comme dans les, comme dans les, comme dans les tableaux du Douanier Rousseau . . .* The words went round and round her head. Not that she minded – it was something of a guilty pleasure.

After seeing Paul, the commissaire had called Denis straight away to book in a meeting. Since then, she had been waiting on that bench, wondering why exactly she had not said anything about her father-in-law's dirty past. Who was she trying to spare? Serge Rufus and any last vestige of his image? Or Paul and his uncertain grief at being orphaned? Herself, as the messenger? Herself, and her last chance at her husband trying to get her back?

"Wah!"

Capestan jumped out of her skin as the beast's hands took hold of her shoulders. She had been too absorbed to hear Denis approach. He still had paper towel round his neck after having his make-up done for his next scene. The man's cheeky charm had only grown since he turned forty. The roundness of his cheeks had disappeared, making way for an altogether tougher, action-man character. Big but well defined, with a shaved head and a hooked nose, Denis looked set to roll over a car bonnet to avoid the next explosion. The advantage of having famous friends was that you could keep up with them in H.D., even if you had not seen them in person for ages. Denis was the big success story of the trio, the shining light whose career had taken off in a way that the other two's had not.

He leaned in towards Capestan and they each pressed their forehead against the other's left temple, then the right one, a habit they had started one day to parody some big comedian who air-kissed so as not to spoil his blow-dry, or something like that. They could not really remember anymore, but the ritual had survived.

"How you doing, old girl?"

"Fine, and you, old man?"

Denis held out his arms to indicate the mega-production going on around them, with him yet again in the starring role. A thriller, part of which was set in the Orsay, presumably just to give the Louvre a rest.

"So long as no-one knocks the ladder while I'm on top, I'm happy. Parents are well, plenty of chicks, holidays not long from now – can't complain! How about you? You called an end to your years as a hermit? Back on the mojitos?"

The actor smiled. The mojitos thing was a reference to their partying days – those were long gone, and Denis knew it. He became more serious.

"Have you seen Paul again?"

"Yes. Actually, that's why I'm here."

Behind them, the booming voices of the directors of photography and the sound engineers tore into the junior lighting guys and the assistant boom operators, while other stressed-out, high-pitched people yelled about timings, budgets and silence.

"Serge is dead. Murdered."

"Oh shit."

Denis turned to the paintings to his right. Several thoughts seemed to be crossing his mind, and Capestan was not sure she would mange to decode them all. Surprise was not one of them. He turned back to Anne.

"Do you know who did it? And is Paul O.K.? How did he take it?"

"Paul's not too bad. Sorry to be so direct, but I do have a question for you," Capestan said apologetically. "For the inquiry."

"I'm listening," Denis said with a frown, his hands in his lap.

"When you came to Paris to perform in that café-theatre, that must have cost money, right? Lodging, fees and all that. You were all co-producers, weren't you?"

"Yes," he said after a pause, avoiding eye contact.

"Who paid?"

Capestan hoped Denis would tell her the truth. They used to be very close, but had not seen each other for a good few years. People are always cagey about money and police matters, especially paranoid celebs.

"O.K., O.K.," the actor said, throwing up his hands. "It was Serge. He made me swear not to say anything at the time, but he gave me a massive sum. In cash."

"How much?"

"Five hundred thousand francs . . ."

Capestan whistled.

"Did that not strike you as odd?" she said.

He prodded a dusty patch on the museum's shiny floor with the tip of his trainer.

"Yes, a little. But . . . in the end, you know what kind of a guy he was. I didn't try to understand, I just took it."

"Did he tell you where it came from?"

Denis let out a sharp laugh.

"No, of course not. He said it was to help launch Paul's career. My first thought was: 'To launch him, or to get him off your hands?'"

"What did he say to that?"

"Oh no, I didn't say it out loud. Serge scared the crap out of me. Paul was the only person who answered back to him, as if to show he had the courage."

"Well, he did."

"Yes, you're right."

The information about the finances matched the commissaire's preconceived ideas, yet she could not shake off the feeling that Denis was not telling her everything, a feeling she would stick in a corner of her head like one of Dax's Post-it notes.

From the set, they heard the director spitting into a walkie-talkie: "Where's the star cleared off to now?"

"Right, I'd better get back to it – they won't ask so nicely next time," Denis said as he performed the same knock of the forehead with Capestan.

He scooped up a replica Taurus Raging Bull from a side table, which he waved at her:

"See, it's not just the cops who get to play with cool guns . . ."

A silly joke to finish – despite the bad news, her old friend was never one to break with tradition.

"Yup, although if they loaded it with live ammo, the recoil would send you flying off-screen, old man . . ."

"Ooooh, that was good – you win."

The joke, yes, thought Capestan. But the truth? That was less certain.

Dax was not sure about the speed-dating thing, but his friend had insisted on putting his name down. Had to be worth a try before the fad petered out, he said.

Feeling uneasy in the large brasserie that been taken over for the event, the lieutenant – clean-shaven and wearing his finest white T-shirt beneath his leather jacket – was greeted by a pretty woman who, although not participating herself, explained how it all worked. A little too fast. Dax caught most of the drift: he was to sit down in front of a girl, they had seven minutes, then the bell would ring and he would move on to the next girl at the next table.

He nervously fidgeted with an unruly bit of hair at the top of his head before sitting down opposite "Doriane", according to the name badge.

"Hi, my name's Doriane," she said.

Doriane was thirty-two and a mobile telephone consultant. She loved sport, sewing and reading epic fantasy novels.

"And what about you? What are your passions?" she asked.

Dax thought long and hard to avoid a foolish answer. He loved his job and I.T. He loved going for walks, too, especially in the countryside. And video games, of course. Birdwatching. Let's not forget boxing. But is that what she meant by "passions"? He wasn't entirely sure . . .

The bell rang. Before he got round to answering, Dax had to leave Doriane.

28

The *métro* from the Musée d'Orsay back to the commissariat moved along in its typical bouncy fashion. Making the most of that rarest of treasures – a free seat – she was rereading *Saga*, a dog-eared old Tonino Benacquista paperback. She always switched off completely on the *métro*. Either she read or she let the time and space wash over her, trying her best to curb her people-watching tendencies. At Palais-Royal, she caught a glimpse of a man in a thick, brown, woollen jumper sticking adverts onto the sides of his ceramic cave. A thousand steps from daylight, he must have had to glue several square metres of grey paper before pasting each one, sheet by sheet, onto the curved wall, gradually unveiling the intense blue of the Pacific, the white sand, the palm trees, and a smiling woman in a bikini. He was brushing an image of happiness without showing any emotion of his own, before moving onto the next one and the one after that.

Capestan emerged at Châtelet where a dry, chilly breeze turned her eyes and nose red. She weaved her way through the crowds of window-shoppers on rue de Rivoli towards the relative calm of place Saint-Opportune. Denis had seen the money twenty years earlier and he must have known it was dirty. Capestan could not keep Paul in the dark about a fact that both she and his best friend were aware of. She would call him when she got back.

In this part of town, the streets are like a maze of little alleyways, most of them pedestrianised. Paris bustled and teemed, forcing millions of people to cross paths and rub shoulders. Some of them were murderers. Had Max Ramier fled the capital after the Plaza episode? The commissaire would put money on not. But where should they look for him now?

Rosière had been on to the management at the Plaza and learned that Ramier had paid for his suite in cash a few days earlier. A casual twenty-six thousand euros. But, contrary to what he had told the prison service, he had only moved in a month after his release. Three days after Jacques Maire's death, no less. He must have gathered up the lucre after each murder. Rather than revenge, his actions were much more guided by money. According to the police file, the sum that the armed robbers walked away with – twenty million freshly printed francs, plus whatever was in the safety-deposit boxes – had never reappeared. Was there still another batch to retrieve? Had Ramier extorted Rufus's share, or had the commissaire spent it all on his son?

If his list of murder victims was complete, then maybe Ramier had skipped town or even left the country. He must have known the B.R.I.'s reputation, which was reason enough not to hang around.

Capestan had asked the team to put everything into finding the fugitive, leaving her to focus on the thorny issue of Orsini. She was missing one piece of information, and finding it meant calling Buron.

Capestan put herself in the capitaine's shoes. If a gunman had shot dead her family in cold blood, she would chase him to the end of every desert, to the bottom of every pit, to the uppermost branches of the tallest forests. She would catch him and string him up like a sandbag. And then she would beat him until she died of exhaustion herself.

Orsini, however, had waited for years. Waited for what? What more did he need to know before taking action? Maybe the identity of the accomplices had passed him by and he had held on for Ramier's release to find out. The D.N.A. tests indicated that the three murders had been committed by the same criminal, but they had not revealed who that criminal was. Was Orsini following behind Ramier, who was simply recovering his money? Capestan had cross-referenced the capitaine's hours with the timings of the murders. Not once had he been at the commissariat. Yet the same vengeful blood that coursed through Capestan's veins clearly did not flow through stony Orsini. Maybe he was hoping to arrest them, but Ramier had pulled the rug from under his feet by killing them first.

The commissaire had brought up the capitaine's H.R. record. He had indeed joined the police after the hold-up. It must have been what lay behind his change of career: something to look into. Did he have any suspicions about Serge Rufus at the time? Had he tried to keep tabs on him?

If this mission had underpinned all of Orsini's decision-making since joining the police, then that in turn asked questions about why he had been posted to the Brigade des Innocents.

Capestan inserted her earpiece and flicked through her contacts until she found Buron.

"Morning, Capestan. Are you calling to explain why the Police Judiciaire has just received a bill for a 'World of Warcraft' subscription?"

"No, but if you feel the need to talk about it, then I'm all ears, Monsieur le Directeur. I have a question for after, though."

Buron sensed her genuine concern and abandoned his supervisory tone.

"I'm listening."

Capestan rotated the microphone between her thumb and forefinger. There was only one way to ask this question.

"How did Orsini end up in our squad? Who sent him?"

"Himself. Why?"

"He demanded to be transferred into the worst division of the entire police service? He deliberately banished himself and you didn't think to tell me?"

"To be honest, his colleagues have loathed him wherever he's been posted. I assumed he was being badgered for some reason or other and decided to take off. Why, what's going on with Orsini now?"

"Nothing new, I just ran into a curious journalist. Thought I'd follow up on it."

The commissaire could almost make out the sound of the directeur drumming his fingers on his Moroccan leather desk-blotter.

"Your lying's got better, Capestan."

"Thank you, but right now I'm afraid I don't have time to perfect it, Monsieur le Directeur. But I assure you, the truth will come out, ready to be buried."

"I'm sure it will, commissaire, I'm sure it will."

Capestan arrived at the foot of the building that housed their commissariat. So Orsini had requested the transfer himself. Her status as Rufus's daughter-in-law must have played a part.

Orsini had come because of her.

He was watching her, weighing her up, maybe even suspecting her.

Capestan wiped the soles of her boots on the doormat, still unsure what to do about the awkward captain. She could understand the battle he was fighting, but why did it have to involve harming her squad?

She turned the handle just as part of the team were bundling out the door. Saint-Lô, Rosière, Lebreton, Évrard, Merlot, Dax and Lewitz spun her round by the shoulders, with Torrez following in his own good time.

"We've located him!"

"Who? Where?"

"Ramier, at the Lutetia."

"He's booked himself into another luxury hotel? Under his own name?"

"No," Rosière said, hitting the lift button like a jackhammer. "Using his name from Velowski's manuscript. I thought it might have been a regular pseudonym and asked Dax to run a search. We must be the only squad with this info. . . ."

Since the meeting, Buron's instructions, though clear on the surface, had left them some room for manoeuvre. That at least was how Capestan had chosen to interpret them in the heat of the moment. With all their G.P.S. technology, tracking devices and C.C.T.V. cameras across the city, if the B.R.I. and Frost had not nailed this address, then it was not up to the rookies to hand it to them on a plate.

Of course, this spiteful logic meant the squad could not afford to screw things up.

"Let's go! We can't lose him this time!"

"Consider it done!" Dax crowed.

"Ah, never say that!" Torrez said with a groan.

29

"I can't come with you now."

"Yes you can, José, come on."

"No, something bad'll happen. Too many signs."

"There haven't been any signs, just a slightly overenthusiastic phrase from Dax. Nothing odd there. Come on, that's an order."

Torrez nodded, his forehead more furrowed than a mastiff's when you try to drag it towards the bath, before jumping into the 306 and slamming the door behind him. Almost as if he was saying I told you so.

The legendary hotel reared up on rue de Sèvres like an ocean liner, its balconies now rather tired-looking and covered in safety nets, reminding Capestan of the bandages on a diva's face after her latest nose-job.

Capestan and Torrez pulled up at the entrance to see Lebreton and Saint-Lô leaping up the stairs four at a time, while Évrard stayed down at reception. Rosière, Pilote, Dax and Lewitz were only just getting out of the Porsche – the brigadier was obviously worried about the unforgiving hooks of the tow-truck, since he had opted for a proper parking space at the foot of the scaffolding that climbed the whole of the palace's western flank. All four set off, with Lewitz bringing up the rear, still clutching the microfibre cloth he had used to wipe away smudges from the bodywork.

A sudden movement overhead caught Capestan's attention and made her look up. The others followed suit. A man had clambered out of a window and was making his way down the scaffolding. Max Ramier.

In his haste, the fugitive slipped on the wet aluminium walkway, colliding with the building's façade. He steadied himself just in time, tearing off a block of white stone as he did so, which bounced all the way down to the ground. Ramier watched it tumble, holding onto a lifeline to keep his balance.

Lewitz was the first to respond. The brigadier tore down boulevard Raspail at such speed it looked like he might collar Ramier before he even touched the pavement. After sprinting a few metres, he leaped onto the bonnet of the Porsche and spread-eagled himself as wide as he could to intercept the stone block, which shattered his tibia. The dull snap of the fracture reached the team, who instinctively turned to Torrez for a split-second before kicking into action. The distraught lieutenant took a step back.

Capestan briefly touched him on the shoulder, then ran to Lewitz's aid with the others. The brigadier was howling in pain, his leg sticking out an unnatural angle. The officers arrived one after the other to assess the damage as Rosière called an ambulance. Lewitz had chosen to save the car. The moment of confusion was all Ramier needed to slip through the netting and hare down the boulevard. Capestan took off in pursuit, supported by Saint-Lô and Lebreton, who had shinned down the scaffolding.

Ramier was confidently quickening his pace, following a true line down the wide pavement and making no attempt to escape down one of the surrounding side streets. At the current rate, he looked like he could breeze all the way to Lyon. Lebreton's long limbs and Saint-Lô's natural élan kept them in contention, while Capestan was having to dig deeper to avoid lagging behind. Even at the junction with the hectic rue de Rennes, with cars and pedestrians swirling in every direction, Ramier sliced through the crowds as if he were the only person in the world. The screech of tyres and honking of horns echoed the furious expletives of the passers-by. The officers followed, holding their arms aloft by way of apology. Ramier had just gained twenty metres on them, continuing the same wild kamikaze approach across rue de Vaugirard, before lurching left onto rue de Fleurus.

For six long seconds, he vanished from their line of sight. Capestan opened up her mental map of the area to reveal a labyrinth of different options. Six seconds was enough to turn left down rue Jean-Bart, or vanish into any number of the little courtyards on rue Madame further along. A removal van, legally parked for once, was so tall it blocked their view, forcing the officers to take a right. Their instincts were rewarded when they spotted Ramier's outline crossing rue Guynemer and hurrying through the black, gold-tipped railings into the Jardin du Luxembourg.

Buoyed by this fresh visual after several seconds of uncertainty, Lebreton and Saint-Lô shot into the park. A few paces behind them, Capestan suddenly wondered if the man was armed. A cold bead of sweat ran down the back of her neck. Ramier was dangerous, merciless and, as they well knew, capable of firing at a child. And the gardens were packed.

Straining to make out any bumps in the fugitive's clothing and assess the freedom of his movements, Capestan considered giving up the chase. But thanks to their second wind, Lebreton and Saint-Lô were virtually on his heels. Ramier zigged down a narrow path that was bordered to the right with the wire fence of a playground. Before the officers could follow, they were cut off by a line of ponies being returned to their post. Even without any kids on their backs, they waddled along as slowly as ever. It took an eternity for them to pass and any hope of getting round them was futile.

Ramier would soon be nothing more than a fleck on the far side of the park.

Lebreton and Capestan were doubled up and gasping for air, their lungs on fire. But Saint-Lô, still on high alert, raced towards the pony-driver and grabbed the reins from his hand without any explanation. Then, making full use of his jockey's physique, he sprang into the saddle of the first pony and spurred it on with a roar. The beast shied in surprise before tearing off ahead like a fury. What with being tied together, the others had no choice but to follow.

After its rider calmed it with a rather gruff stroke on the neck, the pony soon made up the distance between itself and Ramier, goaded on by the joy of being able to gallop at last, as well as by Saint-Lô's booming voice. The others followed rapidly in its wake, crossing the park in record speed looking like a mad string of runaway sausages. Their hooves pounded on the ground, kicking up dust and making an infernal racket. Terrified tourists yelled and dived out the way, while passers-by leaped into hedges or onto benches. Teenagers upped sticks and stubbed out cigarettes with unprecedented speed, then pulled out their smartphones to film the action.

Some of the nags to the rear started to crave the limelight, pulling off in various directions and slowing the progress of the valiant lead pony. Saint-Lô, displaying admirable flexibility amidst this chaotic stampede, turned around to establish the meaning of this sudden loss of discipline. With an instinctive motion of his right hand, he pulled up his trouser leg and unsheathed the dagger he kept strapped around his ankle. In a single swipe, he sliced the cord to separate his steed from the rest of the troop.

Now unburdened, his mount seemed to grow wings and fly forward like a diminutive Pegasus, its mane flapping and its hooves hammering on the sandy path, accelerating after Ramier. At this point, the other ponies scattered into the park in search of snacks and other distractions, except for a dark grey one, who returned to its post, clearly too old for this kind of tomfoolery.

Max Ramier stole a glance over his shoulder and, even at a distance, the shock was visible on his tired face. But he was a cunning man. Rounding the Sénat, he ran down some steps and went full tilt through the traffic of rue de Médicis.

It was over.

Saint-Lô pulled softly on the reins and patted the pony's flank to slow it down, which it begrudgingly agreed to do. Saint-Lô dropped to the ground and, after running his hands through the beast's mane and still holding the bridle, headed for a piece of card that was fluttering at the top of the steps.

It had fallen from Ramier's pocket while he was making his escape.

"Wow, he must have been one of the finest horsemen in his company," Capestan said, full of admiration.

30

Notwithstanding Saint-Lô's spectacular efforts, Ramier had escaped again. The team had returned to the ranch dejected, praying that neither the B.R.I. nor anyone else got wind of this crashing blunder, an unmistakable lesson in the perils of going it alone. Any charge of incompetence would be entirely valid. If number 36 was to hear, it would earn the squad enough negative stripes to see them all through to retirement.

There was just the small piece of card, which had come to them as much by chance as through exertion. Across it were six digits written in biro. Six digits without a name, address or any other clue were their only spoils. Orsini had grabbed it feverishly before shutting himself in his office. His colleagues had been quite happy to leave him to it. While Saint-Lô, Merlot, Lebreton and Rosière sat in silence on the bar stools in the snooker room to drink the drink of the vanquished, Évrard and Dax went to hospital to see Lewitz, whose family had already rushed to his bedside. Torrez had slunk off home long ago.

Capestan was out on the terrace, where she had just called Paul to fill him in on Serge Rufus's inglorious role in the armed robbery. She had also informed him that the money had gone towards financing his first Paris production. Down the line, Paul's reaction to the hold-up had seemed more resigned than surprised. On the other hand, this show of patronage from a father who was as unaffectionate towards his son as he was disapproving of his unworthy career path had overwhelmed him. He would need to distil the news a few times before figuring out which bottle to keep it in, with the right stopper and stored in the right place.

"See you soon," Capestan had said, removing her earphones and jabbing the red dot with her index finger, wondering if she was being overly optimistic in hearing a question mark in his "See you soon?" She would have loved to answer, even with a pause, or with silence, but she had to make do with her blank screen.

She sighed wearily, which reminded her of her other task. She scrolled up to find Buron's number.

"Monsieur le Directeur . . ."

"Capestan, I've been waiting for your call. The ponies in the Luxembourg – anything to do with your lot? Did Ramier get away again?"

The directeur's tone was neither harsh nor playful.

"Yes, I'm sorry, I – "

"This man is slippery, yet you've found him twice, Capestan. That's twice more than the others. Find him a third time. I have faith in you. Oh, and Happy Christmas. I'm sure the inquiry will catch up with you nice and quickly."

Buron gave little away, but he was never one to kick people when they were down.

"Thank you, sir. Thank you for everything. Happy holidays to you."

"Ha, holidays . . ." the directeur said before hanging up.

Anne crossed the large sitting room, empty save for the flashing

Christmas tree, whose lights Rosière switched on first thing in the morning and off as she left to go home. She went through to the snooker room to join her four colleagues having their consolatory drink.

Tomorrow was Christmas Eve and the commissaire had given everyone the day off. A welcome ceasefire that would let them come back with a clean slate and some fresh leads.

31

10.00 a.m. Capitaine Orsini.

For almost twenty years now, Orsini had hated Christmas, and no part more so than the *réveillon de Noël* – Christmas Eve dinner. He also hated the back-to-school period, Mother's Day, Father's Day, birthdays, the beach, tobogganing, parks, markets, Disney and any kind of ball. In short, he hated every aspect of his shrivelled, deliriously unhappy life. He was nothing more than an empty suit clinging on to a mission whose purpose had long ceased to interest him. It was that or nothing.

On this Christmas Eve, a new beacon – the latest in a line of several hundred – had had the decency to distract him from the festive spirit that touched everywhere else. A clue that was now sitting on his desk, namely the five-centimetre piece of card picked up by Saint-Lô.

947091. An enigma. And a whole day and night to solve it.

11.00 a.m. Brigadier Lewitz.

His leg was killing him and the plaster was itchy, but Lewitz was worrying about the Porsche. He may have saved it from disfigurement, but he was terrified that Rosière would take it back to the hire company and that he would never be able to drive it again.

Sitting on his sofa with his foot up on the coffee table, he was waiting for his fiancée and his future in-laws, who had been adamant that they would celebrate the *réveillon* in his front room given his immobile state.

"Don't fret, we've got everything under control – we'll bring drinks, dinner, crockery, folding chairs, the lot."

All the same, Lewitz would have preferred to be in a better position to meet her parents for the first time. Behind the wheel of a Porsche, for instance. Luckily, his one-bed flat was gleaming. He had called the caretaker of his building and begged her to put him in touch with a cleaner who would be happy to come out on Christmas Eve. Money would be no object. Then he had looked out his best suit – a shimmering midnight blue number – and his longest pair of kitchen scissors, before cutting the left trouser leg lengthways to accommodate his cast. Cleanly shaven and hair washed, he looked as handsome as a freshly valeted car, albeit one with a small dent in the bumper.

Midday. Lieutenant Diament.

His hands were so enormous that the broadsheet looked like a paperback. Page thirty, a short paragraph. A police officer somewhere up north had committed suicide at his station. Yet another colleague turning a gun on himself. Before long he would lose count.

"Basile," Lieutenant Zahoui said from the doorway. "I just checked the board, you're on-call tomorrow, the thirty-first and the first. Sorry. And . . . I'm not supposed to tell you, but as of Monday, you're on patrol too."

"Do you reckon it'll go on much longer?"

Zahoui shook his head sadly.

"I'm afraid so, buddy. You didn't expect a quick sulk, did you? You criticised the boss in front of people from another department. He's no pushover – and he holds a grudge."

On November 9, a huge fair had opened on the Champs-de-Mars to celebrate the hundredth anniversary of the Police Judiciaire. Basile Diament had invited his mother along and his heart was pounding with genuine excitement. One of the videos on the big screen was dedicated to Diament's unit, the Varappe Division, and he could not wait to see the maternal pride written across her face. Before taking a seat for the short film, they dropped in to the area where the P.J.'s different departments were being showcased: senior management, the Brigade des Mineurs, the drugs squad, the Brigade Financière, etc. They all had their space to shine, including, of course, the fabled B.R.I. There was a document summarising their remits, along with photographs of each premises to give an idea of the atmosphere at their various offices. On one such sheet, an image depicted a desk where, amid the ashtrays defying the smoking ban, a framed, signed photograph of the former leader of the National Front had pride of place.

Basile's mother winced as if she had been stung by a wasp, before turning to her son with a look of great compassion and gently stroking him on the cheek. The humiliation ran through Basile like a blade, a feeling far more intense than anything a video or a big screen could generate. He had not come here to be insulted, nor to show her what he had been made to endure.

The following day, during the inauguration, Divisionnaire Buron, the directeur of the Police Judiciaire, the Préfet and a few other big cheeses had asked him what he thought of the fair.

Standing to attention and eyes front, Lieutenant Basile Diament had expressed his disappointment at seeing photographic evidence of political partisanship, which was inappropriate at such an event since it reflected the opinion of a single individual, rather than a whole police division.

Diament did not know that the photograph belonged to Frost. Two months later, he was still paying the price.

1.00 p.m. Lieutenant Évrard.

At the market on boulevard Richard-Lenoir, white paper wrappers adorned plump chicken thighs and whole sides of smoked salmon lounged on pieces of golden card. Vol-au-vents, savoury canapés of various sorts and Christmas logs were all around, while the last trees lined the pavement. Soon it would all be gone, allowing the grated carrot and tabbouleh to resume their rightful places. Évrard tugged the heavy tartan shopping trolley laden with vegetables and followed her parents down rue du Chemin-Vert. On the corner, a man was roasting chestnuts on a brazier, their sweet smell warming the air. As her parents passed the window of an estate agent's, they slowed their pace ever so slightly. Évrard glanced to the side, trying to catch a glimpse of the rental prices. One was for a nearby studio and was not too expensive, and Évrard could not help pausing. Her father stopped in the middle of the pavement too.

"Do you want us to come and see it with you?"

She had not gambled a cent for over six months. The squad and her friends had helped get her on the straight and narrow. There were a few outstanding debts, of course, but her salary was coming in. A regular pay cheque. Évrard wanted to believe she could do it. She was back in luck. The lieutenant turned to her father and nodded.

"Yeah, that would be great."

2.00 p.m. Lieutenant Torrez.

José Torrez ducked between the ropes and stepped into the ring, iron in hand. A basket of crumpled laundry was sitting to the right of the board he had been allocated. Opposite him, his challenger, a solid old boy, shot him a look of sheer defiance. Between the boards, the pearly-toothed referee-cum-M.C. was shuffling some cue cards. In a nod to the festive time of year, he had opted for a red bonnet with a white bobble and flashing lights.

When the two contestants were in position, the "Rocky" theme tune belted out of the speakers and the referee grabbed his microphone with gusto: "Ladies and gentlemen! Welcome to the final of the 2012 French 'Golden Iron', brought to you by Philips. It is my honour to introduce the man to my right, joining us all the way from Paris and ironing no fewer than five shirts in ten minutes – José Torrez! Let's hear it for him! And to my left, from Mulhouse in eastern France, the mighty François Sarton, recently off the back of nine shirts in ten minutes! You heard me – nine! Another round of applause, please. The victor in this final bout will have the great privilege of representing France in the Grand Final in Hawaii not long from now. Let's give it up one more time for our contestants!"

Amid the cries and cheers, Torrez made out the voices of his children: "Yes! Go, papa! Smash him!"

3.00 p.m. Commandant Lebreton.

Lebreton contemplated the boot of the Lexus. It was full to

bursting. He and Rosière were off to the house of the commandant's sister in Sceaux, just to the south of central Paris.

"Eva, you're . . . It's too much."

"Yeah, but – "

"I know, but it's too much – you'll make them feel uneasy. Our
family doesn't go to town with presents. It's more of a gesture with
us. And anyway, the whole thing will be over by 11.00 p.m. at the
latest."

"O.K., O.K.," Rosière said. "You can wield the axe yourself,
Mr Sensible."

Louis-Baptiste took out the heaps of parcels tumbling from
the saloon. He read the labels and decided to keep it to one per
person, leaving the overspill on the steps leading up to Rosière's
house. Pilou sniffed at each one with interest, as if to make sure
the commandant was not brazen enough to cull the pâté.

The Lebreton family were an altogether more sober bunch.
Their tastes bordered on the austere, in fact. In temperament alone,
Eva was already rather out of place, and that was before throwing
in her fulsome gifts and abundant gratitude. Lebreton had poked
fun at his family a bit so that Rosière knew what she was in for. He
was glad to have her by his side, what with her explosive tongue
and her unending ability to distract him at any time and from any
heartache, and he certainly did not want her to feel out of place or
be the butt of any potentially hurtful comments. She was his friend,
and that made him the guardian of her happiness for the evening.

With one derisive eyebrow arching high above her mascaraed
lash, she watched him scoop out the presents and the champagne,
the caviar and the salmon. When Lebreton was finished and the
boot was closed again, she turned the key in the ignition and said:

"Like I care – you left the smallest ones and they're the most expensive."

3.05 p.m. Capitaine Rosière.

Rosière had observed her colleague going to and from the car with the same studious gaze she reserved for works of art – a mixture of admiration, respect, feeling and attachment. He was her friend, her pal. The best, kindest man she knew. All wrapped up in a shit-hot bod. And her saviour this Christmas Eve.

Watching the pretty, rejected parcels stack up in front of her door, Rosière felt a pang of regret about leaving them there, cleaved from their recipients. She plucked a marker pen from the inner pocket of her bag, removed the lid with her teeth, grabbed the first present and mumbled:

"We're going to need to take a little detour on the way."

4.00 p.m. Lieutenant Dax.

Weaving in and out of the pedestrians, Dax was stepping on it despite lugging his last-minute presents. He did not want to be late, not for an in-laws' year like this. His brothers and sisters were all with their other halves and children. Other houses and other homes. Dax would be the only son at his mum's this year and he was determined not to keep her waiting. The grub would definitely be ready and she would have cooked enough for all the absentees put together. The lieutenant had put on a smart jacket, but he had chosen trousers with plenty of give in the waist. Tonight, he would be eating for the whole family.

5.00 p.m. Capitaine Saint-Lô.

Saint-Lô had poured himself a small glass of plum brandy that he usually reserved for the small hours. From his sofa bed, he gazed bitterly at his walled-up fireplace.

That was how things were, now. Walled-up fireplaces and lowered ceilings. All flamboyance extinguished; all loftiness curtailed. No desire to go beyond. Life had become even smaller than his body.

Nowadays the *réveillon*, the eve of the birth of Christ himself, was marked with a tree shoved in a pot. Midnight mass was celebrated at 6.00 p.m. Thousands of parcels were tied with a ribbon, but not a single hearth was lit.

Saint-Lô wanted logs and he wanted fire.

There was a proper chimney at the commissariat. The capitaine drained his glass in one and set it down on the side table next to his armrest with a firm gesture.

He stood up, pulled on his long coat and boots, and put on his hat. Then he left.

6.00 p.m. Capitaine Merlot.

Drinks o'clock. Shame being alone (a rat did not make much of an aperitif companion). Merlot stroked the thick fur between Ratafia's ears. He paused for a second. After a while, he heaved himself out of his armchair in front of the blank television and rummaged through his drawers in search of some trinkets, which he proceeded to swathe in recycled wrapping paper. Essential to keep every bit, that way one always had the right size.

He slid the crumpled parcels into the pockets of his jacket and his overcoat. Then, with the rat in tow, he went downstairs to the shop to buy a bottle of fizz, before waiting at the bus stop that took them to the rue des Innocents.

If anyone happened to be lurking at the commissariat, he would be ready to raise a glass.

7.00 p.m. Commissaire Divisionnaire Buron, Directeur of the Police Judiciaire.

The directeur checked his bow tie one last time in the mirror of his vast hallway as he waited for his wife to find her fur. The children were not coming until the following day, the twenty-fifth. This evening, the two of them were eating with friends. A dinner party for six in a beautiful panelled room with elegant chandeliers. Bound to be deathly dull – Buron was dreading it.

11.00 p.m. Commissaire Anne Capestan.

Earlier on, sitting between a niece and a nephew, Anne had praised her brother-in-law for his gorgeous tie, despite it being the same clashing colour that ruined the family photograph every year. He replied that if she was off the wine, then she should just say – it would be easier for him that way.

But she had barely heard him, what with the decibel count of her sisters' combined giggles. This had not put off her mother, who shouted over them for help – the truffle mashed potato was getting cold and no-one was passing the serving dishes or the gravy, least of all her husband, who was busy explaining to his youngest grandchild how to distinguish an Impressionist work from a pointillist painting. The grandchild in question had not listened to a single word and was simply waiting for Grandpa to finish so he could get back to playing "Minecraft" with his cousin.

Anne now set down the empty bowl of potato on top of all the other washing-up on the work surface. In one evening, her kitchen had seen more action than the last two years put together. As ever, her feet automatically took her to her window, where she liked to sit and watch rue de la Verrerie below.

On the far pavement, just in front of a Vietnamese grocery, whose owner was going to get a serious shock in the morning, were four words painted in big, white letters: "ANNE, ALWAYS THE SAME." The smile across Capestan's face was even broader than the one twenty years ago.

The falling snowflakes were not enough to cover the message.

11.05 p.m. Paul Rufus.

The smartphone seemed to take up the entire sideboard. Slumped on a bar stool, Paul was keeping a close eye on the mobile, a drop of white paint still stuck to the blonde hairs on his forearm. Every cell of his body was charged with anticipation. He could not remember the last time he had drunk, eaten, moved. There was nothing around him but a small, dark, rectangular piece of plasma that he hoped would light up tonight.

It was not the most appropriate timing, but Paul could not give a damn about circumstances, about propriety. About anything except Anne.

The ringtone and vibrate settings were both on full, and Paul jumped when the call finally came. He stared at the name on the screen: Anne. A huge wash of relief nearly knocked him off his stool. He stood up and pressed the green icon.

The softness of the "Hello" told him that they were home at last.

11.30 p.m. The commissariat, rue des Innocents.

"You had better wait for us before opening them." The message on the folded piece of A4 sitting in front of the parcels under the tree was quite clear. Saint-Lô and Merlot had been pawing the ground all evening. Even Orsini had prowled around the pile two or three times. In a spirit of convivial solidarity, Merlot had texted the absent colleagues. Dax, like Évrard, had finished early and dropped in to see what was up. They came in joyously, their hair and shoulders flecked with sparkling flakes. With almost magical punctuality, the snow had decided to honour its side of the bargain by turning Christmas Eve a perfect white. Tomorrow it would be slush, but for now, the immaculate coating would cover up the greyness, muffle the noise and reflect the orange glow of the street lamps as well as the neon signs of the sex shops. Lebreton, Rosière and Pilote eventually arrived to a collective "Ahhhh!" and the distinctive pop of a cork. Now they could tuck in. Every corner was suddenly full of ripped paper and snipped ribbons as Merlot's ghastly plonk mixed with the fine Champagne to pour down unfussy throats. The aroma of the tree joined that of the chocolates and the tangerines to cheer up the atmosphere even more.

Gifts changed hands, with Rosière and Merlot's haul mixing with whatever Évrard and Dax had managed to find in the late-night corner shop. Belts from Hermès swapped with ashtrays from some Riviera bistro; Colette tote bags with steel bottle-openers. Each lucky recipient fell into raptures, baying with enthusiasm and chortling unreservedly.

Saint-Lô smoothed his moustache with both hands before teasing Merlot.

"My friend, that belt will need another fifty good inches if it's to buckle that paunch of yours."

"Or eight holes for yours, my fellow!" the capitaine said, patting the musketeer so hard on the back that he almost sent him flying.

After rooting out one of Merlot's presents, Rosière was intrigued to discover that it looked a lot like a stone. She studied it all over before asking:

"What's this, then?"

"Careful, that's very precious," Merlot said, wagging a priggish finger at her. "That there is a piece of the Berlin Wall."

"You've been to Berlin?" Dax asked.

"Yes, in 1960, along with my dear, now defunct parents."

"Are you telling me this is a piece of the Berlin Wall that actually predates the construction of the wall?" Rosière said, her lip already quivering with expectation.

Orsini burst out laughing. The sound surprised even him, not to mention the others, and he turned to check the stone's provenance, before regaining his composure and addressing Rosière:

"No, Eva, I believe it is a piece of *a* Berlin wall, rather than *the* Berlin Wall."

"Have some respect, please," Merlot said, downing a whole glass of Dom Pérignon.

Saint-Lô seemed aggrieved at receiving so much without giving anything in return. On top of that, the general excitement was abating, so after a short silence, he summoned the only thing he had available to him:

"Friends, I have nothing by way of gifts, but if you so wish, I could recite a poem I once committed to memory."

"Wonderful idea!" Rosière said, always keen for a spectacle. "We're listening."

"It is an epic poem, a hellish famous one from the Middle Ages: *La Chanson de Roland*."

By what felt like the hundredth verse, the party realised they were not in for a sonnet and began to display signs of restlessness. Saint-Lô paused.

"Epic poems and songs of deeds last the whole night. There must be a good two hundred strophes yet! You'd be advised to settle . . ."

So the squad, engorged with bubbles and nibbles, made themselves comfortable on the armchairs and carpet, rugs and cushions to listen to the troubadour by the fire, his rich bard's voice lulling along with the crackling logs and Merlot's contented snores.

Midnight. Special Officer Pilote.

Sitting nice and upright with his back warming by the fire, Pilou glared at the rat disapprovingly. This impostor was starting to make itself at home, venturing ever further into territory that was his by right – first come, first served, and all that. It was time to lay down some boundaries.

Indoors, Pilote was prohibited from deploying his urine-jet territory-marker. A furtive glance in the direction of his beloved mistress was enough to dissuade him from trying it out now, despite the gravity of the situation. He aimed his muzzle at the intruder. The rat, out of sheer provocation, volunteered a single paw onto his rival's carpet.

Pilou bared his teeth and let out a deep growl, followed by a single warning bark.

The rat retreated immediately. That would show him who was in charge here.

00.01 a.m. Special Officer Ratafia.

From underneath the sofa, Ratafia's two black, beady little eyes stared at the beast out front. How dim could a dog be?

32

Knocked from side to side by the Antigang officers rushing around without seeming to notice them, having already been moved to one side by the forensics teams and ignored by the Crim. detectives, Capestan, Lebreton, Orsini and Rosière stood in front of Max Ramier's body in stunned silence.

They had lost their killer.

They had three murders and no perpetrator.

Four murders now, in fact.

"It's like Agatha Christie, *And Then There Were None*," Rosière said. "Everyone croaks and by the end, there's no more perp."

"Apart from in the book, the killer only pretends to die. It works on an island – gets more tricky on a pathologist's table," Capestan said.

The night before, she had left Paul's feeling warm but somewhat befuddled, returning home to daydream at her own pace, her own rhythm, without getting swept away with plans. Buron's message bidding her to this latest murder had caught her bang in the middle of her reverie, jolting her back to reality. On her way, she was expecting another player from the armed robbery – not Ramier.

Capestan of course suspected Orsini. Rooted to the spot at the crime scene, the capitaine was scrutinising everything. Searching for some trace of himself, perhaps? He was frowning, reflecting in a sombre mood. Had he forgotten something?

Now that forensics had Ramier's body, they would soon be taking a D.N.A. sample to compare it with the first three murders and obtain incontrovertible proof of his guilt, which remained the most likely theory.

But who had killed him?

Orsini? Capestan asked herself the question over and over again without managing to come up with an answer.

Perhaps they would find another D.N.A. trace at this scene. Someone new blasting their way into the equation. An accomplice who had not shown up in the files. Or a cellmate who had caught wind of the crop waiting to be harvested.

At a glance, there were no warning signs, no theatrics. Either the killer was rushed or a second murderer was involved. Again, the latter seemed the most likely theory.

It was 11.00 a.m. and it felt as if the morning was yet to rise in this corner of the Bois de Vincennes. The bare trees would have let the sun through, but the thick mass of black clouds was squeezing any weak rays of light to the point of strangling them. A thin yet steady drizzle had washed away the snow, turning it to a sludge that clung to the soles of their shoes, taking any fingerprints with it. A few patches of grass were still visible through the broken branches and dead leaves. The light-hearted lawns beloved of Parisian picnickers in the summer had been reduced to a dingy corner where a gangster's thickset corpse did not seem out of place.

"Fresh in this morning! Still warm from Father Christmas's sack, dispatched by special sledge mail!"

The wisecracker was Lieutenant Zahoui from the B.R.I. It was as if he needed to clear some space to make way for the next lot of inane jokes. Behind him, Diament gave them a tiny flicker of acknowledgement.

"Two bullets in the stomach, two in the thorax, one in the shoulder and two in the trees."

"Father Christmas's aim is all over the shop. Either that or the reindeer failed to come to a complete stop," Rosière said, never one to be outdone.

Zahoui burst out laughing, delighted to have found a kindred spirit. He gave the capitaine a pally pat on the back, not that she would ever have been so overfamiliar, but she took it with the sort of aloofness that celebs display when they are mobbed by fans.

In this residential family area on the edge of the wood, the seven bullets had been heard and the police alerted right away. The gunman had, however, had plenty of time to escape. No silencer, no accuracy – this smacked of an amateur, albeit an amateur armed with an automatic pistol and no qualms about offloading half a magazine. They could be looking for a gangster not used to carrying a firearm – a driver, for example – like the one Lewitz thought was missing from the hold-up.

Add to that the heap of enemies Max Ramier must have amassed in his time. He did not like anyone and no-one liked him. He was wild and violent, a man with no respect for life or its obligations. There was every chance that this crime had nothing to do with their inquiry and was simply a settling of scores from a former co-prisoner. Bastards like Ramier left a lot of grudges in their wake, and the police were less than motivated to do anything about them – they had better people to protect.

A few Antigang guys sneered at the corpse, but most of them were just gutted that a stranger had swiped their prey from under their noses. It had been the B.R.I.'s job to bring back the mortal remains of the man who murdered the mighty Commissaire Rufus and hang them from a post. All they had was a mud-spattered body and a cheeky perp. who had vanished into the trees. It was bad enough that the officers from Crim. and the Crapheap were breaking their balls – if everyone joined in, the cowboys would be reduced to sitting around playing their harmonicas.

These very cowboys would get the ballistics report well in advance of the Brigade des Innocents. All they would need was for the weapon to be on file and they would have a massive head start. Either officially or in people's memories, every gang member in the region was recorded. The B.R.I. would just need to nab him.

Judging by the time of the call to the police, the shooting took place at 10.00 a.m. An early start the morning after the *réveillon*. As far as alibis were concerned, Capestan wondered if Christmas made the killer's task easier or more complicated. Only a hermit could head outdoors at that hour without their family noticing.

That narrowed it down to at least half the gangsters. And about a third of the police officers.

No, those were dead-ends. The shooter was an amateur, Capestan remembered.

At first glance, Ramier, despite being riddled with bullets, did not appear to have been beaten. No-one had wanted to make him talk. The murder had not been driven by money. Or maybe the victim had been carrying it on him and it had been recovered directly from there.

What was Ramier up to in these parts? There was nothing in his file about him spending time at the Vincennes. There wasn't a bar for at least two hundred metres in any direction. Why was he here? Capestan stepped away from the crime scene to take a broader look and assess any points of interest in the surrounding area. On the perpendicular street that ran out of the wood, there was a haberdashery, a gym and a hair salon, while the avenue had a bank, a mobile telephone shop and a pharmacy, all shut on a public holiday like today.

A long saloon pulled up on the avenue. Buron extracted himself with greater difficulty than in his younger years, but he smoothed down his coat and walked towards them slowly. A certain quiet fell over proceedings. He spent a while greeting the lead investigators working at the scene, taking on board the various points of view. Then he made his way over to Capestan, continuing to survey the premises with his basset hound's eyes.

"So, Capestan, has this made a mess of your inquiry too?"

"I must admit, this body has turned all our leads into dead-ends."

"All your leads, Capestan? Really? You don't have another little suspect lurking in your case notes?"

Capestan's question about Orsini clearly had not fallen on deaf ears. Buron must have demanded to see the files.

Considering the discretion of the comment and its tone, which was more suggestive than assertive, he was clearly leaving his commissaire a bit of wriggle-room. She noted this and glanced over at Capitaine Orsini, who was taking himself away from the bustle and heading up the avenue too. He was looking for something. And he alone seemed to know what.

33

Back at the commissariat, Lebreton and Capestan chucked on their coats before heading out to the terrace. Louis-Baptiste brought out a packet of cigarettes from his inside pocket and lit one. The red tip crackled as he took a drag – the only sign of warmth on this biting winter's day.

Without exchanging a word, the two officers were mulling over the same thing. Orsini, a member of their squad, still had not mentioned his significant connection to the Minerva Bank incident. This put Capestan and Lebreton in a delicate situation. Either they carried on ignoring the elephant in the station, or they turned him in to the rest of the squad, for examination at the very least.

Capestan, slumped on the parapet with her hands clasped together, watched the occasional passer-by on the street below. The area was virtually a desert after the mayhem of Christmas Eve. The famine after the feast, with nothing in between. One minute people are buying everything, the next, nothing. Back to normality, just with empty bank accounts and exhausted bodies.

Lebreton took another long puff and leaned back against the rear wall of the terrace. As with his posture, the commandant's well-cut overcoat emphasised his natural elegance, his sober, reserved manner asserting a strong presence that was never overbearing.

"He must know that we know. No two ways about it," Lebreton said calmly.

"Yes. The photocopies were incomplete, but he must suspect that at least I have seen the unabridged report."

"Yet he hasn't come to discuss it with you."

Capestan stood up straight and slipped her numb hands into her coat pockets, where one of them found an old *métro* ticket. The commissaire instinctively scratched the corner of it against her thumbnail.

"No, he hasn't come."

"The least we should do is bring it up with the team. Ramier's murder is a game-changer. Before, Orsini was just a victim. With the chance that he was manipulating us and withholding information . . ."

"It was him that put us onto Jacques Maire."

Lebreton picked up the ashtray by his feet and stubbed out his cigarette in a slow, deliberate circular motion, before taking two steps forward to set it down on the table.

"True. But surely he was using us for his personal ends. In any case, we can't protect him if he has committed murder. We can't carry on operating in the dark and bending the rules. Not when there's been a murder."

Capestan had reduced the ticket to a tiny tube which she was now rolling between her fingers.

"No. God, I just don't know . . ."

"How did he find out about L'Isle-sur-la-Sorgue anyway?" the commandant asked, narrowing his bright eyes slightly.

"The local daily, *La Provence*."

"But how did he know that Jacques Maire had changed his name and moved there? Or even that he had been involved in the hold-up?"

"I don't know."

Capestan paused. Rosière was of course already in the know, but the idea of having to tell the others made her uncomfortable. But the time had come.

" . . . There's something other than Orsini. According to Eva's analysis of the manuscript, Rufus was technically an accomplice. He got his cut for hamstringing the police response."

"Although he did arrest Ramier," Lebreton said sceptically.

"Probably because he wasn't expecting him to shoot. That turned their plan on its head – protecting him became too big a task. He must have 'cuffed Ramier and let the others make off with the moolah . . ."

Heavy grey clouds were moving over the commanding Église Saint-Eustache. Still deep in thought, the commandant charted their progress without really seeing them.

"In that version of events, I understand why Ramier was furious enough to beat him up on his release. But why didn't he turn him in when he was arrested? I don't buy that it's anything to do with that old-school gangster stuff about not ratting."

"Me neither. It's about the money. Ramier wanted it and he knew where to find it without the authorities getting their hands on it. It was his best shot at recovering it after prison, even if that meant serving a longer sentence. Either that or Rufus bargained with him in the heat of the action."

"It's a major coincidence that Orsini was sent to the squad headed up by Rufus's daughter-in-law."

Capestan pulled out her long hair caught inside her collar.

"It's not a coincidence – he requested the transfer. He came here for me. He must have been banking on finding some family secret. To see if corruption was passed on through marriage, perhaps."

"At any rate, he was keeping an eye on you, as with all the possible suspects . . . Tell me, was Jacques Melonne ever mentioned in the Lyon case notes as a possible fugitive?"

"Yes, but only in passing. He didn't match the description at all . . ."

"Rufus's description, which was unreliable. Same for the hostages – they were in shock."

"Fair point . . . Maybe Orsini tracked all the names, knowing that one of them would be the man."

"But why would he do that? What did he want? The shooter was in prison, after all. Justice had been done."

"We'd have to ask him."

"Yes. And he would have an answer for you," came another voice.

It was Orsini.

Capestan and Lebreton let the capitaine lead them into the games room, where the rest of the squad had gathered. Orsini sat at one end of the snooker table, leaving the long sweep of the baize between him and his colleagues. The gloomy day creeping through the windows kept the room in almost total darkness, so Rosière had switched all the side lamps on, as well as the one over the table, and the fairy lights at the bar. A warm atmosphere fell over the space, which was in stark contrast to the sudden chill that accompanied Orsini's announcement. He cut short the condolences that followed the revelation of his wife and son's murder, immediately switching the focus to the relevant aspects of the investigation, as if to remind them that their relationship was strictly professional.

Capestan wondered if this was really a form of rejection, or whether it was to keep their consciences clear and avoid clouding their suspicions and decision-making.

"I wanted to find out the brains behind the operation. Who had been the chief organiser."

"Could have been Ramier," Rosière said.

"In all honesty, capitaine, putting any preconceptions aside, do you associate the word 'brains' with Ramier?"

"For a successful hold-up, I agree, probably not. But for a failed one . . ."

"No, a policeman would never take orders from an idiot like that. The plan came from another corner. I wanted to know which one."

"What made you think Ramier would lead you there after his release?"

"The fact he did not denounce his accomplices, for one. Then there were my contacts at the prison in Corbas. I knew Ramier had no money. His cut was out there somewhere. And he would definitely want to retrieve it."

A policeman would never take orders from an idiot like that. The sentence suddenly came bouncing back into Capestan's mind, forcing her to interrupt the line of questioning:

"Hold on, hold on, how did you know that the 'policeman was taking orders'? After all, Rufus was never even suspected of being complicit at the time."

The commissaire turned to address the rest of the team, finally able to put the matter to rest.

"It makes sense now. Lewitz, this explains why there was no driver: they hadn't expected to need a quick getaway."

"It was only ever suspicion on my part," Orsini said. "A pure hunch. I was completely astonished, downright disgusted, to be the only one presuming it. Consider the facts: no consistency in the witnesses' descriptions of the perpetrators, let alone the sequence of events. He managed to arrest the most dangerous man, but let the other one get away? He arrived at the scene of an armed robbery with interns? He was the first there – by a distance – before the alarm had even been sounded, according to the staff? I found that stroke of luck dubious. And that's before mentioning the man's demeanour and the blind eyes of his colleagues, always quick to defend their own . . ."

The officers all shook their heads with a sigh. That was going too far.

"Oh no? You don't think so? Even you, commissaire, you provided our colleagues with a dossier in which my name – there in black and white – no longer featured. Foul play runs in the family, clearly. Today I'm suspected of murder, but you're still protecting me. Is that not so?"

The looks boring into Capestan ranged from unalloyed disdain to complete sympathy. The commissaire gave them a fleeting show of apology. No point dwelling on this point for hours – she would have done the same for each and every one of them.

"Protection is going too far," Lebreton said, still grappling with the issue. He knew it was right, despite running contrary to his convictions. Before joining this godforsaken squad, the commandant would have blown the whistle the moment he came across Orsini's name, no questions asked.

"I know," the capitaine said. "But all the same, let me reassure you that I did not kill Ramier."

With this statement, the waves parted in the room. Half of the officers believed it; the rest did not.

Capestan was alone in the middle, sceptical twice over.

34

The mobile unit that Lieutenant Diament had been attached to was heading down boulevard Sébastopol, the north–south artery that separated the Marais from Les Halles, passing the imposing Théâtre de la Ville before reaching the smaller playhouses on the boulevards of the Left Bank. The broad pavements that threw together tourists and locals were lined with K.F.C.s, banks and furniture stores. The officers, bulked up even more thanks to their bulletproof vests, and their feet clad in thick-soled Ranger boots, were patrolling as night fell.

Just before rue Rambuteau, the doorway to a branch of L.C.L. housed a mattress covered in a jumble of rugs and duvets, with a ragged plastic bag and a bashed-up shopping trolley serving as bedside tables. In it were sleeping a man, a woman and, between them, a little girl who must have been four, maybe five.

Ignazio, the solid if slightly paunchy leader of their unit, let out a sigh.

"Right, let's go. Diament – your treat."

"What?" the lieutenant asked, knowing he had heard correctly, but refusing to believe it.

Basile Diament looked at the family and wondered how they had managed to sleep while from all sides the cold, the light, the noise, the passers-by and the absence of walls assailed them. Habit and weariness, presumably. What level of exhaustion or indifference did you have to be overcome by, what with the endless line of people filing past your feet? How many woolly hats did a little girl need to drift off under a Parisian night sky? The warmth from her parents must have just been enough.

"What do you mean 'what'? Move them on, then that's that."

Diament answered without thinking. A reflex response to a simple command.

"Negative."

There was so little defiance in the lieutenant's tone that his superior opted for leniency.

"Diament, I'm going to pretend I didn't hear that. It's your first shift, so let's start from the top. When it comes to Roma, for the sake of the inhabitants, the tourists, the city's image and all that, we can't let them settle. You know that, don't you?"

"Yes."

"So get on with it."

"No. No, I don't want to."

"No-one wants to, lieutenant, no-one. But we have to."

No. Plenty of people and police officers must have passed by today without seeing them, so why could they not let them have their four square metres of pavement tonight? Diament stared at the girl. He had not trained for hours on end and built up kilos of muscle so he could wake up children.

There was no way. Enough was enough.

Basile swallowed. His head seemed to pound with the impact of all the digs, all the tears that had built up, threatening to break out. His eyes burned. He took a deep breath. He had bottled it for six years – he just needed to resist a little longer, a few more hours. He could not stumble now; in fact he had to lean on the anger and the revulsion, not give way to exhaustion and despondency. To sadness. Burn-out, as the docs call it. Basile rallied himself.

"No. I didn't see them, I'm done here."

"That'll do, Diament. What is this, politics? You all pro-migrants or something?"

"No, it's nothing to do with that! I couldn't give a damn about politics. It's just that – I won't do it."

Ignazio was understanding enough. He was not a bad guy, he was only doing his job. Maintaining order, keeping the juniors in line. Deterring the Roma. He wanted to bring Diament round, not realising that the way into his head was barred.

"It's no biggie!" he said. "You know it won't be a family, they probably barely know each other. It's their job. And its ours too. You know what the deal is – we shake them up a bit, they go ten metres down the road, wait for us to go, then they start over."

Diament suddenly did not want to do his job. The tremors were starting to overwhelm him. Months, years of bullying, of humiliation, and now this? Displacing a little girl. Where was he supposed to draw the line? What next? If he was certain of one thing, it was that there and then, the answer was no. He tried to speak. One last try. After that, he would let go. He would let his body take control. He was not even thirty, but screw it. His mother would understand. Maybe he was old enough not to be her son any more.

"Honestly, what is that going to achieve? Look at that kid. She's just got herself to sleep. They're finally settled and you're asking me to turf them out?"

To his right, Diament saw one of his colleagues was trying to get past him to put an end to this whole kerfuffle, either that or to make a good impression on Ignazio. The lieutenant stood in his way, shifting all of his two metres and one hundred and twenty kilos between the officers and the mattress.

"Not you either. No-one's going to do anything. Let's move along."

"Or what?" the man asked, pushing the button of the walkie-talkie attached to his left shoulder.

"Come any closer and you'll find out."

Having come this far, Diament began to relish the idea of taking a gallant last stand, only for an unmarked car to pull up next to them. Frost, the B.R.I. commandant, lowered the window, a malicious smile playing across his lips.

"You win this time, my boy. Consider yourself transferred."

35

Capestan had to stretch her ears to make out the doorbell, an almost ultrasonic buzz that was over before it had begun. Buron had called to give her the heads up: *He's a big guy but you don't even know the half of him. I think deep down he's damaged. Fix it if you can, please, commissaire.*

Diament made the cardboard box look no larger than a packet of breakfast cereal. The lieutenant stood in the doorway with a frown and a worried look in his eye. His height and his bulging muscles seemed to shrink everything around him.

Despite their poor track record, Capestan kept her sarcasm to one side.

"Welcome, lieutenant. I'm not sure we've got any offices for a man of your size, but we'll see what we can do. Come in."

"Keep out of the games room! No offence, stud-muffin, but I've become very attached to that snooker table," Rosière said, unlit cigarette in hand as she followed Pilou's wiggling hindquarters out to the terrace.

"Ever since she started winning . . ." Lebreton said. "There are two small offices at the back – we could always knock through the partition wall."

"Why not? Or here in the sitting room?" Capestan said.

"He might block out our natural light."

"Sorry if we're making you feel like an oversized wardrobe," the commissaire said to Diament, who was following the conversation without daring to intervene.

"Indeed, even my own enrolment sparked less interest," Saint-Lô said with a tinge of bitterness.

A loud discussion from the direction of the terrace drew them away from their confab. Capestan made for the kitchen, followed by Saint-Lô, Lebreton and Diament, after he had found a spot for his cardboard box.

Merlot and Rosière were at loggerheads again. But this time there was no hint of pleasure – it was a proper argument.

"I'll say it again, I think he killed Ramier," Merlot asserted.

"No, you're wrong – he said it wasn't him. Plus a policeman wouldn't have sprayed a whole magazine around the park before eventually slamming a slug into the target."

"Not sure I agree, Eva," Évrard said. "Orsini never practises his shooting, but he's cool-headed too. Maybe he missed a few on purpose. I'm with Merlot – I think it was him."

"Oh, for Christ's sake! If he'd wanted a 100 per cent hit rate, he would've taken himself off to the range! I'm telling you, it wasn't him."

"Yes it was. This is a murder, for heaven's sake. We'll have to notify the I.G.S.," Évrard said resignedly.

"No, no, dear girl, I'm not with you on that front," Merlot said with an reproachful wag of the finger. "Of course he may have strayed from the straight and narrow, but I can't condone snitching on him. We'll have to settle the matter amongst ourselves, keeping the cursed authorities out of it," he added, determinedly avoiding eye contact with Lebreton.

The debate had been raging since the day before, prompting a subtle division of the squad into rival factions: pro- and anti-Orsini. Or, to put it less radically, those who believed him and those who did not. Two further sub-groups were in even hotter dispute: those in favour of a proper inquiry; and those who preferred to keep things casual. Capestan had remained neutral until now, finding that she was in agreement with everyone; clearly not an ideal stance from a leadership perspective.

She was hoping for some burst of wisdom to emerge from the turbulent, murky depths of her imperfect conscience. Most of all she feared that the issue would damage the squad's now-brittle cohesion. Cracks were starting to form. Since Lewitz's accident on the Porsche bonnet, Torrez was in a new, not just self-imposed, exile. As for Orsini, he was still stalking the corridors, maintaining a silence as icy as a Norwegian glacier. No-one could accuse him of appealing to people's compassion. Whenever he went by, conversations would peter out before taking a more congenial turn.

"There's nothing to settle," Rosière said. "We've got to find the real shooter before the B.R.I. or some other load of thugs come and grab one of our colleagues by the plums."

Dax and Lewitz, who had abandoned the conversation after not managing to get a word in, let out a collective "Oh my God!" as they leaned out over the street.

"Quick, quick, come and see!" they said, twirling their arms at their colleagues.

The team tore across the terrace as one. Down below, a gathering stampede was brewing like a thunderstorm, causing panic-stricken heads to appear at windows all around the square.

It had begun. The invading hooligans surged up the *métro*

escalators as if they had been vomited from the Forum des Halles shopping centre, before spilling into the surrounding streets and rallying on rue Saint-Denis where, for some mystifying reason, they were prowling back and forth like a barbarian horde in sponsored shirts. Within a split second, all the locals knew the score: Paris Saint-Germain were hosting Chelsea that evening.

The fans bellowed with overexcitement, pumped up on beer and beef hormones. At the head of the cortège were three guys with sweat-soaked hair brandishing bangers as big as sticks of dynamite, which they were lighting and chucking at the shops lining the street. The owners lowered the metal shutters as quickly as they could, while café waiters rushed to bring in their chairs from the pavements.

One bloke, who was clearly even more hammered than his pals, grabbed a table from outside one of the bars and, despite its hefty weight, hurled it at some passers-by. A cluster of his brainless comrades adopted the ingenious idea and began throwing chairs and advertising signs in all directions, without the least consideration for the nearby men, women, children, prams and grannies.

"Let's go down," Lewitz said, picking up his crutch.

Capestan nodded and the whole squad hurried back into the apartment. Ratafia weaved in and out of their feet, blazing ahead to scout out the area. As they went, they all grabbed their jackets and slipped on their red "Police" armbands. Just as Rosière made to follow, Capestan stopped her.

"You stay here and call the riot police, the préfecture and anyone else."

The capitaine hung back with a disappointed Pilou and a

stunned Diament, whose gaze was switching between the chaos in the street and his determined colleagues.

"You must be out of your minds!" he said. "You can't go out into that mad crowd without any kit! You've got no vests, no truncheons, no tear gas, no helmets ... Wait for back-up from the pros! Tell them," he said to Rosière.

The capitaine simply shrugged – she knew her colleagues.

"The bystanders don't have much kit either . . . We've got to help them."

Diament stared at her for a second as if she were mad, then swivelled on his heel and followed the others downstairs.

They fanned out on reaching the square, spreading their arms and calling for calm. Their pleas fell on deaf ears – it was clear that any respect for the vaunted 'bobby' had been left at the border. Emboldened by their superior numbers and het up after the long journey, a few of the more malicious supporters sensed a good opportunity for a scuffle and unleashed an endless torrent of provocations, insults and gob.

They needed to be contained. The officers had to stymie this destructive energy somehow, even if that meant absorbing it themselves.

One bare-cheeked youth, who clearly had his sights set on being pack leader, started hassling Évrard, shoving her by the shoulder. Without a second's hesitation, Dax punched him full in the face, knocking him out. That was their cue.

Saint-Lô, impetuous as ever, his head lowered like a furious mountain goat, shot forward into the centre of the sweaty, deafening column that had been drifting aimlessly forward. Merlot, Lebreton and Dax rushed up the flanks to pick off the scattered individuals who were vandalising the property and intimidating the pedestrians pressed up against the walls of the buildings. It did not take long for Lebreton the athlete and Dax the boxer to subdue these men, so surprised were they to come up against any resistance, and too drunk to react in time. Merlot, despite being less well-equipped for physical exertion, made up for it with boldness. He went straight into the fray, issuing stealthy yet powerful jabs into the mob's midriffs, while Ratafia created some helpful diversions by nibbling their heels.

Capestan turned to Évrard, Diament, Orsini and – one rank behind – Torrez. She motioned towards the men carrying the bangers and the officers, acting like a single body, swooped into the mass with a view to neutralising these linchpins.

For Évrard, who was the lightest, it was like running into a brick wall. As she was splayed on the ground, one hooligan grabbed her by her jeans and windbreaker and sent her flying into a newspaper kiosk. She lay there slumped and stunned, half-unconscious beneath a pile of magazines.

They were too powerful, too fanatical and too numerous, raining fists down on the meagre squad and making it seem like a suicide mission. No sirens and no sign of the long, black C.R.S. coaches full of riot police. Without the cavalry, this was turning into a rerun of the Alamo.

Orsini's face was already covered in blood. His eyebrows, nose and mouth were all gushing, but the capitaine still staggered forward with glazed eyes, launching himself chaotically into the blue and white shirts around him. He was clearly no brawler. His cravat was still in place, but the rest of his garb was stained with grubby boot marks.

At the rear, Lewitz was doing his best to trip people up and dent a few skulls, but his dodgy balance left him defenceless when one of the men took hold of his crutch and yanked it, knocking the brigadier over, before letting off a salvo of kicks into his stomach with a mate.

Diament was like a raging wrestler dropped into the crowd, locking any head within range in his giant arms, sometimes three at a time. He was screaming even louder than his adversaries, convulsing his torso in a manner worthy of the haka, and flattening noses that were a good thirty centimetres lower than his own. He fought with the fierce joy of a man who was fed up with punchbags, relishing the sweet crack of bones and the heat of the blood on his knuckles. It was as if he was the only person on the battleground, which was soon the case as a wide area opened around him as his challengers fell back, forcing him to go off in search of prey further afield. He had forgotten all about his new squad – at last he could let rip without restraint, free of codes and protocols. Lost in his own world, he snapped out of it when he heard Lewitz's cries and ran over to help. Diament seized the biggest of the brigadier's assailants, hoisted him into the air and flung him into his fellow thugs, like a weightlifter dropping his personal best to the ground, before delicately picking up his colleague and carrying him to safety.

Torrez was on his own in the fray too, scouring the nearby streets to save his colleagues from his ruinous presence, which was now more shadowy and ominous than a flight of circling vultures. Despite flying solo, his courage was bolstered by the knowledge that the odds were not in favour of his opponents.

The pain of the first blow had set Capestan ablaze with fury.

Redder in the face than the devil himself, she had swung blindly, desperately putting to use the hand-to-hand combat techniques that had been etched into her muscles during training. Now her vision was blurry and the ground swayed beneath her feet. There was no way she could have predicted that someone would attack her from behind and attempt to strangle her. The man squeezed and squeezed and only loosened his grip when she was on the brink of asphyxiation. Capestan collapsed onto the pavement, only to feel Dax take hold of her arms and ferry her to the foot of a building, where Merlot and Évrard were already slouched against the rough wall. The lieutenant was a thoughtful stretcher-bearer, placing the wounded at a safe distance but still facing the mêlée.

Two men were holding Orsini's arms while a third pummelled him with a succession of blows. His cravat was finally askew. Capestan watched as members of both the pro- and anti-Orsini factions ran to his side. Saint-Lô's services were not required – Lebreton was closer and snatched the back of the attacker's strip, stretching it right back. He spun him round and delivered a fearsome headbutt that sent him crashing to the canvas. The other two, their courage vanishing, let go of the capitaine and melted into the throng of their pals.

Rosière pushed open the heavy front door of their building. She had put on a pair of trainers that were better suited to the task than her six-inch heels, even if they did clash with her emerald-green satin dress. She brought with her a thick first-aid kit and a police dog hell-bent on revenge, who started snapping at the enemy's calves the moment he stepped outside.

Dax collected Orsini and deposited him next to Capestan. After a fit of coughing and before Rosière could tend to him, he turned his swollen face towards the commissaire and placed his fingers gently on her forearm to get her attention. Capestan leaned in until she could feel Orsini's breath on her ears. He let out a groan before the words came:

"I've found something. I think I know who killed Ramier . . ."

"What? Who? Someone we know?"

Orsini nodded with difficulty.

"Later, later . . . After all this," he said, pointing to the square that was still in complete turmoil.

At the start of the conflict, the squad had been outnumbered three hundred to ten. Now they were reduced to five, while the mob seemed to be gathering apace. The fountain's stone nymphs surveyed the carnage, smiling nonchalantly throughout.

Saint-Lô was in a bind as three hefty chaps bore down on him. He was backing into the wall to avoid a rear attack. In the corner of his eye, he saw Lewitz struggling to pull himself up on a downpipe to come to his defence. Saint-Lô shook his head and shouted:

"No! Just the crutch!"

Holding the crutch aloft like a javelin, the brigadier launched it at Saint-Lô, who caught it mid-flight. His teeth flashed as he grinned broadly. He tested the weight of the long instrument with an expert gesture and, when he had found the optimal balance, he tightened his grip, flipped the two semi-circular pieces of plastic to the outside, and brandished it with an air of gleeful self-confidence.

"En garde!" he shouted.

The Chelsea fans might not have understood the words but they soon grasped the meaning. Something in Saint-Lô's eyes made them think twice about taking the piss, but it did not check their advance. Before they even noticed it move, the crutch thumped into the chest of the first supporter, whose eyes rounded with shock as he fell to the ground winded. Next it struck the second man full in the throat, sending him spluttering to his knees. The third man was left to fend for himself, his nerve weakened but his pride keeping him in place. With a sharp movement, he pounced at Saint-Lô, hoping to fight him man to man. The capitaine nimbly dodged aside, grabbed his opponent by the arm, sent him off-balance, spun him round one hundred and eighty degrees, took one step back and jammed the point of the crutch plumb between his eyes.

"A thrust worthy of Nevers, my friends!" Merlot said, not surprisingly a devotee of nineteenth-century swashbuckling novels. "Of course the rubber stopper loses a bit of penetration, but still, the aim was true!"

The man had had his fill and sprinted off down rue des Lombards. But the sea of football shirts was showing no signs of abating, either in number or drunkenness. Saint-Lô tossed the crutch back to Lewitz and unhitched the dagger from his ankle. Before Capestan could protest, he calmed her with a wave of the hand – the blade would remain in its leather holster and serve only as a sort of prod.

Diament alerted the agile capitaine to his presence with a roar, holding his arms out in a gesture that suggested he wanted to get things over and done with. Like a J.C.B. on a beach, he gathered up armfuls of thugs and rammed them into each other. Coming in the other direction, Saint-Lô stung them with his dagger, popping in and out of view at lightning speed. The combination of the grizzly bear and the hornet succeeded in herding the beer-soaked beasts together.

Merlot chose this moment to turn to Ratafia:

"Go! Go and help them, little Rata!"

The rodent shot to the musketeer's aid. No longer content with nibbling ankles, it boldly climbed up trouser legs and bit into the men's thighs. The fans screamed and began thumping their baggy tracksuits to get rid of the stealthy beast that had come out of nowhere.

Mimicking Saint-Lô and Diament's sandwich strategy, Pilote rushed forward and started sinking his teeth into the bums of Rata's victims, who were now at a loss as to where to throw their fists.

"Higher, Rata! Higher!" his master howled, goading him on.

With his muzzle pressing forward and his sharp claws digging into the skin, Ratafia managed to gain ground. The onlookers could see the outline through the folds of the material as he made it to the groin area, followed by tell-tale rings of blood that stained the pale cotton. Grown men fell to their knees and wept.

"Yes, go on, my dear ratty! Attack, attack!" Merlot shouted, jolting up to a standing position.

He turned to Capestan:

"I trained a police rat! I trained a police rat!"

"Shh, stop that, not so loud," the commissaire replied.

Just wait for the headline writers to get hold of that – police-trained rats deployed to emasculate football fans. Buron was going to be ecstatic.

Soon after, the throng that had invaded the Fontaine des Innocents dispersed. The mass of fans not so much charged as hobbled towards Châtelet and beyond, wounded and bent double, eager to reach the plastic seats in the stands that for many would be even less comfortable than normal.

The combined efforts of the squad's two newest recruits (three, counting Ratafia) had given them the upper hand over the barbarians.

"Victory! We won! Veni Vidi Victory! And all thanks to my rat!"

Merlot was over the moon. Although his black eye had swollen to double its size; although he was going to need an expensive trip to the dentist; although his battered colleagues barely had a limb intact between them; although Torrez, Lebreton, Dax, Saint-Lô and Diament – the last men standing – were limping towards them with a dog and a red rat at their side, Merlot was acting as if this was his Austerlitz.

"You know, whatever it is they were looking for, I think we might have ruined their evening," Évrard said, smiling in spite of everything.

All around, the jubilation began to prevail over any dents to their pride. Merlot, still beside himself, tickled the rat's neck, bloodying his nails as he did so.

"Oh, I'd say! Didn't we just!"

He paused for a moment before clutching Évrard's arm and adopting his most sincere tone:

"Nothing worse than having your knackers knackered."

36

"No. I don't believe you. It's not him."

Capestan was determined to block out what Orsini was saying.

They were in the capitaine's office. His cravat had been studiously retied. As with the rest of the squad, the two of them were covered in plasters, bandages and antiseptic cream. The bathroom at the commissariat had been transformed into a makeshift field hospital, with Rosière taking charge of boosting the troops' morale. A doctor had arrived and asked them to wait in line on chairs in the corridor before examining them in turn and putting them in order of priority. Évrard and Lewitz had been sent to hospital for precautionary X-rays, while the others had only needed patching up. The doctor had also assessed Ratafia, who was remarkably unscathed. The team congratulated each other with hearty pats on the back, and Dax even shed a little tear at the scale of everyone's gratitude. Capestan had only been able to appreciate the camaraderie for a few short seconds before finding herself in this seat listening to Orsini's nonsense.

"It is, commissaire. All the signs point to it."

"I'm telling you it's not."

"Listen . . . I understand. I'll leave you with my findings and let you reach the same conclusion for yourself," Orsini said, his voice far softer than usual.

On the spotless glass table, he set down, one after the other, the piece of card with the code, a D.V.D. containing surveillance footage, a club membership card and a file. Then he left in silence, taking care not to let the door slam.

Capestan gazed at the objects. She was battling against reason, but Orsini's line of argument was nonetheless making gains. The plausible reality was creeping into the tangle of her mind despite her efforts to keep it at bay. Bit by bit, her denial was being worn away, giving way first to anger, then to despondency. What next? What was she to do next?

So Orsini had not murdered anyone. He had not avenged his wife, nor his son.

But Paul – Paul had avenged his father.

The father he had never loved, the father he had not seen for years. The father whose legacy to his son was violence and *lex talionis*.

Or maybe it was an accident. Yes, an accident. Albeit one he had gone looking for.

Capestan stared into nowhere for a long while, until the whole room became blurry, until her pupils dried up completely.

She did not understand.

Was her husband a killer? He did not fit the profile. There was not an ounce of the malcontent about him. What had led him to behave in a manner that was so out of character? Animal instinct? Association? A sense of duty? Or maybe it was simply a desire to prove to his dead father that he was made of the same stuff, a final appeal to the timeless need for parental acceptance, for love and approval, that no amount of neglect or cruelty can dampen in a child. Paul alone could answer these questions.

Capestan also could not help wondering how her husband could have committed a murder at the very moment that they had finally been reunited. Not exactly before her eyes, but in a way that was bound to show up on the radar of her investigation. How could she ignore the giant red dot that had suddenly started flashing along with the tone of a flat-lining heart monitor?

She would have to analyse everything in the cold light of day. This awful sense of personal waste would have to be put aside in favour of a professional eye.

Paul must have lost faith in her investigation and decided to act alone. He had manipulated her. But why? Did he think she would not realise it was him? That he could get away with this hideous lie, sitting pretty on their sofa for the rest of his days? Or did he reckon that it would be all too easy for his wife, a police officer, to bungle the investigation and let him off the hook? Keeping the personal to one side was not going to be easy. Or maybe he was planning to turn himself in and confess to the murder? Capestan was tempted to wait and see.

To wait. For once, Capestan had no urge to act. She wanted to let life decide for her, let herself bob along any which way, like a desperate dog scrabbling to get out of a stream. For everything to sort itself out for her. For someone to come up to her and say: "Don't worry, it's all under control."

But that wasn't how it was going to be. Orsini had been meticulous.

947091. A backwards date, as he had eventually realised. July 19, 1949.

He had then gone through the case notes of all the murders

with a fine-toothed comb, page by page. Nothing. It was only when he studied Rufus's H.R. file that he found a match. July 19, 1949 – his wife's date of birth. The brute did have a shred of sentimentality. Or was he just being practical?

Having linked the code to Serge Rufus, all Orsini needed to do was figure out its significance.

If Ramier had kept it on his person, it must have been of some use to him.

The money.

A left luggage code, perhaps? Orsini had called all the railway stations, but none of them had a six-digit system. Then he had dug deeper into Rufus's paperwork: was he a member of any clubs – sport, cards, that sort of thing? Or an ex-police officer's association? Was it for an old pigeonhole at number 36? A locker at the shooting range? Nothing. Orsini had come up short.

Until the murder in the Bois de Vincennes.

Since there was nothing to link Ramier to the Vincennes, maybe Rufus had some connection with it. As he was scouring the roads running near the park, the capitaine struck upon a gym. It was one of those fitness clubs where there is just an automatic barrier that opens when you present your membership card, paid for in cash more often than not. Guaranteed discretion. Open daily from 7.00 a.m. to 11.00 p.m.

After forcing a cleaner to let him in, Orsini had tried the code on every locker. One of them had opened. Empty.

Later, the video footage taken from that room had played for hours on the capitaine's desktop. On four separate occasions, Ramier's hazy black-and-white profile appeared after a cautious glance from side to side. On November 28, December 14, December

22 and, last but not least, December 25, the morning of his death, he left the centre with a large bag slung over his shoulder. That must have been his final pick-up before scramming for good, so he chose a day and a time where no-one would disturb him. December 25, 10.00 a.m. On three separate occasions, a different hazy black-and-white profile, this time belonging to Paul Rufus. December 21, 22 and 25. The first time, he went into the fitness room and left a few minutes later. Same drill the following day. On Christmas Day, Paul spotted Ramier exiting the club, visibly hesitated for a few seconds, then eventually followed him towards the park, until the two of them were out of shot.

Capestan gathered her thoughts. It was December 20 that she saw Denis and told him that Serge Rufus was dead. Did Denis have a message for Paul in the event that his father passed away? Possibly. Serge and Denis had managed to see eye to eye in a way that the father and son had not. Serge, what with his love of the old-school, might have given Denis a letter or a package "just in case" something happened to him. Except Denis was not really up to speed with the former commissaire's health: it had taken his chat with Capestan to gee him into action.

And Paul had not said a word to Anne.

Not on the night of the *réveillon*, and not on Christmas morning.

She had left his apartment at 8.00 a.m. feeling giddy with happiness. Two hours later, Paul was tailing Ramier into the Bois de Vincennes.

Bucketfuls of sadness in Capestan's head were snuffing out the flames of her rage, only for the embers to rekindle straight away. She was yet to know which of the two emotions would engulf her.

Did she feel a glimmer of understanding? No – that would be

a sign of weakness. Yet there was still a strong temptation to dodge the issue with some bogus reasoning, to let him off the hook and reprieve herself in the process.

In his shoes, would she have pulled the trigger?

No, not for a man like Serge.

There was a knock at the door and Orsini poked his head in.

"Telephone. For you."

"Couldn't they try me on my mobile?"

"Well yes, but that's in the sitting room too."

Capestan instinctively patted her pockets before admitting that he was right. She sighed, then realised it might be Paul. She searched for an answer in Orsini's eyes, but he narrowed them slightly to tell her that it was not.

"Buron."

Capestan let out a huff. Buron. The last thing she needed now was flak from the directeur. Reluctantly, she heaved herself up.

Avoiding eye contact with her colleagues, she picked up the telephone on her desk and turned to take the call.

"Monsieur le Directeur?"

"Hello, Capestan. I'm calling with regard to the mass brawl that broke out by the Fontaine des Innocents . . ."

"Yes, O.K., O.K. Listen, we did the best we could. We're sorry – there you go. As much as we love being reprimanded, it does seem to happen an awful lot for an anonymous squad like ours."

There was a brief silence at the other end of the line before Buron resumed:

"Actually no, commissaire, I was calling to congratulate you.

Your intervention might have run contrary to procedure, not to mention prudence, but it was a fine act of bravery that certainly prevented a lot of damage. I must say, the local inhabitants appear to have been mighty impressed by the sight of police officers engaging so courageously despite being heavily outnumbered."

"Oh, right. Thank you," Capestan said, somewhat apologetically. "That's nice to hear. And good of you to pass on the compliment."

"Of course, the very same inhabitants are berating the C.R.S. for being so slow to respond, as well as the city council for being so poorly prepared on match days. And there were even some stories about hordes of blood-soaked animals trained to kill. Does that ring any bells?"

"The poor preparation?"

"The blood-soaked animals trained to kill."

Capestan was holding a biro, the tip of which she was rotating on the wooden surface of her desk.

"We might have had a bit of help from Rosière's dog and Merlot's rat."

"I see. Everything all right, Capestan?" Buron asked, a note of genuine concern in his voice.

"Yes, fine, Monsieur le Directeur," she said. "Everything's fine. We're just recovering from our injuries."

"Good. Call me back when you're less the worse for wear."

Lebreton was waiting in the long queue for the counter at the charcutier-traiteur on rue Montorgueil. He served himself some grated carrot and pork rillons, before deliberating whether to try the potato salad, which had chunks of ham in it. Then he dropped in at the greengrocer's to buy a couple of apples.

The commandant, as had become his custom ever since meeting Pilote, could not resist looking at the little dog minding its own business a few metres away from the rotisserie chicken stand. With his resplendent white coat and glassy eyes, he was no longer a puppy. Around his neck he wore a collar with a silver medallion that had no fewer than three telephone numbers engraved on it. This mutt was long past the age of bolting from its owner – but someone clearly could not face the thought of losing him.

37

"Anne, I need to talk to you."

In the end, he did call.

Sitting beneath an outdoor heater on the terrace of Le Cavalier Bleu, Capestan charted the steady, hypnotic motion of the heads ascending the long tubular escalator of the Centre Pompidou. She was very fond of this package of colourful cylinders that her grandmother, a fierce opponent of the project, used to refer to as the "Cultural Colon".

On the damp pavement, the hundreds of droppings courtesy of the square's army of pigeons were being washed away in the drizzle, lulling the tourists into a false sense of cleanliness. With the school holidays still in full swing, the Parisians were nowhere to be seen. Only one other table was occupied on the broad terrace at the corner of the rues Saint-Martin and Rambuteau, so there was no danger of them being disturbed. Capestan had not been able to face the thought of meeting at either of their apartments, so Paul had suggested a café that was close to both the commissariat and Anne's place. A nice show of consideration for a man who was about to confess to a murder.

She saw him at a distance walking down rue Saint-Martin, his hands in the pockets of his navy blue sailor's jacket, his shoulders hunched to protect his neck from the cold. His grey beanie, unable to tame his unruly barnet, had let slip a few strands of blonde hair that the rain had drenched. Capestan wondered if she would ever stop being blown away by his beauty. Maybe in ten minutes' time, if he proved incapable of saying what needed to be said.

He hesitated for a split second before kissing her on the cheek, then sat down across the table from her, hands still in pockets. The waiter appeared out of nowhere, his thumb and index finger jiggling the purse in his waistcoat pocket as Capestan ordered a coffee.

"I'll have one too," Paul said, more to dismiss the question than because he wanted to drink anything.

"How are you? Lovely Christmas weather, hey," he said, keen to engage Capestan.

He was waiting for the coffees to arrive and the waiter to leave before turning to more serious matters.

"What happened here?" he asked with a hint of concern, indicating the bruise on her neck and the plaster on her forehead, before nodding his thanks to the waiter.

"Chelsea fans," she said, not bothering to expand.

She had not come here to complain, and definitely not to be consoled.

Paul took the hint. He could read her well. He stirred his espresso for an age, delaying the inevitable for as long as possible. Please don't mess this up, Anne silently implored him. He took a deep breath and looked out at the pedestrians on rue Rambuteau.

"O.K. I'll put this bluntly because I can't think of a way to sugar-coat it. My guess is you're already investigating it, but you never know. Ramier, the man who murdered my father, is dead. I killed him."

"How did it happen?"

A police officer's question. The only thing on her mind was the question *Why didn't you tell me sooner?*, yet here she was demanding a detailed confession. Paul did not appear surprised. He had committed to this path and was moving headlong into the tunnel. He just had to grit his teeth until he reached the finish line, and not think too much on the way.

"He was strangling me and I was so short of air that I couldn't fight back. So I fired."

Strangulation. Same method as Velowski, Capestan thought to herself. That fitted. Now she needed to figure out why Paul was walking around with a gun.

"Where did you get the firearm?"

"O.K., I know. Let me start from the beginning – that'll make it clearer," Paul said, tapping his teaspoon gently on the table twice. "After seeing you, Denis came round to mine. He brought me an envelope that my father had given him for safe keeping 'just in case'. With his murky past, there can't have been a shortage of 'cases', so it was worth him taking precautions. But because I refused to see him . . . Anyway, you know all that."

Capestan said nothing. With her arms crossed and her back against the banquette, she was content to listen, eager not to sway his testimony with the slightest reaction. Paul took another deep breath before carrying on.

"In this envelope, there was a card for a sports club, another card with a locker code written on it, and . . . a letter. A short one."

Paul swallowed and his eyes went more red, but he frowned and continued down his tunnel.

"I went to the club the next day and opened the locker. It contained wads of cash piled up in a collection of shoe boxes. Six of them. I closed it and left. I fretted about it all night – I had no idea what to do with it. I felt that the least I could do was take one box and figure out how much was in there . . . So I went back. And when I did, there was a box missing. I counted and recounted, then checked and searched again. But I was absolutely sure one was missing. Someone had taken it. Who? I immediately thought about Ramier and the marks on my father's body. He had tortured him to get the code."

Paul spread his arms wide to show Capestan how evident the matter was.

"I knew he would be back, so I decided to wait for him. But a guy like that, I couldn't go and talk to him without at least some form of protection. So I got hold of one of my father's old pistols, one of his 'phantoms', as he liked to call his unregistered guns, or so he told me when he was trying to get me interested in his police stuff. He tried to teach me how to clean and fire them too, but I didn't want to. Anyway, I took the revolver – "

"Pistol. It was a pistol, we found the cases."

"Oh," Paul said, raising his eyebrows. "I took the pistol. Just as a safety measure, I went and tried it out in the middle of nowhere. I didn't want to find myself face-to-face with a killer holding a rev— a pistol that went 'click-click' like in the movies."

Paul ventured a smile but thought better of it straight away. The woman opposite him was not laughing at all. She was grappling with the extraordinary lack of sense that had set her husband down this path. He had thought himself capable of confronting this man – he had mistaken blindness for courage.

"Did you stop to think about what kind of man Ramier was? He had just murdered three people. How could you risk confronting him? Why?"

"I wanted to know more, that was part of it. Was my father really a bent cop? How bad was he? Had he fired too? Had he killed anyone? If so, when and who? Had Ramier killed him to avenge some betrayal? Maybe Serge had decided to come clean? Nothing in his letter shed any light on their history."

Paul shook his head with regret. He was only too aware that his quest for the truth had not worked out too well.

"In the end, I just waded into the mess. I was right about one thing: he came back. You had shown me a picture of him on your mobile. I recognised him coming out of the club with a bag over his shoulder."

He paused, then almost as an aside said:

"I've still got it, the bag. It's yours to do with as you see fit. Anyway, I decided to follow him. When I was a few metres away, I called out to him. He turned round and looked me up and down. I could tell that he recognised something about me. I . . . well, I look like my father, as you know. I confirmed it for him, introduced myself. He came towards me and I was about to ask my first question, but he didn't give me the chance. He went straight for my throat and started choking me like a maniac."

Paul's eyes bulged at the memory of the attack. He was still not over it, still did not understand it.

"I fought back, but at such close quarters and without being able to breathe, I soon realised there was no way I could loosen his grip. I managed to reach into my pocket and bring out the pistol, then I started firing as best I could . . ."

His hand tightened round the spoon, which he still had not put down.

"In the stress of the situation, I must have emptied the whole clip. I was petrified that I'd missed and that he would wrestle the gun off me."

The shooting champion in Capestan was forced to admit that, at point-blank range like that, lodging two bullets in the nearby trees was an achievement in itself. Looking on the bright side, this would play in his favour.

Paul seemed to have reached the end of his story. Now it was up to Capestan to ask the question that had been tormenting her more than any other. She struggled to get the words out.

"Why didn't you talk to me?"

"I didn't want to embroil you in it."

"Is that a joke? Paul . . ."

She and he were embroiled body and soul, down to the core of her every feeling, a link that had slackened for too long but had – on his initiative – only just pulled them back together, snapping them back to their true shape, and he wanted to spare her somehow?

"Knowing all this, knowing your intentions, why did you come and paint that message outside my place? Why?"

Paul looked down. She was right, there was no escaping it. But that was all separate from reason, from sanity. All that mattered there was that they had been together again.

"Because I was only thinking about you. I didn't calculate anything, I just wanted you to come back. You wanted it too, didn't you?"

The facts rendered any response pointless. He carried on:

"I'm sorry, I really am. I had to do this alone, without the police, to get proper answers from the only guy who knew. I didn't expect it to turn out like it did."

With a sociopath like Ramier, it could not have happened any other way. Paul had allowed himself to be misled by a version of criminals that belonged in fiction. And he had run away instead of coming to her.

"You should have called me straight away. We need to go and log this confession right now. The firearm is always going to be a problem, as is withholding information about a fugitive, but the signs of self-defence at the scene will make things easier. Why didn't you call me?"

Paul shrugged then slouched back in his seat. He held up his hands, then gave the most honest answer he could muster:

"Well, because it was you. If you had nothing to do with the case, if it had been any other officer, then I would have picked up the phone, I guess. But I wasn't proud of myself, and when you feel as pathetic as I did, the last person you want to tell is the woman you love. On the other hand, I wasn't going to come clean to anyone but you. It was all a muddle, I was in a state, in shock, you know. So I waited."

Capestan let her eyes drift towards the square. The pigeons had regrouped along the roof of the Atelier Brancusi building. The rain was still hammering down, set in for good in the Parisian sky, making the tarmac even darker as it masked people's faces, even if it did quench the thirst of the horse chestnuts, the base of whose trunks were clasped by metal grates that funnelled the water into the drains and on to the sewers.

38

For a second, Capestan looked at Paul and considered burying the whole thing, just like that. All she needed was another culprit. Not that there was any shortage of shitbags around – her challenge would simply be to find one who fitted the bill.

But no. She could not live with that. Which was a shame.

Then she thought back to Orsini's proposal earlier, back in his office.

"I don't know whether it was for revenge or whether it was an accident," he had said, "but if necessary, I'd be willing to testify that I was there, that he had called me, and that he acted in legitimate self-defence."

"That would be perjury, capitaine."

"Paul committed a crime that I could – perhaps should – have committed myself. It seems reasonable that we share the burden. False testimony and complicity – that should do the job."

"No. It's nonsensical, apart from anything else. Let's not forget that you were with us when the body was discovered, along with half the officers from number 36. You would have been noticed."

Orsini had lowered his head, his jaw clenched.

"True. Listen, if there's anything I can do, just let me know – I want to help."

"Message received. Thank you, capitaine."

On reflection, maybe Orsini could admit to receiving a telephone call earlier that he had not given due attention. That would clear Paul of at least one charge . . .

No. Capestan had to curb her fears about seeing her husband disappear into the grubby walls of a prison. She had to look at everything with a cool head, as if it were any other homicide. Deep down, Paul was no murderer, and the elements would surely demonstrate that so long as she managed to present them like any other piece of evidence. She needed to give herself some time to think – right now her brain was whizzing all over the place.

Still slumped in his seat with his fingertips resting on the edge of the table, Paul was waiting for the information to register and for Anne to say something.

"What am I supposed to do, from where you're sitting?" she asked, more to break the silence than anything else.

"Arrest me. I'd want it to be you, unless you'd prefer not to, of course. Either way, I'm not going on the run – too old for that. And besides, people know my face, so I wouldn't get far. I want to take responsibility for my actions."

Capestan let slip a sigh as she nodded her head. Responsibility. He had no idea what lay in store. But his sincerity was writ large, lighting up all the space around him. This man swept nothing under the carpet.

"So he left you a letter?"

"Yes."

Paul undid his thick woollen jacket and carefully removed a piece of paper that was folded in four from his inside pocket. He handed it to Capestan.

"Here, read it."

Capestan checked her hand as it moved forwards. It was personal. She would have preferred a brief summary instead.

"Read it," Paul insisted, sliding it across the table. "I really want you to."

Capestan unfolded the sheet of paper.

Paul,

As you well know, I've been a bad husband, a bad father and a bad policeman. Before any of that, I was the bad son of a fierce father, as you also know, but I'm not looking for excuses.

You've been a bad husband – just as I predicted – but a good son. I didn't understand your courage at the time. Playing the funny man, being happy . . . there was no better way to rebel against me. By the time I began to understand, we barely saw each other any more. Too bad, that's just how things go.

But from a distance and without you knowing, I wanted to remain your father, to act like one. I took an unconventional measure to find a way to finance your career in Paris. You would definitely have managed without me, but I wanted to do my bit. I saw it as a duty.

The money that wasn't used then will serve as your inheritance today. These funds came via dishonest means, yes, but over the years I've been able to convert the francs into euros, and they're clean. It's all stashed in a locker at a sports club – you'll find the address and code enclosed.

From your father, who is sorry, but could not have been any different. Good luck with everything.

Papa

Anne folded up the sheet, keeping quiet about the reflections that this show of remorse, as belated and curt as it was defiant, inspired in her. One thing had irked her too much to ignore, however.

"You haven't been a bad husband."

"Of course I have. He was right. I wasn't cut out for the role."

Capestan slowly shook her head. The least she could say was that she had had ample time to pore over their relationship since Serge's death. Ultimately, she had behaved like her father-in-law. She had shut herself away and stifled even the smallest glimmer of joy around her. She had let her fury smoulder without any reprieve, just under the surface, like a threat, to avoid talking about anything.

"No-one could have coped, Paul. Because I wouldn't have wanted them to. You leaving was just a formality. It was justified. Your father was wrong – you were an excellent husband."

Capestan returned her focus to the pigeons, the passers-by, the square, the wind, the rain. Then she looked back at Paul. She had to back up her good faith with solid evidence.

"Did you keep the weapon?"

"Yes, I've got everything: the gun, the bag, the card for the club, my muddy shoes . . ."

All of a sudden, Capestan thought about the marks around her own neck. She leaned forward:

"May I?"

He lowered his roll-neck to reveal several large, bluish marks that were already starting to turn yellow in places. It was clear as day – Ramier had had no intention of loosening his vicelike grip. They had no time to lose.

From a strictly factual point of view, the scenario was credible:

the killing was an act of self-defence. The marks were unambiguous. The fact he was carrying a weapon, along with his desire to act alone, could be put down to shock at his father's death, quickly followed by the news of his corruption. After that, he confessed of his own free will, the delay owing to the emotional complexity of the situation: his ex-wife was involved in the inquiry and they had only just patched things up when he confronted Ramier. Disturbed and traumatised, he had not known what to do in the heat of the moment. But as soon as he came to his senses, he had given himself up willingly before returning the stolen money to the authorities.

That held water.

Either Rosière or Merlot would track down the details of the police service's least favourite lawyer, one of those hotshots that ekes out months of gruelling work with the aim of freeing the kind of rogue that they would never want to bump into in public themselves. Some handy opportunist or other.

It held water.

Capestan took out her mobile, flicked through her contacts and hit the call button.

"Hello, doctor, this is Commissaire Capestan. Might you be available for a consultation? It's urgent. At the commissariat. Thank you, doctor, see you shortly."

Capestan stowed her telephone away, gathered her things and invited her husband to do likewise.

"I'm placing you under arrest, Paul. It won't be me questioning you, as you can imagine. But don't worry – stick to the truth and it will all be fine."

Everything was going to sort itself out. They just had to move forward.

39

Lyon, Minerva Bank, 4 August, 1992

Serge handcuffed Ramier, took him outside and flung him onto the pavement. He was gripping the pistol so tightly in his pocket it was as if he might pulverise it. With his left hand, he yanked the scumbag by the collar so he could hiss into his ear. Sweat was pouring into the man's eyes:

"Fucking hell, what came over you? You're sick! You're a piece of shit! Why did you shoot the woman and the kid?"

"It was Velowski's fault – he didn't manage to cut his meeting short. Plus that no good, small-town, bastard banker said my name when I came into his office. It was his fault; he killed them. All I did was fire."

Serge struck him hard on the nose with the butt of his pistol.

"You've got us all in the shit. I can't let you go now, no-one would believe it. We'd all be caught red-handed and never see the money again. So listen to me, dickhead. For the others, we're sticking to the plan. I let Jacques go and Alexis gives a false testimony. We'll keep your cut for you. Shut your mouth, do your time, and you'll get it when you come out. Understand? Do you understand?" he said, shaking him.

Through his own sweat, Rufus's, and the blood gushing from his nose, Ramier managed to summon a wicked smile.

"Understood. See you then. I'll be in touch just before."

Rufus shook him again then let him fall to the ground.

The wailing sirens levelled out and doors began to slam. Rufus felt the rush of activity around him as his colleagues took charge of the scene. It was doable. Tight, but doable.

40

Like a pride of lions prowling the savannah, or killer whales patrolling the ocean blue, the wheelie cases were dominating their natural habitat, the very one they had been designed for: the smooth linoleum of Roissy-Charles-de-Gaulle. After crashing across the city's tricky cobbles and rough pavements, they could finally glide along in blissful silence.

The police officers at their helm were considerably more noisy. Rosière, the flamboyant figurehead, was striding ahead, occasionally raising her arm to bid the rest of the fleet to follow her, like a tourist guide making a beeline for the "Mona Lisa".

Diament's former colleagues had clocked him at passport control. They came up to him and pointed at Capestan: "Your boss in the running for wife of the month, is she? Nothing says 'I love you' like prison. Poor guy should've broken it off for good, because he sure isn't gonna break out . . ." No-one heard Diament's response, but it certainly shut them up.

That put the topic that none of them had dared broach back on the table. Capestan wondered if she was going to have to reel out a load of explanations or excuses there and then in the comfort of the seating area in Terminal 2E.

Back in the Commissariat des Innocents, the squad had

surveyed Paul's arrival with a thinly veiled incredulity, with the exception of Orsini, who greeted him with a long handshake. Having asked Rosière and Lebreton to place him in custody, the commissaire assembled the team to summarise the arrest, the facts and everything else pertaining to the case. The officers went the extra distance to act naturally. Afterwards, Rosière and Lebreton escorted the suspect to Buron at number 36, quai des Orfèvres, who referred him to the public prosecutor. For the moment, everything seemed to be going O.K. and Anne felt able to breathe again.

The squad finally reached the floor-to-ceiling windows of the departure lounge. Lewitz, still with his crutch, and Dax hurried off to bag two free rows facing each other, like teenagers at the cinema. Once they had all found a spot and stacked the luggage, backpacks and bags of duty-free in the middle, Dax stood up to offer the commissaire the seat of honour.

Rosière, who could not stop stroking her handbag in the absence of her dog, what with Pilote not being eligible for travel to the U.S.A., leaned in to Capestan and stuck her high heels in it with characteristic matter-of-factness:

"Don't chew it over too hard, darling, seriously. Paul's self-defence line is a no-brainer. With that slime-ball silk handling his case, I can see it being thrown out, maybe with a cheeky suspended sentence."

"A celeb. in the dock? The media will tear him to pieces," Évrard said, struggling to adopt the same diplomatic tone.

"Nonsense," Rosière said before the lieutenant could go any further. "Quite the opposite – it'll make for a mega-comeback! Plus, as a bonus, that gorgeous face of his will land him every new cop and crook role going. He'll bring in so much cash at the box office the finance jocks won't know what to do with themselves. Especially with his comedy background, he's going to clean up."

"But I'm also worried about the squad's reputation," Capestan said, "that I've dragged you in–"

"Ohhh, water off a duck's back, isn't that right, guys?" Rosière said, like a conductor fronting a gospel choir.

The rest of the team nodded wholeheartedly. All of them knew a thing or two about sticks and stones, and they weren't about to let this latest episode hurt them. At any rate, people had stopped speaking to them a long while ago.

"And anyway, what reputation?" Rosière said, poking her commissaire in the ribs. "It's already at rock bottom! Our findings on Serge Rufus mean we've sullied the name of another one of our own; our commissaire arrested her own husband, who – word in the ear – probably benefited from her information –"

"No!" Capestan said, suddenly riled.

"That'll be in the version doing the rounds, I assure you. Where was I? Yes, a husband who – in the end – will get off the hook thanks to a slippery lawyer and V.I.P. media coverage. Frankly, we've gone beyond reputation into the realm of legend! No-one's going to hold anything against us ever again!"

"*Could passengers on flight AF1810 to Los Angeles please make their way to gate E31, where your flight is now ready for boarding.*"

The officers stood up as one squad before the cases resumed their transit.

"Gee-whizz – thirteen hours to L.A. then another eight to Honolulu . . . That's quite a journey," Évrard said.

"Yeah, but in . . . business!" Rosière said, smiling as she revealed the surprise.

"Oh, fantastic! Are you kidding? I really hope I get to see the cockpit . . ." Lewitz said, overcome with excitement.

"And what about Torrez?" Dax asked.

Rosière handed over her passport and boarding pass, before answering this perfectly legitimate question.

"He took a separate flight with his family. Something about not wanting to crash."

EPILOGUE

With the humidity nudging 70 per cent, the air seemed like you could suck it up through a straw. Completely frazzled by the journey, the time difference and the climate, most of the French officers had spent the first two days wringing out their shirts. Then they had ransacked the shops. Today, their noses already peeling, they were all sporting baggy Hawaiian shirts adorned with huge flowers and small palm trees.

At the side of the open-air ring, drunk on Mai-Tai, they held their arms aloft and stamped their feet as they urged on their champ. with a range of hollers and basic rallying cries. This was the decisive round. The speakers were blaring out fit to explode. Fabulous women dressed to the nines in traditional grass skirts, garlands and floral headdresses paraded around the ring holding up placards showing the scores, along with Philips advertising boards. The grand finale of the 2012 'Golden Iron' was underway.

Torrez's children were displaying the same level of restraint as the squad, in other words none whatsoever. But things were not looking good for their father. He was up against a Canadian woman who had been victorious the two previous years. Standing at one metre eighty, she appeared ready to steamroller her board every time she picked up her iron. She made Bruce Lee's brick-chopping antics look like the unhurried work of a local stonecutter. The opening theme resounded around the full house. Torrez's youngest was quaking with anticipation. The girls were tugging nervously at their plaits, staring at the ring without blinking. The two older boys were elbowing one another, the wait killing them, while their mother, a brown-haired Spanish woman with a classical profile, chewed the inside of her cheek as she kept watch over the flock. The round was about to start.

Torrez closed his eyes for a second before the whistle. He would never have a better chance. This was the final of a competition, which meant not just shirts, so he would have to step it up a gear. But Torrez was ready. He had spent years training for this.

The Canadian started a second early. Deliberate false start. No matter, the lieutenant carried on regardless, picking up shirt after shirt. He lost time on one sleeve, but he did his best to stick to his rhythm. His face covered in sweat and his T-shirt sodden, concentrating harder than a Michelin-starred chef at the stove, Torrez tweaked the collars without letting up for a second. His challenger watched him from the corner of her eye – she had practically emptied her first basket before Torrez had reached halfway. A thin smile flashed across her tense face.

"She's screwed up all her buttonholes, the judges won't miss that," Rosière shouted, focusing hard on the action.

"Keep going, my boy!" Merlot bellowed with pride.

"Yes! Yes! Yes! Hoo hoo hoo! Yes! Yes! Yes!" came Dax's contribution.

"Yes! Yes! Yes! Hoo hoo hoo! Yes! Yes! Yes!" Lewitz echoed.

Capestan, Lebreton and Évrard clapped as loudly as they could to encourage their lagging lieutenant. Even Orsini let out a sudden and speedy "Come on!" before sitting straight back down. A thick gloom had enveloped the capitaine since the case had been solved. He had searched so hard, waited so long, and when it came to it, he had acted so little. The truth might have answered all his questions, but it had also placed him in perpetual mourning, with nothing left to undo his grief.

Torrez was finally onto his second basket. Everyone in the audience could tell he now had his pedal to the metal. The neat clothing was piling up on his table at a breathless rate as he expertly lifted sleeves, turned shirt fronts and directed the point of his iron with pinpoint accuracy. His hair was all over the place amid the furore, the unruly strands flapping at the air. With a quick-fire motion of the forearm, the lieutenant chased away the odd bead of sweat running down his brow, at risk of scalding himself with the steam.

The referee blew the whistle to draw the final to a close.

José Torrez had caught up and, by the end, the two adversaries' baskets had been emptied in the same second.

"Stats! Stats!" the crowd bayed.

The referee took hold of his microphone and tablet.

"Our two challengers have ironed exactly the same number of clothes, so it'll come down to the number of creases! We'll be back with you in a couple of minutes."

The technical experts entered the ring to turn their judicious eyes to the respective stacks of laundry.

The audience hummed with all kinds of speculation as they chewed their nails to the quick. Finally, the judges left the ring and the oily referee grabbed his microphone again with all the relish of the King storming Vegas.

"And so for the eagerly awaited results! For shirt creases: the Frenchman José Torrez has come in at 51 per cent, while Canadian Martha Kitimat has just 31 per cent!"

"Ooooooooh!" came the reaction from the French camp as the Canadians erupted with delight.

"It's not over yet, it's not over yet," the referee said, clawing back the crowd's attention. "For children's clothes creases: Canada, 68 per cent! France, zero per cent! That's right, zero! An incredible feat, ladies and gentlemen. A new record and a perfect finish, which – let's not forget – could only have been achieved with the new range of Philips Pro vapour units, available for purchase in hypermarkets and specialist stores near you. Come and behold the precision!"

The dozens of miniatures folds in the smocks were perfectly in line, the ribbons finely knotted, and not even the tiniest bulge betrayed the poppers on the cotton sleepsuits. The referee was exhibiting them like bona fide works of art, entrusting them to his young assistants who marched them around the ring for the benefit of the awestruck onlookers.

"Without any further ado, we are delighted to crown José Torrez of France our 2012 Philips 'Golden Iron' champion! Let's show him our appreciation, ladies and gentlemen!"

The lieutenant was beaming from ear to ear. His children were elated, jumping about in every direction, one on top of the other, handing out high-fives and howling with joy – their father was a world champion!

The racket from the French contingent of the arena doubled,

then tripled. Between his family, colleagues and the tourists who happened to be in town, the decibel-count was off the chart. A stunned Capestan was watching her partner, who was almost unrecognisable with his delighted face and puffed-out chest. She was genuinely happy for him, not to mention grateful to Rosière, their queen bee, whose generosity had allowing the team to attend this offbeat occasion.

That said, the commissaire was struggling to enjoy the moment in all its glory. She was not sure whether it was the journey or, more likely, the tricky circumstances that awaited her back in Paris, but she felt off-colour. What was more, her nausea was off the scale.

AUTHOR'S NOTE

The final of the 2008 Philips Fer d'Or ('Golden Iron') did take place in Hawaii. For the purposes of the story, the rules and the feel of the competition have been modified. Nevertheless, it was won by a Frenchman – Christophe Hars – now the owner of an excellent restaurant in Issy-les-Moulineaux.

There was indeed a video showing the Varappe Division in action at the fair celebrating the one hundredth anniversary of the formation of the Police Judiciaire. Other P.J. brigades were also part of the exhibition, and the photograph mentioned in Chapter 31 did feature too. The author, however, has no idea which group or person the desk in question belonged to. Attributing it to a B.R.I. commandant is pure fiction.

Rats and pigs really are used by the police. Not in France, but in the United States, Israel and Holland.

ACKNOWLEDGEMENTS

If Marie Curie herself had come back to life and hung out with me for the last year, she'd have thought her Nobel Prize seemed a bit "meh". So, with all my heart, I want to offer my

eternal gratitude and unflinching affection

to Francis Esménard, who turned my little squad from a village team into World Cup winners.

The mighty folk at my publisher Albin Michel, who trained them up, developed their potential and ran them their post-match ice-bath.

Booksellers, booksellers, booksellers! With a particular pip-pip to Fabien at Chantelivre, Christophe at Millepages and Pierre at Fables d'Olonne.

Readers, readers, readers, bloggers, Babeliophiles: the best team-players I could have hoped for. Seriously.

Everyone at the Quais du Polar festival, Hélène Fischbach and the judges of the Polar en séries prize. The Squad could not have asked for a better start.

The judges and organisers of the Arsène Lupin prize – dressing up the Squad in the cape and top hat of one of their heroes has been a source of great joy and pride.

All the fairs, their organisers and their volunteers, for giving me the energy to write another thirty books. A special kiss to Lamballe, which was cancelled at the last-minute on November 14, 2015, in the saddest of circumstances.

Journalists and critics, whose articles I read with bated breath, then framed, displayed, scanned, folded into my purse and/or sent to half the planet.

My bosses and colleagues at *Cosmo*, who without fail have encouraged me, forgiven my absences, had the decency to let me win at pétanque and let me know when there's something good at the cafeteria.

All those I thanked at the end of the first novel – consider this round two, especially you, Patrick Raynal the Great.

All my friends and close/distant/mid-range relations who all raved about the book, hawking it to anyone and everyone with highly biased reviews.

And then – last but not at all least – a big kiss to those checkers who have been there from the start, my very own sounding boards, whose every remark or scribble has brought joy and a flurry of corrections: Anne-Isabelle Masfaraud (official guarantor of plot cohesion and character-tracker par excellence), Dominique, Patrick and Pierre Hénaff (i/c good endings, law, football and animals), Chantal Patarin, Brigitte Petit, Michelle Hénaff, Chloé Szulzinger and finally, one last thank you to Marie-Thérèse Leclair, Isabelle Alvès and Marie La Fonta, whose escapades I have shamelessly pinched and remodelled to my heart's content. I'm not sorry, but I am extremely grateful, if that makes up for it.

SOPHIE HÉNAFF is a journalist, author and former Lyonnaise bar owner. She began her journalism career as a critic at *Lyon Poche*, before moving to Paris to write for *Cosmopolitan*, where she established her own humourous column, "La Cosmolite". *Stick Together* is the sequel to *The Awkward Squad*, which was first published in 2015.

SAM GORDON is a literary translator from French and Spanish. His translations include works by Pierre Lemaitre, Karim Miské and Timothée de Fombelle.